FIRE AND FURY FOR THE TOBACCO GIRLS

LIZZIE LANE

Boldwood

First published in Great Britain in 2021 by Boldwood Books Ltd.

Copyright © Lizzie Lane, 2021

Cover Design by The Brewster Project

Cover Photography: Colin Thomas

A CIP catalogue record for this book is available from the British Library.

Paperback ISBN 9978-1-80048-508-2

Large Print ISBN 978-1-80048-507-5

Hardback ISBN 978-1-80280-873-5

Ebook ISBN 978-1-80048-509-9

Kindle ISBN 978-1-80048-510-5

Audio CD ISBN 978-1-80048-502-0

MP3 CD ISBN 978-1-80048-503-7

Digital audio download ISBN 978-1-80048-504-4

Boldwood Books Ltd
23 Bowerdean Street
London SW6 3TN
www.boldwoodbooks.com

1

Bridget Milligan and Maisie Miles

The ambulance careered through total darkness, bouncing over potholes, missing lamp posts by inches, skimming round corners and passing familiar landmarks barely discernible against a blanket of blackness.

Bridget Milligan, in her capacity as first-aider, clung on with her left hand, her bottom bumping up and down on the passenger seat. With her free hand, she yanked the emergency bell for all she was worth, its loud clatter joining a tumultuous choir of other ambulance and fire engine bells clanging and jangling as each raced to where they were needed.

It might be a bit too much to hope that the raid wouldn't go on too long, that some sleep might be snatched before morning.

Harry Flinders, production operative in the tobacco factory by day but ambulance driver tonight, was hunched over the steering wheel in an effort to better see the road ahead of him in the midst of the blackout.

Street after street of blackness steadily blended to grey, then a pale dirty lemon colour, which in turn exploded to a reddish gold. It got warmer and warmer until the sweat trickled down Bridget's neck and then her spine. At last the heat was there before them, buildings smouldering against a blanket of orange.

'They don't look like flames,' she muttered, her voice sounding unusually small and far away.

'Well they are!'

Harry's curmudgeonly tone put her off saying what she wanted to say: that it was as though somebody had daubed the night sky with a huge brush dipped into a tin of bright orange paint.

If hell could ever be on earth, then this was it. Night had become day and the cold receded with the heat of bombs that had found targets and exploded with grim ferocity. Having been told there'd been indiscriminate bombing on St Michael's Hill, they had gone from Bedminster towards the city centre. They'd heard that other areas of Bristol were also experiencing air raids. It was a big one, the raiders having followed the River Avon from its mouth into the city, leaving a trail of destruction behind them. Harry considered himself a bit of an armchair strategist so had plenty to say on the subject.

'They let loose their main load on Avonmouth and Filton – harbour and aeroplanes – and 'avin' a few left decided to drop them on people. Bloody Germans! Oh God!' Harry's jaw went slack and the cigarette that had been jammed in the corner of his mouth fell to the floor. 'Good God,' he exclaimed. 'St Michael's Hill. Redcliffe. All houses!'

The ambulance swerved to avoid a fire engine and only barely got away with it.

Bridget swiped at the beads of sweat on her forehead. Her navy blue siren suit, so called because it was an item of clothing donned the minute the air-raid siren went off – if not before – felt hot and restrictive. The cold night might help, though thankfully there had been no snow this year, so no vegetables lost to extreme cold.

New Year had been just a few days ago. Some of the residents of Marksbury Road had got together for a party. There'd been a little beer and sherry, along with sausage rolls made without meat and fish paste sandwiches. There was always fish paste to be had. Bridget vaguely wondered how much fish paste would have been eaten by the time this war was over. Thinking of trivial things helped her cope with the scene beginning to unfold outside of the vehicle. She thought of her big family in Marksbury Road, of her friends at the tobacco factory: Maisie who was in another ambulance, and Phyllis who was serving abroad. She thought of the love of her life, Lyndon O'Neill who was far away but still in her heart.

Suddenly the whole horror of war had come home and was there before her.

'Oh God,' she muttered.

The windscreen proved no barrier to the increased heat she could feel on her face. The tight knot in her stomach that she'd had since the moment the air-raid siren had sounded tightened so much that it seemed her stomach was cleaved to her spine. This was her first time as first-aid assistant on one of the ambulances supplied by W. D. &. H. O. Wills. Months of the phoney war when nothing seemed to happen had made people think that nothing ever would. The retreat from Dunkirk had surprised and shocked and the air raids on Bristol had been relatively light until the heavy raid of the twenty-fourth of November. It was on that terrible night that she'd been forced to shelter in a wine cellar beneath St Nicholas Market. Maisie and Phyllis her very best friends and workmates from the tobacco factory had been with her. She sometimes wondered whether the experience had influenced Phyllis into joining up – besides her chaotic personal life. Phyllis seemed to fall in love at the fall of a hat – or what she thought was love. First there'd been Robert her fiancé who became her husband. She might not have married him if she hadn't been pregnant, but as it turned out she'd lost both husband and the baby she'd been expecting, fathered by her typing teacher.

Her eyes misted at those precious moments with her friends.

Once the raid was over, they'd walked home, taking detours as advised by air-raid wardens, remarking sadly that they'd never go shopping in Castle Street ever again. The medieval heart of Bristol had been destroyed, old buildings that had stood for centuries reduced to rubble and dust. Obliterated.

It was back then that W. D. &. H. O. Wills, one of the city's biggest employers and producers of cigarettes, cigars, snuff and pipe tobacco, had organised its own ambulances and facilitated the training of staff to man them, but the writing was on the wall. By the following raids of early December, they were up and running.

Bridget had swallowed the fear and declared the country needed them. 'It's our duty,' she had said to her good friend Maisie Miles. In response, Maisie, younger and slighter than Bridget and brave of heart, had declared that it might be fun, so accordingly they had put their names forward. Maisie had grown up in a tough neighbourhood, neglected by her mother and stepfather. She'd not been keen to work in the tobacco factory, but on doing so had found true friendship with Bridget and Phyllis. There'd been three of them but now there were only two still working in there.

It was certainly a bit different to their day job. Besides, the short six-week course on basic first aid practising on willing patients and despite the serious intent of the training, overall it had turned out to be fun. Maisie and Bridget had taken turns to be patients and allotted a specific injury and bandaged accordingly. Both she and Maisie had learned a lot and giggled a lot, especially when Maisie had drawn the short straw and been given a complete body bandaging.

'I can't move,' she'd spluttered through her bandaged mouth.

Bridget had told her that she'd looked like an Egyptian mummy. Maisie's muffled response had been to say that bandaging wasn't necessary and that all she needed for her injury was a cup of tea.

Such an innocent time, she thought as fear prickled all over her skin. Her courage was diminished and in its diminishment she found herself wishing it had stayed as fun, wished there'd been no more air raids, but there had. A new year had dawned and Bristol was once more under attack.

'I thought they were after the aeroplane works,' she said in as brave a tone as she could muster. Everyone knew Bristol, with its large port, excellent railway connections and, most of all, its aeroplane works, was a prime target.

Harry Flinders scowled through his sweat. 'They was, but their aim ain't as good as it could be. They ain't RAF – they're the boys that do it right.'

Bridget was none too sure about his boast but liked to think he was right. Being in the right and being better at things made everyone feel braver.

'It looks like a rank of houses.'

Harry nodded, said 'yep,' but nothing else. His expression hardened. 'Poor buggers chucked outa their bed.'

Bridget gulped; this was the first night both she and Maisie had become 'operational'. They'd been apprehensive, both fully aware that this would be very different from practising on perfectly healthy people and in a safe environment. All that she'd learned on the course broke into fragments at the sight of the flames.

"Ere we go,' muttered Harry as the vehicle came to a shuddering halt.

He fell out of the door on his side, slamming it shut behind him. Bridget did the same on her side, one shoulder weighed down by her first-aid kit.

The heat hit her. Water gushing from firemen's hoses quickly turned to steam. It was a scene from hell and the air she breathed tasted gritty. She wiped the back of her hand across her mouth and more grittiness transferred to her lips.

Cinders from burning buildings were like fireflies rising skywards, the air full of the sound of water thundering from fire hoses trained on fierce flames, black smoke soaring.

Bridget's attention was drawn to the arrival of yet another ambulance sporting a W. D. &. H. O. Wills logo.

An air raid warden silhouetted against the fire shouted at it. 'Shut that bloody racket!'

Maisie fell out of the new arrival. Like Bridget, she was grasping her first-aid kit.

Her driver, old Fred Winter, who'd retired some years before from driving company vans and lorries but had been brought in to help, climbed stiffly down from the other side.

'Crikey,' exclaimed Maisie as she came to a halt beside Bridget.

They both stared round-eyed at the terrible scene being played out before them.

'Is anyone injured?' Bridget asked an ARP warden who was

bent almost double, hands on knees as he coughed and spluttered, then cleared his throat in an effort to catch his breath.

He looked at them pityingly with red-rimmed eyes in a face blackened from the choking smoke. 'You'll get more than injured.'

Just as Bridget was about to ask him if there was anything she could do to help, a man began waving at them adjacent to where the fire hoses had doused the worst of the fire, though the rubble smouldered like coal. 'Don't stand there gawping. Come over 'ere.'

'On our way,' Maisie shouted back.

'Better leave these here,' Bridget said, laying down her first-aid box where the ground was clear.

'Keep an eye on them, will ya,' added Maisie, speaking to Fred. 'People's lives might depend on it.'

Bridget frowned at her. 'Maisie, nobody's going to steal first-aid boxes.'

'You don't think so? Well, Bridget Milligan, you don't come from where I come from.'

Bridget didn't respond. Maisie had grown up in the Dings, a pretty grim area where the stink of the boneyards and the soap factories fouled the air. Her father, who she'd later found out to be her stepfather, had been a small-time criminal who was currently in prison for selling rotten meat on the black market. As a result of that, two children had died and many others become very ill. He was likely to serve ten years at least. Her mother, downtrodden and abused all her married life, was dead and Masie now lived with her grandmother, Grace Wells, who also happened to be the mother of Maisie's natural father.

One thing Maisie had gained from living a rough life was guts and outright honesty. If you wanted an honest opinion, Maisie was the one you went to. Her courage was indisputable – as she was currently demonstrating.

Arms outstretched so she could better keep her balance, she picked her way over the debris of what had once been the upper storeys of a house of some age, one of a terrace.

'Go careful,' the man shouted. 'The upper floors 'ave collapsed on top of the cellar, but there might still be somebody down there. And no more water. This bit's out. Don't want to bloody drown 'em!'

Bridget and Harry followed on until the three of them joined a huddled band of auxiliary firemen and rescuers silently scrutinising one particular spot.

Harry asked if somebody was trapped.

The man rounded on him. 'Of course somebody's trapped, you big lummock. Now shut yer gob. I can't 'ear bugger all with you yapping.'

'Sorry I'm sure,' murmured Harry.

'Never you mind, Harry,' said Maisie in an extra loud voice that nobody could help but hear – including the bloke who'd told Harry to shut up. 'When somebody needs a big bloke to lift somethin' heavy, you're the man for the job.'

The man was unimpressed and glared pointedly at Maisie. 'I said shut yer gobs!'

'Just pointing out a fact. Just in case,' said an unperturbed Maisie in a smaller voice, though still with a cocky tilt to her head.

All round them, people clambered like ants over mounds of rubble and blackened timbers. Steam rose and mixed with the smoke from fires that were still burning, making the air a claustrophobic fog that was difficult to see through.

The man who'd shouted at Harry now shouted again. 'Well, don't just stand there, grab a shovel!'

'Keep yer 'air on,' snapped Maisie.

Harry was ordered to another area where plumes of smoke were turning to a cloud of hissing steam thanks to the rush of water from a fire hose.

'I can 'ear tapping,' somebody shouted out. 'Give us a bit of quiet.'

The clattering of tools and chatter amongst the rescuers stopped abruptly. Even though the fire wasn't fully put out, the firemen turned off their hoses. The only sound remaining was the hissing of steam from smouldering timbers.

'It's coming from back 'ere,' somebody shouted. 'But I'm warnin' you, it ain't safe. One foot wrong and it's down'ill all the bloody way.'

The man who looked to be in charge surveyed the band of rescue workers. 'Can I 'ave a volunteer to 'ave a go?'

'I'll go.'

'It's Harry,' said Bridget.

Maisie poked at the brim of her tin hat so it was shoved further back on her head. 'That's brave of 'im.'

With bated breath shared with all those round them, they watched as Harry began to make his way across mangled metal, shards of what had been doors, towards where a staircase hung precariously from a wall. Just like the other houses, the upper storey of the house had fallen down and piled on top of the cellar. If anyone had survived, that was where they would be.

A piece of wallpaper had come adrift from the wall and was fluttering like a flag above the staircase to nowhere. It was decorated with characters from nursery rhymes.

'Hey diddle, diddle,' whispered Bridget woefully. *Please God let them have survived.*

'The cat and the fiddle,' returned Maisie, swallowing the bile that accompanied the words. Thinking of the child that might have been sleeping in that room, the family preferring to take their chance rather than go to the shelter made her feel sick to her stomach.

A quick glance at Bridget's tense expression was enough to tell her that their thoughts were running along the same lines. The family might or might not have made the wrong choice. It could indeed be that a survivor was tapping on a water or gas pipe and that the child too was alive and being held in a loving embrace. She closed her eyes tightly and willed that it was so.

Somebody close by suggested that the family might have gone to the shelter and it really was only the sound of water hammer.

A senior fireman pushed his way through, the others making room, their dirty faces tensing as they waited to act on his judgement of the situation.

Hands resting on knees, he bent over and looked and listened, then held up a hand, a signal for everyone to be quiet. There was a sound like breaking glass when he took a step forward, along with two of the others.

'Stop,' he shouted. The raised hand again. 'We need to get closer, but I reckon this is too thin a layer to take our weight. We don't need a heavyweight, we need a bantamweight.'

A man who was indeed a bit thinner than anyone else offered to go further forward and take a closer look.

The fire officer glanced at him before shaking his head. 'If you're any more than about eight stone, you'll go right through before you can get there.'

A lone voice rang out into the fragile silence. 'I'm a bantamweight. More like seven stone in me bare feet.'

Maisie's face was gilded with gold and made Bridget think of the statues of saints in the Catholic Church more richly attired than when they'd been flesh and blood and not painted plaster.

The three men standing at the heart of the desolation eyed

Maisie's slight frame and the fireman, a man of senior office and used to being in charge of such situations, beckoned her forward.

'Now listen carefully,' he said, a thick moustache quivering with bits of soot and grit. 'All you got to do is shine a torch down into the hole and see what's there. I can see the rim of the hole from here, so I know there is one. Got that?'

'I got it.'

'Right. John, fetch a rope and tie it round her waist.' Its use was explained. 'So we can pull you up if you fall through. We shouldn't have any trouble doing that, you being such a lightweight.'

'Good job for you,' said Maisie in her normal cheeky style. Inside she was scared but nicely so. She was going to help someone. It was what she'd always wanted to do. Up until the January raid, she'd been at a distance from this war. Now she was part of it, feeling useful, but also important because people would be depending on her.

'Take this torch. Shine it down into the hole.'

'I 'eard you the first time. I know what I gotta do.'

Heart in her mouth, she showed a bit of bravado at first, stepping forward as though everything was perfectly flat, perfectly normal. Her manner was more to reassure herself rather than impress anyone else – not that she would ever admit it – now or in future.

A sudden shift of debris slowed her progress. Common sense and the will to survive came into play.

Ahead of her were lumps of brickwork; a gas oven lay on its side next to the handle of a pram or pushchair; more evidence of a child. The closer she got to her objective, the stronger the smell of gas.

She paused on thinking she heard something; waved her hand, signalling total silence from those behind her.

The sound was still there: tapping.

'Is anyone there?' she called out.

The sound of her voice started a small avalanche of rubble. She held her breath.

She dared call again. 'Hello.'

There was a sound, not a word as such, but a grunting, snoring, bordering on a squeal.

Toe then heel, she took one step, paused for the sound of more falling rubble. Took another step, again toe forward, then heel following. It was such a tiny advance, but she knew it to be necessary. Her life, and perhaps also those trapped, depended on it.

She allowed her mind to stray on how it would be with these people when they heard she'd been instrumental in saving them. That would be a very glad day indeed, and her mind dwelling on a positive outcome helped keep fear at bay.

The rough ground, the broken woodwork, the stones and brick and busted furniture posed obstacles, but she judged she was close to the tapping and the other sounds she could hear.

Suddenly her foot slipped and she cried out. In response to her shout, the rope round her waist became taut.

'You all right, me love?'

She swallowed hard. Her heart was racing like a train, but she hadn't fallen. A few more steps and all would be well.

The beam from the flashlight bounced over all the things that made a home: a broken teapot, battered saucepans, the ragged fringe of a rug, twists of cloth and linoleum. After that there was nothing, the column of light disappearing into a gaping hole.

'I'm there,' she shouted over her shoulder. 'Just give me a bit of slack.'

They'd been holding her too tightly, wary lest she disappear out of sight at any moment. The tautness eased. Taking a deep breath, she took another step, another and another, and finally a fourth one.

'Hello,' she called, her voice dropping down the hole, along with the light she was levelling down there.

That odd sound again, somewhere off to her right.

First there was only a jumble of items. Most prominent amongst it was a cast-iron fireplace, a huge Victorian one. Steadying her hand, her gaze followed the light from the torch. A little cry escaped from her throat. It looked like a gas pipe had come loose from fixings that had kept it firmly attached to a wall. Nothing held it now; the whole length of pipe was swinging backwards and forwards, tapping the mantelpiece of the fireplace.

She chose to believe that they weren't all dead and reminded herself of the grunting, snoring sound she had heard.

Determined that someone should come out of this alive, she tried again to locate someone – anyone – who might have survived.

Suddenly there were two faces. She gulped and in doing so breathed in some of the thick dust that was lay heavy on the air. The dust coated her tongue and she needed to spit. In an act of reverence, she turned her head so that whatever she spat out would not land on the pale faces beneath her.

Chilled but determined, she dragged her gaze back to the job in hand. Not job. People. They were dead but still people.

Taking a firm grip on her emotions, she took in the details. One was an adult – a woman if her fine cheekbones were anything to go by. The other was a child. Their eyes were closed and their faces shone whitely, which she guessed was dust from the plaster of fallen ceilings and tumbled walls. In a way, they looked peaceful, but it did nothing to take away the sheer horror of the scene. They might just as well have been in bed together, buried as they were beneath the surround of a marble fireplace, their dust-covered faces framed by an inner band of decorative tiles.

Her breath caught in her throat before she whispered to herself, 'No. I heard something...'

Someone behind her was asking loudly if she had found anything.

She stared down at the two faces which didn't look real. They were too still, too lifeless. The child's head lay on its mother's chest. The mother's arms hugged the child close in a useless act of protection. She became vaguely aware of another face behind both of them, the face turned slightly away. It was hard not to sob, hard not to cry. With her free hand, she brushed at the wetness trickling down her face. She heard nothing and saw nothing except white, dust covered faces.

'Are you ready to come back?'

She felt the rope tightening round her waist. They were preparing for her to back away, reeling her in as they might a fish on the end of a line.

'Yes,' she shouted, her voice strident and oddly confident.

Bit by bit and very slowly, she retraced her steps, though backwards instead of forwards. It wasn't easy, but she had faith in the men bringing her back to the surface and all she had to do was place her feet as close as possible to the steps she'd taken earlier.

She was shaking like a leaf when her feet finally found solid ground and the rope was being untied. She'd seen her mother die, but not like this. Never like this.

Bridget pushed her way through. 'You all right, Maisie?' She sounded worried.

It was obvious to everyone from her expression that nothing was all right.

She sniffed and wiped her nose on the cuff of her sleeve.

'They're dead. Two for definite, though it could be three. I thought I heard something, but...'

'It's a pig! It's a bloody pig!'

The interruption came from Harry, who, although he'd been told he was too heavy for the route she'd taken, had gone his own way.

A crowd headed in his direction.

'Finders, keepers,' somebody shouted.

One of the rescuers, she couldn't tell who, patted her on the back. 'Job well done,' he said solemnly. 'We'll get them out as quick as we can. Got yer stretcher 'andy?'

Maisie nodded.

'No need, I'll do it,' said Bridget.

'No.' Maisie was shaking but adamant. 'I found them. I'll get them to the morgue.'

He shook his head. 'Poor sods. They stayed in the house to keep their pig from thieves.'

Maisie looked at him in shocked surprise. 'A pig? A real pig?'

He rubbed at his face, making white patches in the sooty sweat that covered it then nodded. 'Everyone's got to eat and takes care of their own. By the looks of it, the family were keeping a pig in the back garden – probably a joint ownership between neighbours. They couldn't risk leaving it alone and it not being there when they got back from the shelter. So they stayed put to guard the pig. Even in the middle of a bombing raid, there's thieves about. Didn't do them much good though did it.' His voice and expression was sombre. 'They ain't lost their bacon but they've lost their lives.'

2

MAISIE

After such a stressful ordeal, sleep came but fitfully. Maisie tossed and turned all weekend, a vision of waxen faces staring up from out of dark earth and rubble. Every sense replayed the details, the sight, the smell, the heat and the taste of ashes in her mouth. No matter how much she tried to get some sleep, their lifeless faces remained fixed in her mind, the dream refusing to shift.

The tapping she recalled so well roused her to half-consciousness and became a knocking, louder than she recalled.

'Maisie, child.'

The knocking ceased and a warm hand lay on her shoulder. Though her face was implacable, there was concern in the failing eyes of her grandmother, Grace Wells.

Maisie pushed herself up onto her elbows, aware that she was bathed in sweat yet also shivering.

'I had a nightmare.'

Grace's face was never softly smiling. She wasn't a cosy grandmother who sat in a rocking chair knitting, but she was caring and pragmatic with it. 'Let it out, break the dream and it won't come back.'

Maisie told her the dream, which mirrored her baptism of fire, except in her dream the rope that had been her safety connection to the volunteers gathered behind her had snapped. Screaming at the top of her voice, she had fallen into the hole, landing on those who had died in their house rather than go to the shelter. She also told her the reason why they hadn't gone to the shelter. She waited for her grandmother to raise her eyebrows at the mention of the pig, but she didn't. Instead she sighed and shook her head.

'Who can blame them? It was bad enough trying to put a meal on the table during the thirties and the Great Depression; worse in a war when nobody knows what's round the corner. Family comes first whatever the risk. People will do anything to feed their family.' Her grandmother's gnarled hand patted her knee. 'I'll go down and get you a cup of cocoa.'

Maisie knew better than to suggest that *she* went down and got it, that would only result in a sharp rebuke, a reminder that Grace had lived in this house for years and knew her way around without the need for sight.

Instead, she lay back against the pillow, feeling more at home than she'd ever felt in her life, yet things could have been so different. It had come as a shock, and also relief, to learn that Frank Miles was not her natural father. She'd hated him. Before she'd died, her mother had told her to seek out her natural father's mother, Grace Wells. It was the best thing her mother had ever done and the best thing Maisie had done in taking that advice. Grace Wells was tough, but then so was she, plus she'd grown up without affection so didn't expect it. What she got from her grandmother was a support she'd never received from anyone else. Grace Wells was by no means perfect, but her heart was in the right place.

The only other person she'd been close with was her half-brother, Alf. Not that she heard much from him. He was away serving with the merchant navy, mostly on the beef and grain ships coming up from South America, and he wasn't much of a one for writing letters. Every so often, a card arrived, some with pictures of exotic places like Rio de Janeiro, Caracas and Montevideo. In time, they'd meet up again, if his ship came into Bristol, or if the war finally ended and he had managed to stay safe.

She wondered what he would make of her grandmother – if she should ever tell him the absolute truth that is. On the first occasion she'd visited her grandmother, Maisie had been appalled to find out that she practised abortions on girls who had got in trouble. She'd vowed never to go back but had found herself drawn to this strong woman after finding out that her true father had been killed by Frank Miles, her stepfather.

A known small-time criminal, Frank had been married to her late mother with whom he'd been too free with his fists. Seeing her mother with black eyes was a regular occurrence. Maisie had been too young to do anything about any of it. Despite Frank Miles making money from anything illegal, none of it had been spent on her. Shabbily dressed and smelling of the foetid air round where they lived, she'd been shunned by many of her peer group. Spending much time alone had made her what she was: independent, outspoken and tougher than she looked.

Maisie had left school at fourteen and worked for some time at the Royal Hotel on College Green in the centre of Bristol. It was whilst there that she'd heard from her old teacher about a live-in job at a country house. To her, it was like the answer to her dreams. A life away from family and from York Street sounded too good to be true, something that if not tightly clasped could fly away like the feathery seeds of a dandelion clock.

It turned out the dream was not to be. Frank Miles insisted Maisie took a job in the tobacco factory – for his own ends of course. She'd hated the thought of working in a place like that because its smell would remind her of him. Frank Miles smoked heavily, spent cigarette ends spilled from ashtrays and saucers, littered the fireplace and dusted the few rugs that were in the house. The smell and the mess sickened her, would always be connected with him. It was very much the reason why she didn't smoke herself.

As it turned out, though, she didn't regret joining the workforce at W. D. & H. O. Wills. For the first time in her life, she made good friends there. Phyllis Mason, Bridget Milligan and Maisie Miles; she still couldn't help smiling at their decision to call themselves the three M's. 'Like the Three Musketeers,' Bridget had declared. She'd warmed to them both and thus the factory she hadn't wanted to work in had become central to her world.

Bridget was clever. She read a lot and knew a lot about the history of Bristol. Phyllis was a different kettle of fish entirely. She loved looking glamorous and being admired. She'd had an effervescent personality, except when her fiancée, Robert was around. He liked to be in control, tell her what she should wear, how she should behave. Two weeks before he was due to be posted, they'd married. Both Maisie and Bridget had known that their dear friend was pregnant, though not by Robert. Wanting to improve herself, Phyllis had taken typing lessons and fallen for the man who taught the class. Whilst Robert was away, she'd lost the baby and also received a telegram saying he was missing in action, believed killed. No word came and so it was that she'd joined the Women's Auxiliary Air Force. She was a WAAF.

Sometimes Maisie longed for those early days when the three of them had been so close. It beat what she had at home and the likely prospects in life.

Stepfather Frank had also had it in mind that at some stage she would progress to working in a nightclub owned by a big-time gang leader called Eddie Bridgeman. Eddie had come to their house, and the way he'd looked at her had turned her stomach. She hadn't needed her brother's advice to stay out of his way. She had every intention of doing so, not even shopping him to the coppers when she knew full well that he'd been up to no good. That way, she'd hoped to keep him at bay and enjoy life with her mates at the tobacco factory. The only time she would shop him was if he did something that was totally unpalatable – which he eventually did. Two children had died as a consequence of him dealing in rotten meat on the black market. She'd wanted revenge without being implicated – which was where her grandmother, a known money lender and property owner, had come in. It was Grace Wells who had called in a favour from somebody who owed her money, who also happened to be the grandmother to the two children who had died.

So Frank Miles had been put away for a very long time and Maisie couldn't have been more delighted. The only bugbear was that Eddie Bridgeman was still around. Somehow he'd escaped being called up. She'd heard that a medical could be fixed. He'd likely not gone for the medical but sent somebody unfit in his stead. All she cared was that he stayed out of her way. In the meantime she was happy, though Grace Wells was a strange woman and not altogether whiter than white. She looked just as one expected a grandmother to look with white hair, a round face and a kindly smile. But that was as far as being a typical grandmother went: she was tough as old boots, owned properties, lent money at high interest rates to those who had never stepped across the threshold of a bank. In the past she had also charged unlucky young girls and women with too many mouths to feed for her services but due to her diminishing eyesight abortion in the back room of the house was no longer an option. Maisie liked to think she regretted having carried out such procedures. It helped her live under the same roof more easily and pretend she really was no different a grandma than any other.

The slow creaking of the narrow staircase preceded the arrival of the woman she'd come to both love and respect in equal measure. Both of her hands were wrapped round a mug of cocoa. 'Gone 'as it?'

'Yes,' she said and managed to smile as she took the mug and wrapped her hands round it. 'You were right about the dream. Talking about it helped a lot. But then, you're always right, Gran.'

3

MISS CRAYFORD

Miss Cayford, recruitment supervisor, was thinking about Maisie Miles as she ran through the normal format for the interviewing of school leavers for the tobacco factory. She had three files on her desk, each one relating to the three new recruits sitting in front of her. First things first, though.

'Right. Let me see your hands.'

Two of the girls exchanged surprised glances. The third, who had rarely looked up from her tangled fingers, offered her hands.

'Turn them over.'

The girl, Jane, a homely-looking sort without a trace of make-up on her face, dutifully did as requested.

'Good clean nails,' said Miss Cayford as she looked fixedly at each of them in turn. 'Tobacco is a form of food. You wouldn't prepare food with dirty fingernails and hands, would you now?'

'S'pose not,' said the blonde, Carole.

Miss Cayford had already decided that this girl, who looked far older than her fourteen years, was a know-it-all sort and would need to knuckle down if she was to keep her job. The workforce had been slightly reduced, but if cigarette production was to be maintained, new blood would always be required.

It took time to train people, and what with the call-up, it made sense to take on the younger ones to fill the dropout rate of those joining the forces. Hence the fact that Maisie Miles's file was also on her desk. Maisie was about to be promoted. She was young, but my goodness, she was of strong character.

On first being employed at the factory, she'd been a little shabby, but her hands and face had been beautifully clean. W. D. &. H. O. Wills had very high standards and encouraged improvement. Maisie had certainly improved during her short time with the factory.

The other girl, Pauline, followed Carole's lead, looking at her as she offered her own hands, turning them over in the same casually impudent way as her new colleague was doing.

Her attitude did not go unnoticed by Miss Cayford. 'Do you two know each other?'

The two girls exchanged smiles that fitted their attitudes.

'No. She ain't no friend of mine, but that ain't to say we won't be. Ain't that right?' Carole smiled and winked at Pauline, who seemed to bloom at this easily endowed privilege.

'Do any of you knit?' The sudden question took both Carole and Pauline by surprise.

Carole giggled. 'No.'

Jane querulously raised her hand. 'Yes, Miss.'

The other two sniggered.

'Ah! Good to know that you've got dextrous fingers. We like dextrous fingers here at Wills.' She turned to the others. 'And what about you, Pauline?'

'Yeah. A bit.'

Miss Cayford fancied she saw a tiny flush and knew the defi-

ance in Pauline's lofty head shake was in direct response to
wanting Carole to feel she was on her side; she wanted a buddy
and somebody to lead the way. Pauline was a follower and
easily led.

Carole met Miss Cayford's look with a shifty one. 'Ain't got the
patience. Prefer reading.'

'Oh really,' said Miss Cayford, pleased. Perhaps this girl wasn't
as rebellious as she'd thought. 'What sort of books do you like to
read?'

Carole smirked as she replied. 'Not books. I likes magazines.
Picture Post. Film stars and stuff.'

'I see,' said Miss Cayford, somewhat disappointed. She'd
hoped for some sign of Carole being open to further education.
Her hopes were dashed. 'Right,' said Miss Cayford, closing the
personnel files of the three girls. A decision regarding the super-
vision of the new girls had been made. Maisie's experience from
the air raid had flashed round the factory from one girl to
another. Her heart went out to Maisie. It seemed to Miss Cayford
that the girl needed something to take her mind off things. With
this in mind, she placed the three files to one side and added
Maisie Miles's file on top at a right angle. 'Let's get you settled in,
shall we?'

* * *

It was two weeks following her harrowing experience of being
dangled on the end of a rope, that yet another Monday came
round, and Maisie was thankful that it did. Two weeks wasn't that
long, but enough to ease her nightmares and resume being her
old self.

Tea and toast sat on the breakfast table, there was a fire in the range, and her grandmother seemed perfectly happy providing for the granddaughter who had only lately entered her life.

Whilst running the brush through her tangled locks, Maisie caught sight of her face. A haunted look remained in her eyes and her complexion, usually a warm coffee colour, looked a little paler than usual.

She felt her grandmother's eyes on her. 'You're doing too much. Work and this ambulance driving.'

'I have to.'

'Of course you do.'

The statement was very matter-of-fact. Grace Wells understood where others would not. Like her, Maisie was the sort who fought her way through problems and coped with them. Neither were the sort to crumble into helpless self-pity. Maisie wanted to be busy and do all she could for the war effort.

After swallowing a slice of toast and gulping down sugarless tea, Maisie said a swift goodbye to her grandmother, and headed for the bus stop. Some in the queue for the bus were grumbling about the rain. Some just put up with it as they did everything in this war.

The bus from Totterdown to Bedminster Bridge was packed, the windows steamed up thanks to the wet clothes of those who'd been caught in the morning shower. She heard people talking. Most of it was personal: how difficult it was to stretch the rations, how one of the neighbours was being over friendly with foreign troops.

'There was blacks in the pub the other night from the West Indies. Very polite they were and didn't get drunk.'

'I likes the Canadians meself.'

'Met any Australians 'ave you?'

'No. 'Ave you?'

'No. Bumped into some Polish though. Couldn't understand a word they was sayin'.'

Threaded through it were comments about the latest air raid.

'Fifteen killed, I hear.'

'I heard it was more.'

'Somebody said a black-market pig was found in that raid back at the beginning of this month.'

'Wouldn't mind a pound of bacon from that, no matter the price.'

'Bet that all got fried and roasted weeks ago.'

Laughter followed.

Life went on. People had died, but life went on.

The factory was the same as it always was. Ordinary things were going on there too. Her workmates' chatter was all around, plus the music and news on the wireless.

Announcements came over the factory tannoy system about air-raid duty and a request for volunteers to hoist the barrage balloons in Victoria Park. The lunchtime menu was also announced; yet again liver and onions with mashed potato followed by bread and butter pudding – margarine substituting for butter.

Maisie sighed. She felt strangely alone. The place where Bridget used to sit was unoccupied, as were four other stools. Two of those who'd sat there had married and at their husbands' insistence had left. The other two had been called up and had gone gladly. No more tobacco for them, they'd giggled. Their exuberance at going into uniform had melted away once they'd been told that reveille – getting-up time – was around 5.30 in the morning and that square bashing – marching up and down in ill-fitting shoes was outright torture – not that they'd had a choice.

It had come as no great surprise that Bridget, who had worked at the factory since she'd left school, was trained and promoted to cigarette checking and packing. Before the war, it had constituted two separate jobs, but as the workforce had shrunk it was now a case of one operative carrying out two jobs.

At the same time as Bridget was given promotion, just a few weeks ago, Miss Cayford had approached Maisie about supervising new recruits to the factory.

She was as prepared as she ever would be for the new employees who were starting today. Miss Cayford would bring them along when all the paperwork was in order, just as she'd done when Maisie had started work in Wills's back in 1939.

Being given responsibility for her section hadn't come as a great surprise. When asked what she'd thought of the idea, she'd assured Miss Cayford that she would do her best. Miss Cayford had responded that she didn't doubt it. 'I have great faith in you,' she'd said. 'I know I'm placing a big responsibility onto your shoulders, along with my reputation for delegating to the right people. Please don't let me down.'

'I won't let you down,' returned Maisie, shaking her head emphatically and standing straighter and taller, as though that in itself would make her seem even more deserving of Miss Cayford's trust.

Nothing much fazed her and dealing with immature young girls straight from school who no doubt thought that they knew it all was no exception. Like everything else in her life, she would face it head on and take the new responsibility in her stride.

She had left Miss Cayford's office with a spring in her step. She was no longer the new girl, and although she looked young and slender enough for a good wind to blow her away, she was far from that. She grew up in a tough area of the city and could stand up for herself. Woe betide anyone who thought otherwise.

Entering the stripping room was like taking command of a ship – or what she imagined it was like. She bent over and whispered into Aggie's ear whilst passing. 'I've got to oversee the new girls.'

'Of course you have,' returned Aggie, showing no sign of surprise. Although it was Miss Cayford who had introduced Maisie to working at the factory, it was Aggie who had kept an eye on her, as she did most of her 'chicks', as she called the younger women and girls she worked with.

The lack of surprise was disappointing. Maisie had so wanted her to be surprised and burst with congratulations.

'I know I can do it. I'm not too young or too small,' Maisie said as if that was the reason for Aggie's less than enthusiastic response. Though she harboured few misgivings, she craved Aggie's encouragement.

Aggie Hill was a big person with a big heart. She was motherly towards all the girls, but especially to Maisie, who had lived with her for a while at the Llandoger, the pub she ran with her husband Curly– before local gangster Eddie Bridgeman had dropped in. That was when Maisie moved in with her grandmother – anything to avoid Eddie. But Aggie still had a soft spot for the girl who had looked forlorn and lost when she'd first come to the factory.

Aggie reassured her. 'No, you ain't too young or too small. You might be only pint-size, but I wouldn't cross you,' laughed Aggie, her big belly wobbling, her arms holding up a sack of tobacco leaves as though they weighed no more than a few ounces. But then Aggie could do that. She was a big woman with big arms and hands that could just as well wring the neck of a man as that of a chicken.

Now alone at her workstation waiting for the new arrivals, Maisie pondered on all the changes that had happened. Bridget now worked in the packing department and Phyllis had joined the Women's Auxiliary Air Force. The factory workforce had been reduced to coincide with its falling supply of tobacco. The Atlantic was crawling with enemy submarines. Ships carrying tobacco from America, Rhodesia and India were all fair game for German torpedoes and although they were receiving some supplies, they were greatly reduced, food and armaments having priority. It was agreed by all that they were having a hard time.

The letter that had arrived from Phyllis had lifted their spirits:

'I'm aiming to be stationed abroad, hopefully somewhere warm where there's plenty of food and no air raids. I'd like blue seas and warm sunshine...'

The letter had been passed round and it was agreed by everyone that life outside the factory walls sounded wonderful. But Maisie wasn't so sure. The factory was like a second home, definitely a big improvement than the one in which she'd grown up. Perhaps if she'd had Phyllis's life with Robert – the husband from hell as far as she was concerned – she might have thought differently.

Maisie looked up as Miss Cayford approached, the three new recruits trailing in her wake. Smiles were exchanged and it occurred to her that Miss Cayford had not been left untouched by their present circumstances. She was definitely looking a little older now, thick shanks of grey wiry hair threading back from her forehead into the original dark brown. She was a very private person, so nobody really knew anything of her personal life. However, she was a good sort. It was her who had initially inducted Maisie when she'd first arrived at the tobacco factory and now instructed her to oversee the new girls.

'Carole, Pauline and Jane are new here. I know I can trust you to show them the ropes just, like Bridget and Phyllis did when you first started.'

Miss Cayford's smile was warm, but Maisie sensed flattery in an effort to encourage her to take on extra responsibility. There would be a slight increase in wages, though not enough to compensate doing her job. There was also, of course, the extra responsibility of war work. Miss Cayford was also required to put in the same effort, holding down her day job plus doing whatever else in the way of war work required of her. It was rumoured that she was also looking after aged parents.

Miss Cayford, a gold ring with a red stone flashing, waved her hand towards Maisie by way of introduction. 'This is Maisie Miles. She'll get you settled in and show you what you must do. I've already shown you the cloakroom and canteen, but Maisie will point you in the right direction should you get lost,' said Miss Cayford. 'Over to you, Maisie.'

Maisie managed a weak smile.

'Don't hesitate to come along to my office if you have any problems,' Miss Cayford added.

Maisie took the list detailing the girls' names and thanked her. For a brief moment her eyes met those of the older woman before she was left to her own devices.

'Right then. Let's all get to know each other, shall we? I'm Maisie Miles. Now this isn't a hard job, it's just a bit boring. Same thing over and over again; strip tobacco leaves, throw the stalks to one side and put the leaves into a basket.'

They gave no sign of whether they'd understood or not, though one of them looked totally bored even before she'd done anything.

A varied bunch, she thought as she studied the new arrivals. One girl shivered like a blancmange, so was obviously nervous. Another looked bewildered and the girl with the folded arms looked hostile. All three were not long out of school, just as she had been when first starting, and she couldn't help but empathise with each of them and their feelings. All the same, she knew they would try her – or at least one of them would.

Here goes, she thought, glancing at the list Miss Cayford had handed her. She took a deep breath and fixed all three with a very firm and direct look.

'Right. Which of you is Carole Thomas?'

'Me.'

Ah. Miss Hostile!

Carole Thomas was the only one of them who didn't look like a frightened mouse about to scamper into the nearest hole. She stood defiantly, a snooty, disdainful look on her face. Light blonde, almost white curls, escaped from her scarf and framed her face too prettily to be by accident. From what Maisie could see of the colour, it didn't seem natural.

Surprisingly, she was wearing lipstick, which brought a frown to Maisie's face. She couldn't help recalling her first day, when Miss Cayford had insisted Phyllis go to the cloakroom and wash hers off, but that was before the war. Like everyone else, Miss Cayford was too busy to worry about trivialities. Without meaning to, things were getting overlooked and of late she had seemed distracted – even a bit shabbier than of yore. Word was that her house had been hit back in the January raid, but she was a very private person and not one to share details of her home life.

It was patently obvious to Maisie that the would-be blonde bombshell was setting her stall as ringleader of this little clique. Nothing new about that, of course.

The second girl wasn't blonde but she was similar in build, had mouse-coloured hair and perhaps could look pretty if she dabbled in make-up. If ever a girl was destined to be a disciple of Carole Thomas, it was this one, and that, thought Maisie, will be trouble.

Swinging her hips, Carole threw a challenge. 'Ain't you a bit young to be in charge of us?' Her expression was truculent and she spoke in a tone that suggested a mistake had been made.

Maisie was prepared that they might presume that she was not much older than they were – which was true, but Maisie had the experience of work.

She adopted an air and a tone of authority. 'I ain't as young as you, an' I know more than you do.' She purposely fixed Carole with a warning look. 'Got any objections to that?'

Still folding her arms in a defensive manner, Carole held her head to one side, a rebellious pose meant to intimidate, though if she'd known anything of Maisie's background, she would realise she was going up a dead end. 'Worked 'ere long, 'ave you?' Her tone was close to contemptuous.

'None of your bloody business, but since you ask, long enough to tell you how to do the job,' returned Maisie. 'Unless you bin 'ere before and know what to do.'

Carole didn't actually quell at the rebuke, but for a fraction of a second there was a touch of rancour in the flashing eyes and a flickering of the heavily mascaraed lashes.

She wasn't to know, and was not likely to find out, that Maisie had grown up in a rough area amongst rough people, where bullying was a given side effect of poverty. Everyone wanted to be cock of the walk, the one who grabbed it all, the one who'd fight for what was due to them, the one who would steal from his or her neighbour to have a better life – or even just to survive. She could most definitely cope with the likes of this little madam.

Carole wasn't the sort to give up easily. It wasn't long before she yet again stood on her own self-importance. 'So we're to sit here,' she asked in a lofty, rebellious manner. Her gaze flicking over the table and stools with nothing short of contempt.

'That's the idea,' said Maisie. She curbed the urge to smile.

Carole, like others before her, thought their defiance something new. She was wrong. Young girls like her were nothing new. In time, they'd settle down and work here for years or decide they hated it and move on. Some never left until marrying, though because of the war some were staying on even after marrying.

Looking thoroughly bored though beaten, Carole tugged a stool from beneath the table. She turned up her nose and flicked at the seat.

'It is clean,' said Maisie.

The pert and perfectly formed nose sniffed with undisguised disdain. 'Well, I don't know who's bin sitting on it, do I.'

'My best friend used to sit on it,' said Maisie. She clenched her fists and maintained her calm expression, though, goodness, she would so like to wipe the contempt off Carole's over-made-up face. 'You can work standin' up if you like and 'ave the varicose veins that go with it. Not very pretty; makes you look old and ugly before yer time.'

A chewing of lips preceded Carole giving in, though she couldn't help offering one last dig before she did. 'Don't look very comfortable, though I s'pose it'll 'ave to do.' She sat herself down heavily and began drumming her fingers impatiently on the table. 'For now, until I'm old enough to get called up.'

'If the war's still going by then,' said Maisie. 'You reaching eighteen is a bit far off yet.'

'Then I will as soon as I can. You can bet on that.'

I wouldn't bet on it, thought Maisie whilst fixing her with a hard and incisive look. Things could go either way with any girl as time went on. The options were clear; get knocked up in the family way or knock off because you're too old to work. For no discernible reason, her mind went back to the mother and child buried alive in a bombed-out house. The presence of the pig would have lightened the moment if it hadn't been for the dead bodies.

It was with difficulty that she shook off the dark thoughts and forced herself back to the present. She reckoned she had Carole sussed. She was the sort who could twist men round her little finger. Not only that but she influenced those less intelligent and more gullible than herself. And that was it, thought Maisie, and tried not to frown as she considered the reason why. Carole seemed intelligent enough, but why did she act like she did?

Memories of her own home life intervened. She'd had a defiant streak when she'd started here and a terrible home life. Perhaps so too did Carole Thomas.

Well, she ain't one to open up to the likes of me or anyone else in a position to tell her what to do – boss her around! Her private life's her own business. Never mind. Let's see how we go on and cross them bridges one by one, Maisie decided.

Pasting on a warm smile that matched her businesslike expression, she swallowed and went on to the next name.

'Pauline Goddard? Not Paulette then,' she added with a smile that felt too stiff and contrived to be real, but she had to make the effort. Throwing in a little humour would make everyone feel better. The joke and inference was that with a surname like Goddard, she might have been named after the film star, Paulette Goddard.

None of them smiled, though Jane did glance up and for a moment Maisie was sure she saw a slight tweaking at the corners of her mouth.

The joke was lost on the person she'd aimed it at. Pauline looked totally blank.

'Nah. It's Pauline. *Pauline* Goddard.' She threw a 'aren't I clever' kind of look at Carole. The smallest vestige of a smile lifted the sides of Carole's mouth before she folded her arms. Maisie wasn't that surprised to see Pauline follow suit.

With mousy brown hair and blue-grey eyes, Pauline was taller than the other two and although she had looked a little nervous on first arriving, she wasn't now. What she was doing, and Maisie could see this very well, was copying everything Carole did.

Silly girl, thought Maisie, who'd never been one for copying anyone. *And not that pretty*, she decided. Pauline's face was an overlong oval and completely devoid of make-up. Judging by her expression, she was craving approval from the blonde girl she'd only just met.

'Take a seat, Pauline.'

Pauline looked at Carole, who had deigned to sit down after brushing imaginary dirt off the stool. The fact she'd done that irritated Maisie no end, because it had been Bridget's stool, in fact she still thought of it that way.

'No need to look at Carole. She's not the one in charge 'ere, I am.'

Pauline gulped but after a sidelong look at Carole flicked at the seat of the stool.

I've got you taped, thought Maisie, her eyes narrowing as she took in every detail suggesting rebellion. The arched eyebrows, the plump lips that curved at the corners in a way that suggested the world didn't meet up to her design.

Jane Goode was the third girl. Slightly plump with rose-red cheeks and big frightened eyes, she was the sort of girl who was never sought out by others on the basis of friendship. Her hands were buried in the pockets of her overall, which was hanging in a lopsided manner, buttons in the wrong buttonholes.

Maisie pointed it out to her. 'You've got your buttons in the wrong 'oles.' Then wished she hadn't.

Carole had heard her. She made a snorting noise. 'I used to do that when I was five.'

A slight sniggering came from Carole. Yet again, Pauline followed suit, which confirmed to Maisie that one girl would always be pliable to her charms and likely to ape her behaviour.

On seeing an intense flush come to Jane's already pink cheeks, Maisie attempted to repair her mistake. She addressed Jane in a gentle and sympathetic tone. 'Never mind, love. I was nervous on me first day too and did the same. Even worse, I was wearing me slippers! How daft was that, eh?'

It was utter nonsense of course; she'd not owned a pair of slippers back then, though she did now, thanks to Granny Wells. She was just attempting to put this girl at ease.

Schoolgirlish sniggers continued from the other two.

Maisie immediately rounded on them. 'You,' she said, pointing a finger at Carole. 'You ain't a film star. You're 'ere to work, so tuck them curls back under yer scarf and wipe that lipstick off yer face. It ain't allowed.'

'Nobody said I couldn't wear lipstick,' Carole replied defiantly, her features no longer pretty but twisted with what Maisie could only interpret as hate. 'I won't stay if I can't wear me lipstick.'

'Why are you here then?'

The question caught her off guard and for a moment she looked stumped. 'The money,' she said at last.

Maisie smiled. 'Yes. Wills's pay factory workers better than any other firm in this city. So think yerself lucky. Keep the lipstick an' all that make-up and lose yer job.' She nodded at Carole's painted nails and snapped. 'I only 'ope them nails is clean beneath that finger paint or you'll be leaving this job before you've even started it. For now we'll begin with the lipstick. Get to the lavs and clean it off or else.'

The pugnacious thrust of Carole's chin said a lot and if her eyes had been daggers, Maisie would have been skewered to the wall.

Pauline looked a little bewildered, as though considering which way to fall.

Maisie recognised Carole's power. In time, as an acolyte to the glamorous Carole, Pauline too might be trouble. In the meantime Jane looked a bit happier. She had someone looking after her and she was glad of that.

Thanks to the blackout, it was pitch dark, so nobody saw Carole Thomas sitting there crying her heart out.

Other people hated the blackout, but she didn't. It meant she could air her emotions without anyone seeing her. She would hate anyone from the factory to see that although hard on the outside, she was soft as butter inside. She had no friends and no real social life outside of the factory. Staying at home in Sally Lane was fine when her mother wasn't 'doing business', but a nightmare when she was. Sometimes a client gave her some money to make herself scarce; sometimes her mother did. Of late, the eyes of some clients had lingered on her young body, her pert breasts and flowing hips. Her mother wasn't liking that.

"Ere's sixpence. Clear off and get yerself some scrumps from the chippy. I ain't 'ad time to do you any tea.'

Carole had always accepted that her mother was not the same as other mothers. That didn't mean to say she didn't love her. Her mother was very different when the men weren't around.

'Come 'ere, darlin'. Let me make you up to look like a film star.'

She'd worn make-up from a young age and was used to it. Once her figure started to develop, her mother had dressed her in some of her own dresses. They were far too adult for a young girl, but her mother encouraged her and Carole would do anything to please her.

The trouble was that things had changed recently. Of late, Carole had the task of retouching her mother's greying hair. At one time, it had been only a shade or two darker than white blonde, but threads of grey were showing through. Deep wrinkles round her mouth had become deeper, more so when her once full lips were pursed round a cigarette. Red nail lacquer clashed with fingertips tarnished yellow by nicotine.

In the past she'd looked up to her mother. Despite everything she'd been the centre of her world. Things were changing fast and so was Carole. Her reflection in the mirror told her that she was better looking than her mother and it gave her confidence. She was now aware that her mother was becoming more testy than she used to be. The daughter was becoming a threat.

Tonight one of her mother's 'friends' had looked her up and down as he'd taken off his hat and coat. 'Blimey, Carole. Ain't you grown.' He'd turned to her mother and said, 'So when you retiring, Mav? When's the little lady takin' over?'

Ignoring the tense tightening of her mother's expression, Carole had laughed and posed like her mother did when it was just the two of them. Placing her hand on her hip, she'd sashayed in front of the fireplace. 'Come on in, stranger. Make yerself at 'ome.' She even threw a wink at the man who was one of those she'd been obliged to call 'uncle' in the past.

'You little tart!'

The slap and name calling had shocked her so much she'd burst into tears.

It stung. Nobody at work would have believed how she'd

reacted, how hurt she'd been. At work, just as when she'd been at school, was where she was confident and like a flame to a host of dull-looking moths. Not butterflies. Butterflies were pretty. Just moths.

'I didn't mean anything. I was just playing about...' she'd cried, tears running rivers down her face.

Her mother had stabbed a finger in her direction, eyes ablaze with anger. 'I want you out the 'ouse.'

Where to go?

Nowhere until her tears had dried, then, taking note of her rumbling stomach, she spent her sixpence at the fish and chip shop. Wrapped in newspaper, the bundle warmed her hands. If she wasn't feeling so hungry, she might have continued to hold it.

Angry more so than hurt, she made her way to an alley off East Street, down two steps to a ridge of rough stone set into the wall. The alley was her refuge, pitch black, a denser blackness than the blackout, where she was rarely disturbed.

Though she heard people walking by, nobody could see her and she couldn't see them. Before the war, the muted flame of a Victorian wall-mounted gas lantern would have thrown out enough light to see by. But not now. The blackout was total. Nobody could see her here; nobody could see the little girl that still lurked beneath the hard surface.

As a child, she'd been nothing more than a kid to be sent out of the way whilst her mother entertained men who gave her money. The neighbours might turn their heads when her mother walked by, but she held hers high, wore nice clothes and still had her own teeth.

Carole reckoned that was what rankled most with the neighbours. Many women of her mother's age were old before their time worn out with childbearing, husbands who didn't always earn a wage and drank the money away when they did.

It was only a short while ago that Carole realised things had changed. She was growing up. The men were no longer thinking of her as a nuisance but comparing her youthful freshness to her mother's fading beauty.

From a very young age, her mother had told her to be nice to men. It was their world; they earned the best wages and were to be looked up to. With the total trust of a small child, she'd hung on to every word her mother said and did everything she encouraged her to do; to sway her hips, pout her lips as though ready for a kiss, to wink as though she had something very secret to share with them.

It had seemed nothing more than a game back then and she'd bathed in her mother's approval, her laughter as she'd played at being an adult. The laughter had stopped. Where there'd been encouragement, there was now jealousy. She was no longer a child but a rival.

Once the last chip and crispy scrump was gone, she crumpled up the paper with both hands. Just as she was about to throw it on the ground, she heard footsteps.

It wouldn't be the first time that somebody had entered the alley. It was a well-known short cut between East Street and Dean Lane. Most footsteps just carried on through, though on more than one occasion a couple had stopped and she'd heard them breathless with lust.

The footsteps landed flat and even, lacking the tap-tap-tap the heels of a woman's shoes would make.

When the sound stopped, Carole held her breath. He was close by. She couldn't so much hear him breathing, but she could hear him sighing impatiently, as though he was waiting for someone.

Intrigued and a little fearful, she kept absolutely still, hoping all the while that he didn't know about the place where she was sitting.

She heard him grumble about somebody being late. 'Come on, Eddie, for chrissake!'

Eddie. The name struck a chord. Wasn't that somebody her mother had known? The man she used to work for at the night-club? That was back when she was younger, when Carole hadn't been turned out on the street at night. She'd stayed at home, mostly alone, because her mother had worked nights.

It was only minutes before another set of footsteps, just as even and heavy as the first set, entered the alley.

'Eddie?'

Carole held her breath. Eddie. She recalled the rest of his name: Eddie Bridgeman. Everyone had heard of Eddie Bridgeman.

'You're late.' It was the first man speaking.

'I'm a busy man, Claude. You ain't the only business I got tonight.' The tone of the second man was surly and dark with menace.

Aware he might have overstepped the mark, the man referred to as Claude sniggered nervously. 'Course you 'ave, Eddie.' Another nervous chuckle. 'You're an important man. Got yer finger in a lot of pies. I appreciate you coming along to see me. I really do.'

Carole sensed a brittle flattery fused with fear. There'd been times when she'd heard that same tone in her mother's voice. Not all customers were kind. Some liked raising a fist to a woman. The trick was to massage their ego and thus hope the blow would never fall. That's what Claude was doing to Eddie.

She sensed they were facing each other, not much distance between them. This was confirmed by the glow from a lit cigarette and the smell of smoke. It barely lit their faces enough to see their features, but enough to make them out.

Eddie, the second man, was standing between the first and the alley entrance behind him.

'Don't s'pose you got a spare fag...?' Claude asked.

'No I ain't. Let's get down to business. So what you got?' There was no denying Eddie's tone, sharp enough to cut stone.

A torch was brought out and shone onto a leather bag which Claude opened.

Carole barely breathed. The slightest sound and the torch would shine on her.

A fistful of jewellery dripped between masculine fingers sparkled and twinkled in torchlight. A thick bracelet was picked up and held up for closer perusal. Both the beam of light and everyone's eyes – including those of Carole – were trained on glittering items dripping from Claude's fingers. The details were indistinct, but she caught the creamy luminescence of pearl drop earrings held between finger and thumb, plus a tangle of gold, silver and pearl necklaces wrapped round a thick wrist.

She fancied a moment of scrutiny on the part of Eddie. 'Not a bad haul. Seems you was doin' your duty the right night, Claude.'

'I was lucky,' Claude chortled. 'It was that posh 'otel where all the knobs go. Lying all over the place, they were.'

'Auxiliary firemen to the rescue, eh, Claude. The rescue of valuables, I mean.' A malignant humour suffused Eddie's tone.

'Well, they wouldn't be wantin' 'em, would they? Their dancin' days were over.'

Carole tried hard not to gasp at what she was hearing. She'd heard rumours that some auxiliary rescuers were a bit light-fingered, looting anything they could from property – even the dead. It was hard to believe, but hearing what she was hearing now confirmed everything.

'Right. We'll say fifty.'

'That's a bit tight, Eddie. I was thinkin' more of seventy-five.'

'Fifty. Take it or leave it.' His voice was clipped suggesting that was as far as he was going to go.

'You're robbing me.'

'I might not be able to shift 'em for some time. They're a bit 'ot and I don't just mean because they'd got caught in an air raid.'

'OK, OK. I'll take it.'

There was a sudden rushing of movement, the stolen jewellery going in one direction and a roll of pound notes passing from Eddie Bridgeman's hand into that of the thief named Claude.

Sickened and scared by what she'd heard, Carole stayed hidden in the darkness. What could she do about it? Who could she tell? Her thoughts were confused. For now at least she would keep things to herself.

BRIDGET AND MAISIE

First there was the announcement that the huge bomb that had fallen on Creswicke Road, Knowle, but failed to explode back at the beginning of January was the largest ever to be dropped in England. It had been safely defused, christened Satan and placed in storage until a decision was made on what to do with it.

The next announcement to come over the factory loud-speaker was just as interesting, perhaps more so.

'As many of you will be aware, W. D. &. H. O. Wills have supplied two ambulances to help in the aftermath of bombing raids. Many of our male drivers have been called up, so we're calling on women willing to learn how to drive an ambulance. It's open to anyone over the age of seventeen, though preference will be given to those of nineteen or more.'

Maisie's ears pricked up. 'Well, that's me sorted!' Down went a bunch of unstrapped leaves, slap bang on the table. 'Now I can really help.'

Up until now, women had only been required to act as assistants, lugging the first-aid equipment round, deemed the most suitable job for a woman. Anyway, not many women drove anything – but they were fast catching up. More and more women were driving emergency vehicles, buses, even trains given half the chance. Rumour was that there were women driving under-ground trains in London and women were fast replacing men on the buses, especially clippies. This was the first time the factory had asked for volunteers to drive the ambulances they sponsored to help in the emergency.

'I'm going for that,' Maisie said out loud, then addressed the three young girls under her charge. 'Fancy taking my place doing the first aid?'

'I ain't got the time,' said a haughty-voiced Carole. 'Anyway, I don't fancy tramping round bomb sites. They're not nice. Bits of bodies everywhere.'

Pauline glanced at the more outward-going Carole with almost hero worship before following her lead and stating that she too hadn't the time.

Jane was the odd one out, blushing profusely before saying she would love to. 'I'll put my name down. Six weeks' training, isn't it?'

'Only four weeks now,' returned Maisie with a grimace. 'The faster we get people trained up, the better. I'll make sure you get a place.' Her expression hardened when she looked at the other two. 'Glad we got somebody 'ere who ain't afraid of goin' into the thick of things. Still, not everybody's that brave, are they? There's always the girly girls!'

Carole's jaw dropped, and although her face flushed with anger, she held back.

Pauline looked confused, unsure of what was insinuated but reluctant to relinquish her position as Carole's loyal sidekick.

Carole had a more petulant look this morning and although she was still offish with Jane, she didn't seem to have quite so much to say.

At tea break, Maisie met up with Bridget in the canteen and asked if she'd heard the announcement. Bridget said that she had and her eyes were bright with intent.

'Shall we? I mean I'd love to drive and let somebody else pull on that ruddy bell. Wish we had an electric one like proper ambulances.'

'We are proper ambulances,' snapped an indignant Maisie. She frowned. The raid of January the third had lasted for twelve hours. There'd been a few others after that and likely there would be more.

Bridget shrugged and made so-so movements with her head. 'You know what I mean. Anyway, the word is that Harry's been called up and Fred's opted out. He's willing to teach driving but reckons he's getting too old to do active duty during a raid. And my eyesight's better than his. Oh, this is so exciting,' gushed Bridget, her face bright with enthusiasm.

Maisie sighed. 'I did try and convince my new girls to do the first-aid course. Jane was the only one willing to give it a go. The other two seem to be in their own worlds.' She frowned. 'Carole was a bit more subdued than usual this morning. Haven't asked her why and don't intend to. Likely only get me 'ead bitten off. You know what, I get the impression that the more I ignore Carole, the more she tries to please me.'

'You think she admires you?' asked Bridget.

Maisie frowned. 'Something like that.' She grinned suddenly. 'Makes me feel like I'm 'er mother.'

Bridget laughed. 'Well that'll be a first!'

'Oh well. At least they're not picking on Jane. Things seem to 'ave evened out in that respect. I reckon it won't be long before they do the first aid course too. I'll be pleased if they do.'

'I hope they do. We have to do our duty – all we can to get this blasted war over with as soon as possible.'

They exchanged looks that portrayed their mutual willing-ness to do whatever they could to help. By choice, at least for the time being, they were not in uniform, though that didn't mean they wouldn't be called up at some stage. The older they got and the longer the war continued, the more chance there was of that happening and neither of them would shirk their duty.

Maisie took a deep breath. 'I'm no soldier, but I'll damn well do all I bloody well can to beat this bloke Hitler. Damned devil he is and 'as got to be stopped, so I'm up for it if you are.'

'I'm up for it,' said Bridget. 'One for all and all for one,' she said and clinked her tea cup with Maisie's.

Maisie pointed out that there were only two of them now, not three. 'We ain't the three musketeers any more. We're only two. It's quiet without Phyllis.'

Bridget's eyes shone with secretive energy. 'We are still the three M's, but not all in the same place. And even when the time comes and we're called up, it doesn't matter where we are, we'll still be the tobacco girls.' Suddenly, as if remembering something, her pale pink lips curled into a cheerful smile. Still bright-eyed, she reached into her overall pocket and pulled out an envelope. 'It's another letter from Phyllis.'

'Give it here!' Maisie couldn't wait to read it.

Dear Bridget and Maisie,

This is your old mate, Aircraftwoman Phyllis who used to strip tobacco leaves alongside her very best friends at W. D. &. H. O. Wills, but is now doing things she never felt herself capable of as a member of the Women's Auxiliary Air Force, the WAAF for short.

I'm missing you buckets but so wanted to share with you how I'm getting on in this new and so different air force life. As if it wasn't enough to have had two names in my life – the one I was born with and my married name – I now have a number which I had to memorise. I won't give you that number for now; truth is, it's been stressed on me to remember it. Because of that I've come to fear letting anyone know what it is, almost as though it was part of the crown jewels and likely to be stolen by thieves and cut-throats. Can't tell anybody including you two.

I feel I'm changing into somebody different than what I was, or perhaps I always was that person but nobody let me out of the box, determined to keep me in my place.

I mentioned in that short note I sent you that I wanted to serve abroad. Well, I kept on and it's happened. Everyone told me there was no chance, that it's only officer rank. Well, that's what I now am – an officer, and it's all thanks to my typing speed, though it isn't just typing I'm doing. Fast fingers are required to do a lot of things in the Royal Air Force. Us WAAFs are there to support the men with paperwork and ground communications. The fact that I can type at ninety to one hundred words a minute brought a lot to bear on their decision.

So that's it. I'm off to my posting in three days. I'm not allowed to tell you where I'm going until I get there or at least some of the way there. Part of me is relieved to be leaving my past behind, though that doesn't apply to my best mates at W. D. &. H. O. Wills of course. I'm missing you like mad. I'm also hoping that my mother-in-law got run over by a train on that day when you two came to see me off and she turned up like a bad penny. Anyway, although being in uniform is exciting, I do miss my old life. I never considered tearing apart tobacco leaves as hard work, not when I had all that friendship, gossip and laughter going on around me. I certainly didn't get orders barked at me every two minutes as I do here.

I'm in a strange new world but will write frequently to tell you what it's like and what I'm doing. In the meantime, I would appreciate you, my very best friends, telling me what's going on in the factory, especially the stripping room. Is there any juicy gossip? Naughty goings-on? In which case please let me know by return of post. Newspapers are all very well, but they stick to reporting about the war. I am starved of news of good old Bristol and the people I call my friends.

Please take note; you two might remain in Blighty and me wherever I end up, but we're still the Three Ms, Mason (I still am that at heart), Miles and Milligan – the Three Musketeers. All for one and one for all. I've got that right, haven't I, Bridget? Miss all your book-reading cleverness, Bridget. Miss your cheekiness, Maisie.

Stay safe.

Your old mate, Phyllis!

'Crikey,' exclaimed Maisie. 'Wish I was with 'er.' She rested her face in her hands and gazed off into the distance. 'I ain't never bin abroad. Don't know that I want to though.'

'Not many people have.'

'I might go one day, but fer now I'll stay right 'ere in Bristol.'

Bridget thought about what her father had said about his wartime experiences, how frightening it had been and so terribly cruel. Abroad might be a very nice place, but in a war? She wasn't sure it was a very good idea. It was dangerous enough being at home. 'I'm happy staying home. We do our bit and we'll be doing a bit more if we learn how to drive.'

Maisie's response was hesitant. 'Driving an ambulance is all very well – the next step to a uniform if you like – but nothin' like what she's doin'. It all sounds so glamorous.'

'You're not usually into glamour – not like Phyllis is. Nobody ever measures up to her,' she added quickly, not wishing for one minute to upset the girl who was now her dearest friend.

Maisie stirred the single lump of sugar allowed into her tea. 'I've only been as far as Weston on the firm's coach outing. Never been on a train or a boat. As for an aeroplane... well, fat chance I'd say.'

'You mean Weston-super-Mare.' Bridget had a thing for using proper names.

'I ain't a posh person and I'm Bristolian, so it's Weston to me. Wessen, if you wants it proper.'

Bridget laughed. 'Anyway, we were talking about Phyllis. I don't think anywhere abroad is safe.'

'Still she's 'ere for now, I suppose at one of them RAF stations. In the countryside, ain't they? That's where lady RAF's go ain't it?'

'Not all of them.' Bridget had a head for geography – in fact she had a pretty good knowledge of most things. She knew the big bomber stations were mostly situated in East Anglia where the land was flat and thus suitable for heavy aircraft to take off. To some extent, Phyllis would be out of harm's way, but there were no guarantees. She frowned suddenly. 'As glamorous as it might sound to go abroad, she could end up somewhere dangerous.'

A sudden frown creased Maisie's face. 'Shame we can't find out where she is.'

Bridget's mind switched to things closer to home.

'You're thinking of your chap,' Maisie said suddenly. 'You get a faraway look in your eyes when yer thinkin' of 'im.'

Bridget felt her cheeks warming. Maisie had a knack of reading people's expressions. It was unnerving but also a bit like having a second train of thought that cared where your reflections might be heading – just in case they shouldn't be.

Her blush deepened as her mind went back to that first time, the sweet innocence of it; the first man who had stirred something inside she'd vowed would not be stirred.

'I still remember when I first met him. I was lying there in the medical room pretending to be a patient when a whole host of VIPs came round – including Lyndon O'Neill.'

Meeting him had happened shortly after being present at her mother's miscarriage and vowing that she would never give birth, which also meant that she wouldn't fall in love and neither would she marry. Things had gradually altered after meeting Lyndon.

My, but how often had she read 'Finest Virginia' on a tin of tobacco or a packet of cigarettes? A lot of times. Never in her wildest dreams had she ever expected to meet up with anyone from America, especially the son of a plantation owner.

He'd gone back to the States at the outbreak of war, and even though his mother had done her best to end their friendship and even to propose he married the spoilt daughter of an old friend, it hadn't worked. Lyndon had got his father to assist him in his crazy plan to return to England. Luckily for him, his father had friends in high places.

'How long will it take us to learn how to drive an ambulance?' Maisie said suddenly, choosing to change the subject, partly because the letter from Phyllis had made her more determined than ever to get involved. The other reason was that Bridget had got that far away look in her eyes; she was thinking about Lyndon, missing him, wishing he would come back to England.

Bridget's head jerked up sharply. She had been thinking of Lyndon but also attempting to read the headlines on the newspaper in the hands of a charge hand at the next table. Reports of air raids on other British cities dominated the headlines. There was also something about fire-watching being mandatory – well, W. D. &. H. O. Wills had certainly jumped the gun on that! Both of them had done a stint up on the roof armed with a bucket of sand and a stirrup pump.

Maisie's lips fixed in a firm line that ultimately turned into a smile. 'Could be I might even 'ave me own car after the war. What do you think of that?'

Bridget smiled. 'I'll believe it when I see it. Hello,' she said in a quieter voice. 'Looks as though we've got company.'

Carole had a purposeful look about her as she marched towards where Bridget and Maisie were sitting. Pauline was right behind her, just beyond her shoulder like a permanent shadow.

'I'm putting me name down for the first aid course. So's Pauline.'

Maisie feigned surprise. 'Really? I thought you were too busy. Had second thoughts, 'ave you?'

'I can fit it in. Anyways, got to do our bit, ain't we.'

'Very commendable of you,' said a smiling Bridget, doing her best not to laugh whilst thinking what Maisie had told her and how pleased she'd be.

'Well that was a turn-up,' said Maisie after they'd shoved off.

A more serious expression turned Bridget's eyes a more greenish blue. 'Let's face it: if we get any more air raids like the last few, we're going to need all the help we can get.'

Before the war, Sundays in the Milligan household in Marksbury Road constituted a relaxing routine despite it being crowded with her two parents, Bridget and her four sisters and two brothers

Things had changed. Bridget's younger brothers and sisters had been evacuated to South Molton sometime ago in the days after the defeat of Dunkirk and the onset of the Bristol Blitz, which had begun in earnest in November, followed by two more raids in December. There'd been an odd hope that a new year might bring some improvement, but unfortunately there'd been more raids.

Despite them missing their children, Bridget's parents had decided it best that they stay where they were. One thing that did lift their spirits was that their eldest boy, Sean, was shortly to turn fourteen and would be home to start work. Not that he wanted to come home and get a job. According to his letters, he wanted to stay on at the farm as an apprentice labourer, but both his father and mother advised caution. Farm work was hard and there was no future for a labourer.

Bridget had seen her father standing behind her mother, his

hand on her shoulder as she fought to stop her tears falling on the paper.

'It's for the best, Mary me love. He's not a baby. He'll be shaving before very long.'

Mary Milligan's grip on the fountain pen that had once been her father's tightened. 'That's a silly thing to say.'

Patrick Milligan sighed. 'Could be worse. He could be eighteen.'

The meaning of his words hit home. He was saying that if he was eighteen, there would be no argument about what he would do for a living. He would be called up.

Bridget's mother got to her feet, put the top on her pen and shoved both it and the writing pad into a sideboard drawer. 'I'm going to mass. A prayer or two won't come amiss.'

Her father rolled his eyes, not disparagingly but helplessly, as though there was nothing more he could say or do. 'I could do with a pint,' he murmured and headed to where his hat and coat hung from a peg in the tiny hallway at the bottom of the stairs which led to the three bedrooms.

The sound of Mary Milligan's footsteps sounded from the stairs and then overhead.

Bridget smiled sadly to herself. It was Sunday, so her mother wouldn't dream of going to church wearing her everyday coat that she wore for shopping.

Once back down, she pulled on her gloves and told Bridget that she was welcome to come if she wanted to.

Bridget shook her head and declined. 'You go, Mum. I've got everything under control.'

'You're a good girl, Bridie,' her mother said, using the pet name that only the family tended to use. 'I don't know what I would do without you.'

Once she was alone in the kitchen with only the Sunday meal for company, Bridget brushed a tear or two from her eyes.

'Just the onion,' she muttered to herself. Their next-door neighbour Mr Grimes had brought it in at the same time as a cabbage, plus a bunch of sage. He was a good gardener. It was a shame her father wasn't, but bartering had become a way of life. Mr Grimes gave them what he could, in exchange for her father mending an old pocket watch that had once belonged to Mr Grimes's grandfather. Everyone helped everyone else. That was how it was.

Getting lunch ready passed the time. Roast potatoes and a stuffed ox heart both covered in the skin of a bacon joint they'd had during the week were soon spitting away in the oven. Even once it was cooked, the fat it generated would be saved for pastry or adding a bit of flavour to more off-ration offal. Cabbage, carrots and dried peas cooked on the gas rings. Even though the lids were on each saucepan, as per government guidance in order to use less gas, steam still escaped and hit the ceiling, where it hung in droplets until running down the walls as condensation.

She cooked everything in the manner her mother had taught her and although the meat was hardly the best and cooking fat was rationed, the smell was appetising. No matter the deprivations, the Sunday roast would be enjoyed and nothing on earth could prevent that.

* * *

Sunday mass usually went on for an hour and half and on this particular morning Mary Milligan saw old friends and stopped for a chat at the church gate before heading for home.

The wind was cold and she was forced to hold her hat on her

head with one hand whilst her good Sunday coat flapped round her legs.

She was thinking of Bridget and her relationship with the young American, Lyndon O'Neill. It was easy to approve of his name of course, but the fact that he was both American and rich worried her. There'd been a young man in her own life like that once whom she'd thought was the love of her life. It had come to nothing – except heartache.

No point dwelling on it, she thought and ducked her head into the wind and quickened her steps.

The Methodists were also coming out of the functional grey stone building, heads bowing as they scurried out. One or two were known to her by name, and she was known to them, but on Sundays both she and they went their own way, divided by a mutual faith. Eyes were averted – except one set.

Just for a moment, Mary Milligan fancied a hard stare and dark menace flung like a lump of coal in her direction. The woman's attention – and it was most definitely a woman, crow like and all in black – was diverted.

Nothing to do with me, Mary said to herself and hurried on. She was looking forward to the warmth of her own house and the Sunday roast that awaited her.

* * *

Once her mother had taken off her hat and coat, Bridget said that no, she didn't need any help with the dishing up, but if she'd care to set the table.

'Are you bossing me about now, Bridie Milligan?' There was laughter in her voice, joy at being home and having the daughter she had.

Bridget responded. 'Yes. It's Sunday and I'm in charge.'

They chatted about simple things: food, clothing and the amount of mending that needed doing. Mary Milligan didn't like talking about the war. 'It lays the best of spirits low,' she'd stated to her daughter.

Bridget understood and kept talk about the bombing raids of December and January to herself. She could talk about such things with her father, workmates or Lyndon. Not with her mother. Her parents had been promised a better deal after the last war. They certainly hadn't expected their happy life to be interrupted by another.

Just as Bridget opened the oven door to check on progress, the front door reverberated to the sound of the cast-iron knocker banging against it.

Mary Milligan looked up from stirring the dampness from the salt cellar. 'Your father must have forgotten his key or had too much to drink and can't find it. I'll go.'

Patrick Milligan drinking too much would have been somewhat surprising. He rarely had more than three but liked the camaraderie and memories shared with men like himself.

Hand poised on hip ready to give him a telling-off that was usually delivered with a quirky smile, Mary opened the door ready to repeat the same old ritual.

Her jaw dropped and her words were swallowed when she saw who was standing there.

Back in the kitchen, Bridget was busily basting the ox heart. Tomorrow it would be cut into small chunks and mixed with onions and carrots into a pie filling flavoured with beef extract and a spoonful of rolled oats to thicken it, flour being in short supply.

There was something about the muted conversation coming from the front door that made her look up.

There was the sound of the front door closing, the living room door opening and her mother saying, 'Such a surprise.' It very much sounded as though she was speaking to someone she hadn't seen for a very long time.

Bridget paused halfway to standing straight. A strange feeling – as though somebody had walked over her grave. The steamy atmosphere had plastered her hair to her head. She pulled at it with her fingers at the same time as trying to push away the apprehension she was feeling.

The door between the living room and kitchen was already open and instantly filled by her mother – and someone else.

'Look who's here,' said her mother. Her cheerful voice was tinged with something else – not quite surprise, but something.

Her mother came into the kitchen. The gap behind her was filled by a man in army uniform. His face was gaunt and the uniform he wore hung rag-like on his spare frame. Even if he hadn't lost weight, there was no mistaking that Hilda Harvey's dearest wish had come true; her son, Phyllis's husband, Robert Harvey had come home.

Although shocked to the core, Bridget tried to put a brave face on it. The atmosphere was charged. Her mother helped alleviate it by offering a cup of tea. Robert, a haunted look in his sunken eyes, blinked, nodded and sat stiffly on the chair pulled out to accommodate his gaunt frame. It was, thought Bridget, as though he was ready to take flight.

The eyes of mother and daughter met. Bridget sat at the table, whilst her mother retrieved the boiling kettle and made tea.

Making and serving the tea was done in almost complete silence except for asking how much sugar and did he take milk.

Finding the right words that weren't just about tea proved difficult.

'Thank you,' said Robert. With great care, he lifted the cup with shaking hands. Some of the tea slopped down onto the saucer and stained the tablecloth.

Bridget's eyes again caught those of her mother. There was no need for him to tell them he'd been through a lot. All the signs were there.

'So when did you get back?' asked Bridget's mother.

He put the cup down before answering.

'I got back two weeks ago to England. I got here yesterday. I wanted to see Phyllis. Is she around?'

It was the worst thing he could have asked but also the most pertinent.

Bridget gathered her thoughts into some sort of cohesive order. She had to tell him, but only the things he could cope with.

'She joined the Women's Auxiliary Air Force. She needed to get away after she got the telegram saying you were missing believed dead and she lost the baby.'

As he took it in, he stayed silent, his downcast eyes fixed on the tea swimming in his saucer. 'That's a shame.'

He said it without emotion, so matter-of-fact that Bridget wondered whether he had heard what she'd said.

The silence ended abruptly when Bridget's father arrived home, talking too loudly that he'd seen Tom Harvey, who was out looking for his son, Robert.

'He's survived but gone out. Old Tom and Hilda are looking...' On seeing Robert, he stopped abruptly. 'Robert... you're here...'

'He's having a cup of tea.' There was anxiety on Mary Milligan's face and Bridget still looked and felt shocked.

Bridget's father nodded. 'So I see. I could do with one meself,' he said before turning away to hang up his coat in the hallway.

When he came back, he nodded at his wife and daughter, concern in his eyes.

'Well,' he said as he sat down and took a cup of tea from his wife. 'Glad to see you back. I had a quick word with your dad. He's out looking for you. So's your mother.'

Robert hid his eyes behind his hands. 'They don't understand. They think everything is going to be as it was before. That I'm going to be as I was before.' Hands still covering his eyes, he shook his head.

Bridget opened her mouth to say something, but her father noticed, his eyes met hers and he shook his head in warning and then turned to Robert and said: 'Tell you what, why don't we finish our tea and I'll walk you home. Your mum and dad are going frantic. Better tell them you're all right.'

For a moment, there was no response until Bridget's father began relating his own history of war.

'You go off full of vim and vigour; sure, it's an adventure. Then there's dying all round you. A sense of helplessness.' He paused, pretending to drink the last of his tea, glancing at Robert to test his response.

Robert looked calmer almost surprised that somebody else had harboured the same thoughts as himself.

'There's no glory in war. That's what you find out. The blood and guts is real – arms, legs and guts – real guts.' He sensed a flickering of Robert's eyes. 'Nobody can talk about it because they can't see it like you can.' Bridget's father stabbed a finger at the side of his head. 'You can still see it. It's still in here. Mark my words, son, it always will be. But it's your memory. Nobody else's.'

Bridget covered the sob that threatened and pressed her hand flat against her mouth. Tears sprang in her eyes. She'd never cared much for Robert, but today she felt immensely sorry for him. It was at this point that she felt she should have offered him Phyllis's address, but she held it back. Phyllis needed to be informed before landing that on her.

Robert dropped his hands from his face and raised his head. 'I got separated from my battalion. A group of us were in Belgium, just over the border from France. There weren't many of us left. One of my mates got badly injured. I tried to help him, but a blast knocked me off my feet. I don't know what happened next. I woke up in the cellar of a farmhouse. It was bedlam all round. They hid us for months. I couldn't walk and didn't know who I was. Once I was strong enough, they got a group of us together and we were passed down the line a few at a time – one safe house after another, until suddenly I was at the coast. Two fishermen took me on board. They tried a few times to leave the shore without attracting attention. Eventually, I don't know how, they made it. Landed us near Hastings. Brave pair they were and had no intention going back. I don't know where they are now. All I recall is waking up in a hospital, tired to the bone and wanting to go home.'

He looked down at his hands and seemed about to brood again. On seeing the likelihood, Bridget's father suggested once again that he walk him home.

'Home is where you want to be and home is where I'll take you, Robert. Come on now. I'll get me coat on.'

As he got to his feet, Robert smiled a thin, wan smile that left his eyes fish cold. 'I was looking forward to seeing Phyllis. It seems such a long time since I saw her. Never mind. I'll write to her, tell her what's on my mind.'

He didn't ask outright for Phyllis's address, but Bridget knew that in time he would. First things first, she had to get word to Phyllis. It was going to be a bit of a shock, one that wouldn't be well received.

BRIDGET AND MAISIE

Bridget had been hit sideways when Robert had knocked at the door and she couldn't wait to share the news with Maisie. If Maisie had lived just round the corner, she would have gone there that Sunday evening and told her then. As it was, she had to wait until first thing on Monday morning before they clocked in for the day.

'He was looking for Phyllis,' Bridget explained as she filled Maisie in.

'Of course. And there was us thinkin' 'e was dead. Seems that old witch of a mother of 'is was right. Wouldn't surprise me if she'd sold 'er soul to the devil – even though she's supposedly a Christian. So what did he say?'

'He wanted to know where she was stationed. I said I didn't know.'

'And?' asked Maisie, her eyes round with surprise at this incredible piece of news.

Bridget frowned as she considered how he'd been quieter than ever before. 'I've never known Robert Harvey to be lost for words, but he was.'

Amazed by the news Maisie eyed her cautiously. 'What else did you tell him?'

'Nothing much.'

'Did you tell him about 'er writing to us?'

Bridget shook her head. 'I thought it best not to, though surely he must guess.'

'Hmm,' murmured Maisie. 'We'd better warn 'er, ain't we?' Like Bridget she was shocked. Everyone had thought him dead – including his wife, Phyllis.

Bridget took a deep breath. 'We'd better indeed.' They made a decision to take it in turns to write.

'What about Sam Proctor? Did you notice she don't mention 'im?'

Son of the landlady where Phyllis had lodged for a time, a romance had burst into flame but just as quickly burnt out again.

Bridget brushed her hair back from her face before answering. 'I don't think that was ever on the cards. Phyllis is a bit of a butterfly when it comes to men. One day she really will find the right one. I hope she does.'

'In the meantime she'll keep searching!' said Maisie with a cynical smile.

'That's our Phyllis for you. She's happy-go-lucky. Not much can dampen her spirits.'

A slight smile lifted one side of Maisie's lips together with the forthright look she was famous for. 'Hearin' she's not a widow will.'

* * *

It was two days later when another letter from Phyllis arrived at the house in Marksbury Road. Bridget waved it to Maisie as she passed the stripping room entrance on her way to her own work-station in packing.

Maisie gave a quick jerk of her chin in response. The message was clear enough. They'd catch up at tea break.

Until that much-favoured break in the middle of the morning, Maisie thought about how best to break the bad news to Phyllis – once she and Bridget had sorted whose turn it was to write. In the event it was her turn, she practised the opening sentence time and time again as she stripped leaf after leaf.

Dear Phyllis,
Please don't enjoy yourself too much – Robert's back.

No. That was too blunt.
She thought again.

Dear Phyllis,
I hate to break the news, but...

That wouldn't do either. She wanted to break the news but not to break Phyllis in two. Phyllis didn't need that. She was in a war zone for God's sake!

A third try.

Dear Phyllis,
There's a war on. We all know that things are not what they used to be. The world is topsy-turvy and none of us know what's going to happen from one day to the next. Our lives are being turned upside down and I'm afraid this means I've got a bit of news for you that you never expected to hear...

Her musings on what to write were rudely interrupted.

'Well, plain Jane, you ain't the only one signed up to do first aid. Me and Pauline 'ave signed up an' all.'

Maisie's head shot up at the sound of Carole's voice. Hands on hips, both provocative and intimidating, Carole was leaning into Jane and almost spitting the words into the girl's reddening face.

Carole looked her usual smug self and her deadbeat mate Pauline copied each and every action, sticking nose in the air, folding arms and grinning from ear to ear.

'That's all three of us, though I reckon there's some that will fly through all the stuff we've got to learn and some that might be a bit slower.' Her smug gaze slid sideways to where Jane was stripping leaves as though her life depended on it, her cheeks still burning.

Gritting her teeth, Maisie just about resisted the urge to slap her face. 'Ever 'eard the story about the tortoise and the 'are? That slow can sometimes win over fast?'

Carole looked at her blankly. 'What the bleedin' 'ell's that got to do with the first aid course?'

Maisie flung her answer back. 'A bleedin' lot! The 'are – a kind of rabbit with long legs – was racing the tortoise. Everybody was sure who would win. But the stupid 'are was too bloody cocksure of 'imself and the tortoise won the race. Get it, Carole? Stupid, that's what 'e was. Plain stupid.'

'I ain't stupid,' cried Carole. Her lashes, thickly blackened with mascara even though Maisie had specifically told her make-up was not to be worn, blinked.

Did tears threaten? Maisie couldn't be sure. She tried to read the situation but could barely control her own anger.

'I've already started the course. Sister Parker gave me a gold star last week. Said I'd be ready to go out on an ambulance in no time.' Just for a change, Jane sounded full of confidence and pleased with herself.

'Well, good for you, Jane,' said Maisie. 'Once I'm passed to drive an ambulance, I'd welcome you aboard.'

Jane blushed despite the foul look Carole threw her way.

'Tea break,' exclaimed Maisie as the bell sounded. 'Let's 'ope and pray there's more than one sugar cube per cup today – though somehow I doubt it.'

As she made her way to the canteen, Maisie gave further thought to the situation and the fact that she was angry with herself as well as being angry with Carole. She needed something else to concentrate on, something to make her smile and think pleasant thoughts. Bridget supplied it.

'It's from Phyllis. Only a card this time. The writing's small but she gets more in that way.

Over tea and a slice of bread and jam, Maisie read through it.

Hello old friends,

The sea is blue the sun is shining and there's a ruddy big cliff here. That's about all I can tell you. Mustn't mention the name of the place. The local bars are well attended AND THEY HAVE DRINK! Apparently it comes from over the border, though I can't possibly tell you the name of the country over the border.

I'll be in touch as soon as I'm settled.

Missing you as always.

Take care of yourselves and don't do anything I wouldn't do.

Love, Phyllis.

Maisie chortled into her tea. 'Not do anything she wouldn't do? Do what we like then?'

There was truth in what Maisie had said, but Bridget made no comment. For a few minutes as the canteen bustled with life, grumbles and the gobbling of much-appreciated meals, they both sat silently.

Finally, Bridget leaned forward across the table, her hand cupped round her mouth so nobody else could hear what she said. 'She's got to be told about Robert.'

'She's not going to like it.'

Bridget folded her arms across her chest and looked down at her tea which was slowly going cold. 'And it may not reach her just yet. She's more or less said that she won't be able to write to us until she's settled.'

'Sounds as though she's going somewhere a long way away.'

Bridget eyed the BFPO mark as she toyed with her teacup, stirring what little tea was left as she thought disturbing thoughts. 'She mentions the bars are busy and there's no shortage of drink.'

'That it's coming across the border,' Maisie added, her gaze fixed on Bridget's face. 'Have you any idea?'

Bridget was trying not to have an idea of where it might be because to do so was even more frightening. She weighed up the description; a border, the sea and a huge cliff in the heart of the place. A cliff, or was Phyllis being security conscious and meaning rock? Adding all the clues together, one place above all others sprang to mind.

Bridget took a deep breath. 'She's in Gibraltar. I'm sure of it. She mentions a big cliff. What she means is a rock. The Rock of Gibraltar. Oh my God! It's only a stopping off point. My dad told me...' She paused hardly daring to say what was on her mind. 'The WAAF support the RAF which suggests she's going somewhere in need of air defence.' The fierce look in her eyes held Maisie fast.

Bridget swallowed. 'My dad was at sea in the Great War and long before then. He knows Gibraltar. I mentioned it to him that

Phyllis had stopped off there but was going on somewhere else.' She paused on recalling the sudden alarm that had appeared in her father's eyes. 'He wasn't going to tell me what he thought, but I kept on. I told him I wouldn't faint off or anything. He said it was likely Malta and Malta is under constant attack. It has to be there. It has to be.' Bridget took a sip of her lukewarm tea, then grimaced at its tan-coloured surface. 'Did I really put a sugar cube in this? It doesn't taste like it.'

'Never mind the sugar or where she's likely to end up. We need to write and tell 'er the bad news.'

Bridget rubbed her face with both hands. 'I never thought I would ever say that I felt sorry for Robert, but I do. Perhaps we should suggest that she gets posted home to be near him.' She shook her head. 'He looks very sick.'

'I did 'ear that leopards don't change their spots. What I mean is that once he's better, poor old Phyllis might be back at square one: married and living with her husband's terrible parents. She'd been almost a prisoner living there with them. Awful people. I'd run away too if I was 'er.'

Bridget nodded and took a thoughtful sip of her tea. 'I still think we should suggest it.'

Maisie shook her head. 'I don't think we should. The world's upside down at the moment. Take me and Sid. He writes when he can and I write back when I can. We're both doing our bit in this war and so's Phyllis. Bet she needs to concentrate 'ard on what she's doing.'

Sid was a lad with whom Maisie had more of a friendship than a romance. They wrote to each other spasmodically both promising to meet up when Sid got back. She hadn't heard from him of late, but he was in the Far East and she knew it was a long way.

Maisie remained discomfited. Perhaps it had something to do

with her experience in the air raid, but she felt duty-bound to dissuade Bridget doing anything that might disrupt whatever it was that Phyllis was doing. 'Her letters are cheerful enough and so far there's no mention of a man, though that don't mean to say there ain't one. You know what Phyllis is like. Mind, she's been through a lot what with losing the baby and all and living with Ma Harvey wasn't easy.' She laughed. 'I can't get over the sight of 'er face at Temple Meads when we were seeing Phyllis off. And telling the stationmaster that we 'adn't paid for our platform tickets. Cheeky cow!' Maisie played with the spoon tapping it onto her cup, then her saucer.

'Are you doin' anythin' tonight? If you're not, p'raps we can go to the social club. Aggie says there's a dance on.'

'Is she going?'

Maisie laughed. 'She reckons she was a good dancer in 'er time and could shake it with the best of them. Should think she'd only shake the floor nowadays. She might be rationed like the rest of us, but she sure ain't no lightweight!'

Bridget had turned her attention to Carole, who was head to head with her friend Pauline. Jane sat alone at another table as Maisie looked over.

'There's something going on with that Carole,' Maisie remarked.

'She looks a lot older than fourteen.'

Maisie agreed with her. At the same time, she frowned thoughtfully. 'I don't know much about 'er 'ome life.'

'What about her father?'

Maisie shrugged. 'I've read her file. No sign of one and her mum don't work. She wears nice clothes though. Wonder 'ow they afford that?'

'Rich uncle?' Bridget suggested.

Maisie frowned. 'I know where she lives. Sally Lane. It do 'ave a bit of a reputation...'

'You can't know that for sure,' said Bridget, somewhat disapprovingly.

Maisie agreed with her. 'No. I can't.'

In her mind, Maisie recalled when she was younger, passing the darkened doorways of shops in Midland Road, the sounds coming from them. When she'd asked her mother what they were up to, she'd said: 'Working nights to bring up their kids.'

'I'd like to get to know Carole a bit better, but she ain't easy. Get too close and she clams up. Still, I'll give it a try. If I can 'elp I will.'

Carole and Pauline arranged to meet up and attend the dance together. Carole pulled all the stops out, wearing a dress that her mother could no longer fit into. Pauline was wearing a simple blue dress which made her look as though she should still be at school.

Carole felt like a million dollars and loved seeing Pauline's jaw drop.

'Like it?' she said, twirling to better show off the slinky royal blue dress. The skirt was tight, the neckline low and the very high heels of her black court shoes made her legs look longer and emphasised her wiggle when she walked.

'You looks like a film star. Where'd you get that dress?'

Carole returned that it was one of many that she had in her wardrobe; that her mother spoilt her and was always buying nice things. It was far from the truth. Her mother had grown too fat to fit in it but had turned jealous on seeing how well it suited her daughter. Her look had darkened, her eyes green with envy.

'Little tart!' The nasty words had been accompanied by a slap across her face, plus telling her not to bring any trouble home. 'I don't want no bastards in this 'ouse. One's enough.'

Carole knew that she was the bastard, the product of a first love that had ruined her mother's life. Details were sparse, her mother refusing to talk about her past, to say anything much except that unending refrain about how Carole's coming into being had ruined her life.

'He would 'ave stayed with me otherwise. We'd 'ave got married.' The outburst had been followed by a scowl.

Pauline was very impressed and at this moment in time, that was all that mattered.

'Are they real stockings you're wearing? Did yer mum buy them for you too?'

'Of course.'

As if! She'd sneaked them out of the sideboard drawer when her mother had been otherwise engaged with a client. There'd be hell to play when she found out – especially if she got a ladder, but for tonight she didn't care.

Heads had turned the moment she'd taken off her coat. Her face was piled with make-up, her blonde hair was pinned up in a style she thought made her look older and far more glamorous than anyone in the room. Judging by some of the dropped jaws, the effect was working and it wasn't long before she was being twirled round the dance floor. At first it was foxtrots, waltzes and sambas. The tempo quickened and it was jitterbug time, the fast, crazy dancing that was sweeping the country from America.

* * *

Maisie and Bridget did their share of dancing, followed by a couple of drinks bought from the bar. Because so many male employees were serving in the forces, outsiders had been invited. Some of them wore uniform: Canadians, Australians, Polish, Scottish and Irish. A few, exempt from military service for whatever reason, wore suits.

At roughly nine o'clock, the double doors into the social club opened and let in a draught of cold air.

Feeling a bit warm anyway, Maisie waved a hand in front of her face and was about to say something funny to Bridget about it being as warm as where Phyllis was but stopped.

Three men had entered, one slightly in front of the other two as though he were leading them in. All three wore suits, the quality and cut of that worn by the main man of better quality and cut than the other two.

It was suddenly as though Maisie had been smothered in snow. Eddie Bridgeman had arrived.

She touched Bridget's arm and turned slightly away, blood racing and hoping against hope that Eddie Bridgeman hadn't seen her.

She whispered his name to Bridget, who glanced furtively, then turned her back, purposely standing in front of Maisie to hide her.

'Has he seen you?' Bridget whispered.

A minute ago, Maisie had sipped half a cider. Her mouth shouldn't have felt dry, but it did. She peeped around Bridget. To her great relief, Eddie wasn't looking her way but was eyeing every female there as though they were a bag of chocolates from which he would choose the one he most fancied.

'No,' Maisie whispered, shaking her head. 'Not so far.'

The piercing eyes that had searched the social club settled on his chosen prize.

Maisie gulped. No! It couldn't be. But it was. Eddie was making his way towards Carole.

Carole noticed him and froze, staring at him as though he was the only man in the whole place, yet she wasn't smiling. Watching her, Maisie got the impression that she wanted to step back, to run even, but her feet were nailed to the ground.

'Scared,' she whispered so only Bridget could hear. 'Carole's scared.'

The band started up again. Eddie was now with Carole. Neither rouge nor lipstick could disguise Carole's youth or hide the sudden pallor that came to her face. His arms were round her. There was a moment when it seemed she did try to break his embrace, but Eddie hung on firmly.

'She's just the right age,' murmured Maisie. Some time back she'd been the right age for Eddie. He liked them young. Nineteen was young and not to be ignored, but Eddie preferred them younger. Fourteen like Carole suited him fine. 'I'm not letting him have his way,' Maisie growled.

Bridget looked at her aghast. 'What are you going to do?'

Anger glowed like burning coals in Maisie's eyes. 'Whatever I can,' Maisie snapped grimly.

Carole was squirming, smiling nervously up at Eddie at the same time as trying to free herself. All the bravado Maisie was used to seeing had evaporated.

Out of the corner of her eye, she glimpsed a confused-looking Pauline, who couldn't seem to make up her mind whether to smile or to grimace.

Carole didn't see what else was happening until Maisie was on the dance floor and had grabbed her shoulders and jerked her backwards.

'Ouch!' Carole rubbed at her arm but stayed there, watching the diminutive Maisie Miles facing down the wider physique of Eddie Bridgeman. His brow furrowed with anger.

'What the 'ell do you think yer doin', you stupid cow?'

Maisie stood her ground, hands on hips glaring up at him. 'Spoiling yer fun.'

The music stopped. Musicians, dancers and onlookers stopped to see what was going on.

Eddie laughed. One stubby finger poked at her shoulders. 'You can't stop me from doin' whatever I wants to do.'

Maisie hadn't really considered her own lack of stature. She had nothing like his strength, but she did have a loud mouth – and a quick mind.

'You're right, Eddie. I ain't got your strength. You could swat me like a fly. Carole is only fourteen years old.'

'I knows she is,' he said, his face coming in close so there were only inches between their respective noses. 'I knows 'er mother,' he said, his voice dropping to a whisper. 'All I got to do is pay the old tart and I can 'ave 'er kid any time I like.'

Maisie could barely believe what she was hearing, but even if it was true, she wasn't going to let it happen. Just as much as she was responsible for training Carole in the factory, she also felt a responsibility for her welfare. It was hard being young and vulnerable, and didn't she know it! She might have gone the same way herself if her stepfather, Frank Miles had had his way. She was going to do all she could to prevent any harm happening to Carole.

Carole safe behind her with Bridget's arm round her, Maisie faced him down, more angry than she'd been for a long time. He was right in that she couldn't force him to do anything. She didn't have the masculine strength, but there were plenty around her who did.

Seeing that something was going on, conversation had become subdued and eyes hard with curiosity had turned their way. Maisie saw this and jumped in with both feet.

'We don't want blokes in this club who like little girls. It ain't natural and we ain't 'avin' it. She's only fourteen and 'e wants to 'ave 'is wicked way with 'er. T'ain't natural, is it?'

Her voice rang out. There were instant rumblings amongst those gathered round the dance floor and at the bar.

Men whose broad shoulders pressed like rock against their jackets pushed their way forward.

'Come on, pal,' said a very large Canadian with hands like shovels. 'It's best that you leave. We don't want your sort round here.'

Eddie's expression turned black as thunder as a group of servicemen caught hold of both his arms and those of his companions. All his venom was directed at Maisie. 'You bitch! I'll 'ave you. I'll bloody well 'ave you!'

Cigarette smoke wafted into the centre of the room as the double doors opened. The group were only gone for a few minutes. On their return, they were grinning from ear to ear. Bridget and Maisie were standing with Carole and Pauline. Bridget asked them what they'd done with him.

An answering grin spread on the face of the biggest Canadian. 'We shoved his driver and the other guy into the front seats of the car and England's answer to James Cagney into the trunk – oh, boot as you folks say.'

The punishment handed out to Eddie Bridgeman was met with a great roar of approval.

'Let's get a drink,' another serviceman shouted.

A surge of people headed for the bar. Both Bridget and Maisie were offered drinks.

'You're a brave girl,' one said to Maisie. 'That guy looks like trouble.'

'He is,' said Maisie as a sliver of icy coldness trickled down her back. Shaking herself, she turned to Carole. 'Are you OK?'

Carole shook her head avidly and sucked in her lips. 'I'm OK fer now, though I can't say how I'll be when I'm by meself.' Her eyes locked with those of Maisie. 'He knows me mum. Knows where I live too.'

Maisie grimaced. 'Yeah. I 'eard Eddie say so.'

Not far from crying, Carole sniffed and swiped at her nose.

'Me mum used to know 'im years ago when 'e was just a small-time thief. He's a bit of a gangster these days and dangerous – or according to me mum 'e is.'

One of the Canadians brought over some drinks and set them down on a table. 'You OK, girls?'

He had kind eyes. Maisie couldn't help noticing.

'We're OK. Thanks for the drinks.'

'Two more coming up. Hey, that guy looked a nasty piece of work. Will you be seeing him again?'

'Hopefully not,' said Bridget, taking a sip of her drink. She noticed that Carole had shrugged off Pauline's sympathetic pat. 'You OK, Carole?'

Carole frowned. 'That bloke makes me sick. What 'e gets up to makes me sick.'

'Yeah,' said Maisie with a long drawn-out sigh. 'He likes the young girls too much.'

'No. Not just that,' said a softer Carole, one that had escaped the brittle shell she wore and showed her true vulnerability. 'I saw 'im the other night in that alley that goes through from East Street to Dean Lane. He was doing a deal with some stolen jewellery. I saw it. Dead posh stuff it was.'

'I haven't heard of any jewellery shops being robbed,' said Bridget.

Carole shook her head. 'Not a shop. They got contacts who go about after a raid, stealing from the dead and injured. There was a ballroom got bombed a while back, weren't there? A dead posh one up Clifton way.'

Bridget's jaw dropped. 'That's horrible. Surely it can't be true. The place swarms with volunteers after a raid, firefighters and all that.'

'Yeah,' replied Carole, her youthful face now returned to its casual bitterness. 'Firefighters and all that.'

Maisie cringed at what Carole was implying. It was becoming common knowledge about thieving from damaged houses, but stealing from the dead and dying? It was hard to swallow – even of Eddie Bridgeman.

Bridget was just as horrified.

And things could get even more terrible, thought Maisie but said nothing until Carole and Pauline were safely out of earshot.

'I made a fool of Eddie in front of everybody and then 'e got stuffed into the boot of a car.' She grinned. 'Mind you, it was worth it just for that, but...' Her eyes met those of Bridget. 'He won't forget it in a 'urry and then I'll be for it!'

9

PHYLLIS

The sea journey to Gibraltar had passed quickly and without incident. The next leg to the island of Malta she'd been told would be more dangerous.

'Enjoy the journey, love. All you can do, innit?'

Gunners going to join the garrisons there sounded cheery enough up front. She'd taken on their advice. For goodness' sake if the army wasn't scared, why should she be? Perhaps the newspapers had been exaggerating.

Doubts intensified when she'd seen the same chirpy bloke heave his last meal over the side of the ship.

Enjoy the journey.

How enjoyable it would indeed be if the world was not at war, she thought as, during those first days out from Gibraltar, she breathed in the salty fresh air of the Mediterranean. Everything she could see was blue, the darkest strip being the horizon, a line marking the convergence of sea and sky.

'Alright, miss?'

Determined she wouldn't be seen as afraid, Phyllis composed her features, smiled but kept looking at the horizon they were heading for as though it was truly where she wanted to be.

'Fine,' she replied brusquely, her gaze fixed on a spot where she'd seen beak-nosed dolphins break the surface. She slid sideways into a shadow thrown by the coning tower behind her. Being of fair complexion and reddish hair, it wouldn't be wise to stay too long in the sun. It was March and the day was as warm as a June day in England.

Lieutenant Brian Crabbe slouched over the rail beside her. 'No *Malade de Mer?*'

His cut-glass accent she could cope with, but the pompous tone and using the French description left her in no doubt that he'd surmised her as a working-class girl.

'Seasick. That's what you mean.' Her tone was purposely sharp and she couldn't help herself from speaking slowly so her accent was less discernible.

From the very first time she'd donned the smart blue uniform of the Women's Auxiliary Air Force, she'd noticed that officers of all the services had a tendency to talk down to anyone who clipped their aitches and spoke with a strong accent. They ordered their men around and talked down to the few women on board – even the half a dozen fresh-faced members of Queen Alexandra's Imperial Nursing Corps who they might depend on if they became injured. She was the only female who wasn't a nurse and that alone was worrying. Perhaps all that about only officers being posted abroad was all guff and she'd walked into a trap. They wanted skilled female personnel out there, but only if they chose to be there. Her mind went back to when she'd finally been given the news.

'We're making an exception, Harvey, because your skills are exceptional. You're being posted abroad to work alongside plotters and telegraph operators. Don't think it's going to be a sleigh ride. Wherever you are, you'll be under pressure, even those places where the war has not yet reached. On the other hand, you could find yourself in the middle of a very hot spot. Are you willing to take the gamble?'

Initially, she'd had it in mind to find Sam, but the more she thought about his mother and his marching off, the less important he'd become. She'd never really given doing her bit much attention, but now she did. Perhaps it was when she had first put on the uniform. Something had changed inside as much as outside.

It hadn't stopped her from using Sam as an excuse that she wanted to be posted near to him and made out they were closer than they actually were. 'We're engaged.' An outright lie and one she hoped she wouldn't come to regret.

'We'll see what we can do.'

So they had, and here she was sailing across an azure sea with an azure sky attached to it.

Leaving England meant getting away from all she'd ever known, all her problems, her in-laws and even the shift in her relationship with her mother. She could cope with all that. What she found more difficult to cope with was leaving behind her work mates at the factory, principally Bridge and Maisie.

Keeping her gaze fixed on the horizon and ignoring Lieutenant Crabbe did no good. He didn't leave but stayed with his elbows resting on the guardrail, hands clasped together. She felt his eyes on her. His eyes were always on her, though from the start she'd ignored him.

He rolled his shoulders, an action designed to impress, his muscles bulging against his short sleeves. 'So what made you join up?'

'To serve my country.'

'Really?' He laughed. 'Don't kid yourself, love. It's off back to the kitchen sink when this is all over. Best place for a woman is at the sink or in bed.'

Phyllis gritted her teeth. 'I may choose to stay on after the war. Being a housewife doesn't appeal to me.'

Her mind went back to Robert and living with her in-laws.

Brian Crabbe slapped a hairy-backed hand onto the guardrail and laughed as though it was the funniest thing he'd ever heard. 'You're in the services for the duration only, girl! Mark my words, there won't be any women in the forces after the war. They won't be needed. They can go back to their kitchens and their knitting. It's where they belong.'

Phyllis clamped her mouth tightly shut. Never mind wanting to tear him off a strip, she wanted to bite him – draw blood even! But he was an officer and therefore might mark her card for retribution – at least for the duration of this voyage.

'So what skill are you bringing to the party?'

Aware of the sarcasm in his tone, she swallowed a cutting response and told the truth. 'I type fast.'

He laughed derisively. 'Typing? You mean like a secretary? Ever got to sit on the boss's knee, did you? We've all heard the rumours.'

She replied through gritted teeth, though in a tone respectful to a senior officer, 'Typing is a great advantage if you're operating a teleprinter.'

She took great pride in the fact that she'd been trained in double quick time and was an extremely proficient typist. Already possessing the skill speeded up the process. The teleprinter received and sent information gathered from observers and radar stations to aid the apprehension of incoming raiders. She'd been as quick picking that up as she had typing. Her superiors had been so pleased, they'd given her a stripe and made her a Senior Aircraftwoman – a fast promotion born of necessity.

'It's no garden party in Malta, don't you know?' His manner carried on in the aloof vein it had since the beginning.

Phyllis bristled. 'I do know that.'

Yes, she knew very well and although she was terrified, she wouldn't let Lieutenant Crabbe know that. To admit as such would only serve to confirm his opinion of women in the services. He'd definitely hit on a raw nerve, but there was no way she would let the side down – that of women stepping forward to do what they could in this great matter.

Gibraltar had been agog with the news from the tiny island squashed between North Africa and the island of Sicily. Prior to attacks from the Italian air force, the opinion had been that Malta and its people be abandoned and to leave it open to invasion. That was until somebody who could read a map pointed out its strategic importance.

'Whitehall pushes pens. It don't read charts.' That was the statement she'd heard from a humble rating back in Gib who *could* read a chart. 'Halfway between Gib and Alex and with some bloody big deep-water harbours,' he'd said, frowning over the fourth pint he held in his fist. 'And two Italian islands between them and North Africa.'

Winston Churchill, who had been First Lord of the Admiralty before becoming prime minister, could also, it seemed, read charts and had noted the island's position. After due considera-tion and noting the island was only one hundred and ninety miles from the North African coast where a mighty battle between British forces and the Afrika Corps was shifting back and forth across the desert, he'd insisted it be protected at all costs.

Phyllis became aware of Crabbe closing the gap between

them. Their bare elbows touched. In response, she shifted along a bit. He instantly noticed. She didn't need to see the sour downturn at the corners of his mouth.

'No need to be testy.'

Phyllis stiffened. 'Isn't there?' Getting annoyed with officers was basically trivial and not worth the effort, but trivialities helped her not to worry about what was to come or to deeply regret the friendships she'd left behind. 'Why is it men who spend a great deal of time with their own kind think they are irresistible to women?'

'Because we make the extra effort?'

'I would hardly call you a great charmer,' Phyllis said sourly.

Officers, she'd decided, were so used to giving orders to other men, they weren't so good at charming women as they thought they were.

'You would. It's just that you won't admit it.'

She took a great breath and clasped her hands tightly. No matter that she'd gone out of her way to be standoffish, the lieutenant remained standing beside her, his legs a deep brown beneath his baggy shorts and above his long white socks. The arms he rested on the guardrail, hands linked in front of him, were just as brown.

'Are you sure you're not going to throw up, my dear?'

She saw through the façade of concern to the underlying condescension.

'I'm fine. It's just the heat. And the company,' she muttered.

'Perhaps I could escort you to a cool bunk in the hospital wing. There's nobody there at present. It'll just be you – and me and I'm very good at soothing a worried brow.'

She told him that she was fine and didn't need his company. She made a sideways move to emphasise the fact, enough to put a gap between them. 'I'm looking forward to getting to Malta. I've got somebody waiting for me there.'

'Do you really? I'm not sure I believe you.'

'I don't care whether you do or not.' She caught her hair as the sea breeze tumbled it about her face hiding her less than confident expression. She so wanted to slap his face and tell him to get lost.

Crabbe lingered.

Use him, said a small voice inside. *He won't easily budge so why not make use of him?*

She recalled him saying that he'd been to Malta before. A few details might quell her fear and take his mind off trying to seduce her.

Recognising that he was getting nowhere with his ongoing seduction, he turned away just as she found her voice.

'What's Malta like?'

She guessed he would like her asking.

'Ah,' he said, golden hairs glistening in the sunlight as his brown arms returned to their resting place on the guardrail. 'Quite a fortress and a long history. At one point, it was Arabic, then later on was handed to the Knights of St John after they were turfed off the Greek island of Rhodes. The rent was said to be one Maltese falcon. Falcons were very prized back then, so I understand.'

'They hunted with them,' said Phyllis and felt some pride that her old friend Bridget had encouraged her to read. She'd done a lot of reading in those awful months living under her in-laws' roof. 'I did read something about Admiral Nelson, that he captured the island from Napoleon's forces.'

'Clever girl. You know more than most people.' She could tell by his surprised tone of voice that he'd expected her to know absolutely nothing. She loved that. Finding out otherwise was one in the eye for him!

He went on trying to impress her, but stuck to the present, which doubtless he knew more about than the past. 'As of this moment in time, we hold it and the Axis powers want it. It's of strategic importance.'

'I'd heard back in Gib that it was being bombed quite heavily, as much as London in fact.'

He almost laughed. 'More than London, though only by the Italians at present – that was the last I heard anyway. Just the Italians!'

Noticing that his fingertips were edging towards hers, she retracted her hand. Let him get his kicks elsewhere. He wasn't that good-looking and was married, if what she'd heard from the nurses was true.

Memories of Maisie's outspokenness fresh in her mind, all pretence at being anything other than what she was shattered like breaking glass. Suddenly her bravado was as big as that of her workmate and her accent, the one she'd been trying to hide, came flooding back. She faced the smug-faced Crabbe.

'I got some mates back in Bristol. Wish they was with me now,' she said, laying on the Bristolian accent loud and strong. Folding her arms, she cocked her head. 'My mate Maisie should be yer now and she'd 'ave yer guts fer garters! Go along to the sick bay, eh? And 'ave yer mucky 'ands all over me? I may be just a factory girl, but that don't mean I'm up fer a bit of 'ow's yer father with the likes of you! Now push off and try yer luck somewhere else or I'll report you. Better still, I might find out a bit more about you and let yer wife know what yer up to. Dirty old sod!'

It was with a great sense of satisfaction and a grin that could have been picked from the face of little Maisie Miles that she strode off, the sea air fresh on her face. This war, she thought, ain't just about battles between armies, there was also one growing between the sexes. Women were doing men's work and learning new skills that would stand them in good stead for the future. There was something else happening too. Cracks were showing in the old class system. If she had her way, they'd split wide open.

He didn't follow her.

10

PHYLLIS

There were other service personnel around, a few sailors off duty, soldiers looking hot and overdressed in battledress, some who'd thrown caution to the wind and were down to their shirtsleeves. There was laughter and comments as the smiling Phyllis marched by, but they weren't so bloody arrogant about it as Lieutenant Crabbe.

'Fancy a fag, love?'

That was what most of them offered, along with a bit of cheek she could easily cope with.

'Is that Woodbines?' she asked them. When they replied that they were – which most seemed to be – she told them she used to make them. 'Thousands of 'em,' she added, totally open about how she spoke and who she was.

'I'd be like a kid in a sweetshop working in a place like that,' one of them said.

Some of them asked if she'd brought a few hundred with her.

'They're on ration in Malta and I don't fancy running out.'

'Calms me nerves, hen,' said another, who obviously hailed from Scotland.

She stopped and chatted. They were good-natured enough when she told them she hadn't brought a big supply with her, that she was just like them, dependent on War Office rations.

'But I don't mind you having mine,' she said. 'After all, you're the ones who'll be doing the real work. I'm only a backroom girl.' She didn't know whether that was true or not, but describing herself as such did make her feel better.

Her offer was swiftly accepted, relaxation and chat coming with it. Conversations centred on families, wives, children and sweethearts. Try as they might to suppress it, their homesickness showed through the cheery façade and Phyllis felt terribly sorry for them.

She found out the guy from Glasgow was called Gordon McDodd and he was married with four children. 'And another on the way,' he added. 'No wonder I drink and smoke too much.'

There was much laughter, and their unbridled and honest merriment put Phyllis at ease. She told them about Robert, that she'd heard nothing except that he might be missing and probably dead so considered herself a widow, though it hadn't been officially confirmed.

'Could take years,' somebody said. This fact was sombrely agreed by everyone.

She also told them about the mother-in-law from hell.

'I used to have one like that,' declared Gordon. 'Gave the old witch some hemlock from the allotment one day and told her it was cabbage.'

More roaring laughter and Phyllis laughed with them.

Despite the danger that lay ahead, she felt braver in their company. These men were off to an army base on the island and then on to North Africa. They didn't know whether they would come back, yet they were mutually supportive, truly brothers in arms united against whatever came their way.

She crossed her arms across her crisp white blouse, drew on the cigarette and blew the smoke forcefully as if by doing so all her concerns about the past blew away with it.

'You have a searching look in your eyes, Phyllis Harvey. Do you think you might find what you're looking for on Fortress Malta?'

She smiled. Whatever these rough, tough men might be, there was sensitivity too. They saw more than you thought they did. They asked her more about Robert and for the first time in a long time she told them what she could. They were mainly interested in the battle that had laid him low. She had to confess that she didn't quite know for sure, but it was around the evacuation from Dunkirk when he'd gone missing.

'Look to the future, hen,' said Gordon as he lobbed an extinguished dog end into the sea. 'Some of us are going to fall by the wayside. We've all come to terms with it. You have to come to terms with it too.'

He didn't look at her when he said it but kept his eyes fixed on the current moving along on the surface of the water, his jaw rock hard.

'Yes,' she whispered, and nodded in agreement because he spoke sense and, in a way reminded her of Bridget, who spoke words of calm, and Maisie, who gave advice far in advance of her years. She wished she was more like them. Neither fell in and out of love as she did. They'd been sceptical about Robert, and although they hadn't said so, they had disapproved of her liaison with her typing teacher, Alan, perhaps too of Sam.

She'd decided she fell in love too easily – or perhaps it had never been love – not with any of them.

She thanked Gordon and his mates for the cigarette and their uplifting company, then squeezed her way through more servicemen, stepping over kitbags and other stores for which there was no more room in the hold or the cramped crew's quarters. The crew had priority for sleeping quarters; after all, they were the ones who had to get the destroyer *HMS Vendetta* to their destination.

The captain had been kind enough to provide the females on board with a few wooden chairs set in the shade, where they could gossip, read and write letters home. This was where Phyllis headed after collecting from her belongings a notepad she used for writing letters and another one she used as a diary which she now carried in one hand, along with a fountain pen and a straw hat in the other.

Two of the nurses, Megan and Barbara, were already there. Megan sat in the shade hunched over a book. Barbara's very brown legs were stretched from the chair she was sitting on to another, her sandalled feet moving from side to side in time with the gentle roll of the ship.

Because the brim of her sunhat shaded her eyes, it hadn't looked to Phyllis that she'd been scrutinised, but Nurse Megan Hughes was sharp-eyed. She didn't miss a thing.

'What was the Crab Nebula saying to you?'

Megan had a regular habit of giving people nicknames. The captain was Fuzzy Wuzzy by virtue of his copious ginger striped beard. One of the petty officers was called Cough Drop because he was always covering his mouth with one hand and coughing nervously whenever Barbara, buxom daughter of the lord mayor of somewhere or other, passed his way.

Phyllis pulled up a free chair and, seeing there were no other takers, did what Barbara was doing, glad to stretch her legs.

'He asked if I was feeling seasick.'

The other girls laughed and remarked that he was all heart – not seriously meant of course.

Phyllis flattened her letter-writing notepad with one hand.

She intended to write one letter to Maisie and one to Bridget, for whom she had a very important question. So when are you going to marry that handsome American?

What would I do, she wondered, if a rich and very handsome man insisted we marry and leave England forever?

She had no hesitation in answering her own question. She would throw caution to the wind and go with him. New horizons might beckon for a lot of people once this war was over, though Bridget was a member of a very large and supportive family. She had roots.

Whereas you do not, she thought to herself. Not really. Her mother had told her she had itchy feet – just like her father.

'*Had to go off to Canada. Couldn't settle with what he had.*'

Megan noticed her heavy sigh. 'Don't sigh like that. The Crab Nebula will think you're sighing for him and in need of his sexual expertise. Thinks all women in uniform are on rations and need him to make up their quota.'

Phyllis laughed. 'I've known better than him, thank you very much.'

So far, she'd seen nothing of the enemy. Since leaving Southampton, she'd scoured the sea and was beginning to wonder if the enemy would ever put in an appearance. Or perhaps this war was not real.

She remarked on this to the two nurses. 'I was scared of getting shot at all the way from Southampton, but all I've seen is the sea and sky. No sign of the enemy – not that I want to see them.'

Barbara answered, 'According to Ned, my fiancé, that's the way it is. He serves on a cruiser and said that sometimes you wonder whether there's a war on at all, though not to go looking for it because it will come to you soon enough – more often than not when you're least expecting it.' She tapped the headrest of the wooden chair she was sitting on. 'Touch wood, we see nothing.'

Phyllis found herself hoping it was true; a little old magic wouldn't go amiss, along with the ping ping of the echo sounder and the watchful eye of the ship's radar.

Get on and write this letter, she said to herself, though the voice yet again sounded very much like Maisie's rather than her own.

Be calm, Bridget's voice added, which made her smile. Strong characters both of them and if they weren't sitting beside her, they were definitely inside her head.

It was hard to describe why she suddenly became aware that something different was happening. Sailors on watch stiffened. The ship picked up speed. Phyllis and her companions got up from their chairs and exchanged worried looks with the gunners who had heaved themselves up from shady spots to look over the ship's sides.

Standing up straight became more difficult. Legs did not respond to commands. For some odd reason, the words of the old shanty, 'What Shall We Do With The Drunken Sailor', popped into Phyllis's mind and wouldn't be silence.

The deck was heaving one way and then the other.

She looked at Megan and Barbara. 'What's happening?'

Both stared at the sky and she did the same.

'Hey up,' shouted one of the soldiers she'd been speaking to earlier whose name she could not recall. 'Looks like we've got company,' he shouted.

The repeated clarion call of the ship's klaxon was accompanied by shouted orders for action stations. The ship that had merely ploughed its way through the sea, a formidable and immovable fortress, now bristled with life, things that had seemed fixed moving up and down and side to side.

When the forward gun turret swung in a semi-arc and began

releasing its pom-pom shells, Phyllis and her companions grabbed their personal things before retrieving life jackets and tin hats from beneath their chairs.

Second Officer Crabbe came racing through, his tin hat somehow incongruous when worn with shorts, his features ugly with responsibility.

He was all action, waving arms, animated fierceness emanating from the training that might save him, save the ship, save them all. 'You women. Get out of the way. Go below decks. That's an enemy sub out there.'

For a moment it was as though a bucket of cold water had been tipped over each of them. Bewildered looks were exchanged as they sought to retain their balance as the ship zigzagged through a sea heaving from its own making.

A single thought was instantly voiced and agreed.

'Heave your guts up down there you will,' said Megan.

'This will be the first time I've disobeyed an order since I've joined up.' Defiance gripped Barbara's strong jaw. 'Never mind your stomach. If this ship gets a torpedo in the belly, we get it too. We'll stay up here,' she shouted when Crabbe, running and giving orders in one direction, now came back.

At first, fury was writ large on features pink, sweaty and fierce with intent. He stared at them, waved dismissively and dashed off.

'He's got more important things to do,' said Phyllis.

Keeping close for comfort, they cowered back against a bulwark, clutching their tin hats tightly to their heads, trusting to the steel to protect them from blast.

Rough the gunners might be, but with gentlemanly grace, they gathered round the three women, standing facing outwards and three deep, a redoubt of flesh and blood.

The deck beneath their feet trembled as the forward gun burst into life, sending shell after shell into the sea. Fierce spouts of water towered upwards as the ship sped on through, a cradle of flying spray.

Phyllis clapped her hands against her ears in a vain effort to keep out the worst of the thunderous barrage. The air was filled with shouted orders and the pounding feet of men running in all directions. Senior officers shouted at lesser officers, who in turn shouted at ratings. The chain of command was born of tradition, tried and tested for hundreds of years. Everyone seemed to know their job. Everyone was determined to win through.

Following an almighty crashing sound, another group of soldiers came rushing round in a tight-knit group, heads down, metal helmets wobbling on their heads. Two of them were carrying another man between them, blood spurting from his neck. Phyllis recognised Gordon as one of the two men.

'Ship's hit on that side,' Gordon shouted. 'Alistair took a piece of shrapnel.'

Phyllis wondered why she didn't feel scared. 'What can I do?'

Barbara showed her. 'Place your hands over the injury. Like this.'

Phyllis placed one hand on top of the other, screaming silently as the blood filtered through her fingers.

'Don't faint, don't faint,' she murmured.

Nobody heard her and for that she was grateful. This man's life depended on her not fainting.

Keeping up the pressure on the wound as instructed, she raised her eyes to sky and then to sea. She nodded dumbly. Her mouth felt too dry to swallow, but she did anyway. No saliva. Just fear.

Water spouts shot skywards with each fired shell, followed by a lull, a moment when the ship seemed to zigzag through the water.

Her anxious eyes met those of Gordon as he explained what

he thought she wanted to know. 'She's trying to outmanoeuvre the sub whilst her gun turret reloads. There's been damage. They need a bit of time.'

Phyllis gulped more and more breaths of air and blinked away her fear. The sound of more men screaming came from where Gordon and his men had come.

Through the deluge of spray from a sea that had recently been flat and tranquil, she tried to sight the position of the submarine, as all the while fear lay heavy in her stomach. All these brave men; it made her feel braver to believe that they too were scared but going about their duty regardless. Doing something helped, she thought, and knew she had to do the same.

Megan had found a box, a big heavy thing painted in camouflage green with a big red cross on the side. Out came bandages, then a syringe, then a small bottle. Foreheads frowning in concentration, they worked quickly.

Barbara's eyes met Phyllis's over the injured man whose blood she was trying to dam. 'Morphine,' she mouthed.

Phyllis pressed for all she was worth until the throbbing she'd felt beneath her fingers stopped. The bandages had soaked up most of the blood, but some still flowed into the collar of his shirt.

Barbara shook her head and there was desolation in her eyes.

'You can stop now.' Barbara had a strong voice, absent at present.

Megan called from the gap between a twisted piece of metal and the guardrail, 'I need help here.'

Barbara got to her feet and, between the three of them they heaved at the medicine chest.

'I'll take that,' said Gordon, lifting it as though it was a quarter of the weight it actually was.

Phyllis didn't wait to be asked to go along. She'd felt the pulse of the dying man's life beneath her fingers before he'd given up.

She didn't want anyone else to give up – not if she could help it. At that particular moment, she was overcome with the feeling that to help someone in pain was the most natural thing in the world. Not everyone would make it, but if nothing else, it was her duty to give all she had, even if it was no more than to hold a hand or whisper that everything was going to be all right even if it was not.

The next few hours were horrendous; depth charges were jettisoned from the rear of the ship and those guns still able were blasting for all they were worth. There was carnage and chaos in this horrendous game, but suddenly the game changed.

Fingers pointed skywards at three black dots that became bigger as they flew out of the sun.

'Biplanes,' somebody exclaimed. Hands shielded eyes against the glare. 'They have to have come from Malta. We're not too far away now.'

Phyllis knew nothing much about planes; WAAFs were taught only the most basic rudiments of aircraft observation and identification, but even she knew that these three were old biplanes. Each had two sets of wings, one above the other, that looked as though they were connected with piano wire.

Gordon saw them too and creaked to his feet, one leg bleeding from what he said was only a scratch but did in fact look much worse. His mouth widened into an uplifting smile. 'Here come the knights in shining armour.'

Megan, presently ministering to yet another broken man, shielded her eyes with one hand. 'Stringbags,' she said, somewhat contemptuously. 'My dad flew one years ago,' she said by way of explanation.

Gordon added more information. 'Stringbags they might look, but it's what they're carrying under their bellies that matters.'

Barely a minute after he said it, a torpedo fell from the first plane, its progress mapped by the white feathery tail it left in the water. There was a huge explosion.

The next plane did the same.

Those men able to stand clung to the guard rail, faces lit with the fire of hope and revenge. They cheered loudly.

'The first one got its bearings.' An exuberant Gordon kept up a running commentary. 'The second one will confirm.'

Phyllis didn't ask what the third would do. One achingly sad thought surfaced that those men in the submarine were somebody's husbands, lovers or sons. They would never be going home.

The RAF set great store that it would be air power that would win this war and these fragile-looking planes, ancient though they were, looked to be proving it.

If the cheers were loud before, they were even louder when the third one found its target and a great plume of water, far larger than the others, shot skyward, to be followed by a thick black lake of oil.

A strange silence fell; one or two men crossed themselves.

Barbara hung her head and said a little prayer. *'Please God forgive us.'*

Gordon heard her. 'Either them or us, lassie. Them or us.'

* * *

Battle-scarred and patched up for now, the *Vendetta* sped on as fast as her engines would allow. The closer they got to Malta, the more likelihood of other attacks. As a consequence, everyone seemed to be holding their breath and frequently looking seaward or skywards for signs of further attack.

'Thanks for your help,' said Megan, handing Phyllis a cup of tea and a rather scorched-looking buttered bun.

The three of them agreed that it was all a bit close for comfort. They also agreed that they would meet up once they were settled in their Maltese billets. Deep down, each of them shared a dread of how that might be. There would be more aircraft cover once they closed on the island and came under the umbrella of their defences, meagre though it might be. Until then they were running the gauntlet.

Quivering with aftershock was not acceptable. Finding strength she didn't know she had, Phyllis forced herself to think of something else. Taking up the diary she was forbidden by the service to keep – but would anyway – she wrote about the quay-side tavern in the shadow of the rock at Gibraltar where she'd seen cockroaches run along the length of a shelf at the back of the bar.

'Roaches behind the bar and roaches in front of it.' The barman had been referring to the customers who were a hotchpotch lot at the best of times. They had all laughed, all glad of the humour and beer to quell their fear.

'Is that a diary I see before me?'

Barbara looked tired but not so tired that she couldn't quote her own version of Shakespeare.

Everything helped to ease their tension.

'I want to keep a record, just in case... I forget anything.'

An unspoken truth flashed between them as their eyes met. There was another more obvious reason for keeping a diary; a record of all you'd been through just in case you never went home again. They both knew it wasn't allowed on the basis that it might fall into enemy hands.

'I have to,' Phyllis said softly.

Once her diary entry was finished, she turned her attention to writing a letter. No hint of where she was or what had happened was allowed. She had to keep to more general and even personal things. Thinking of that brought the raid on Bristol to mind when she and her friends had sheltered in the wine vaults of St Nicholas Market. It had been terrifying, though not as bad as what had just transpired. More raids on Bristol had occurred since and despite all that she'd been through, she felt for her friends and wondered how they were coping.

Life had to be hard for them, a lack of food and working hard – carrying out their normal everyday work and extras such as fire-fighting, voluntary nursing and working with the ladies of the WVS distributing buns, tea and general help to those who needed it.

So far, she thought, this war has been a catalogue of disasters. The exception was saving an army of almost 350,000 from the beaches of Dunkirk, but it was hardly a victory. The country was giving its all and so far not seeing much in return for their consid-erable sacrifices. The last thing she wanted to do was tell them how it was out here, not that the censors would allow it anyway. So, as that was the case, she would be upbeat and paste on a cheerful veneer that hid the horrors beneath.

Just as she was about to put pen to paper, a rating came in to say that the service for those who had fallen would happen that evening as the sun went down. It sounded an almost romantic scene, canvas-wrapped bodies slipping from the flags that covered them and consigned to the sea. The 'Last Post' would sound.

The tea in her mug was getting cold and the margarine spread on her bun was congealing to a greasy shine. Phyllis had almost forgotten they were there.

Barbara gave her a nudge. 'I suggest you eat what you can whilst you can. I hear food is very short where we're going.'

It took some effort to overcome the sickness in her stomach, but common sense prevailed and, bit by agonising bit, she gulped it all down. Like everything that had happened today, it gave her a taste of things to come, things she was obliged both by the censor and concern for her friends to keep to herself. And so she wrote...

Dear Bridget and Maisie,

Have called in and left our first port of call. The sea is very blue and the sun is very warm.

I'm keeping a diary of everything that happens and the places I visit, then you can read it when at last this war is over.

Love to everyone at Wills. Keep your peckers up and I'll do the same here!

Her eyes fluttered and her hands shook slightly as she replaced the top onto her pen, lay back and closed her eyes. In her mind, she was back in the stripping room laughing with her mates.

She missed Bridget Milligan's cool and unflustered presence, the happy and proud way she'd spoke about her family. She could see her flawless complexion, the clear blueness of her eyes, the silky lustre to her hair. She was one of those naturally attractive young women, face unadorned with make-up. The funny thing was she didn't seem to notice the admiring glances from young men, certainly not like she did. Phyllis admitted to herself that she loved to be admired, loved flattery and that, perhaps, was her undoing. She sighed at the thought.

Her antidote of choice was thinking of Maisie Miles. It was Maisie who brought a smile to her face. She was slender, dark-haired, and big dark eyes shone from a heart-shaped face. Curls untamed by even the most vigorous brushing sprang round a complexion that erred towards coffee with only the minimum of cream added.

She turned her attention to the diary and the truth for posterity that she wanted to record there. The words would be for her eyes only – or for those who came after her should she not survive and find what she'd written:

Attacked by a U Boat. Coning tower hit. Many men injured...
some dead...

* * *

At sunset, the whole compliment of officers, crew and military personnel of other services were standing to attention on the aft deck. The sun was a fiery ball in the west behind them. No breeze fluttered the white ensign hanging at the stern. Only the very slightest wisp of hair fluttered round the girls' faces. Like everyone else in uniform, they stood with gaze directed towards the setting sun as the padre intoned the familiar words... *Ashes to ashes, dust to dust...*

One by one, the bodies of the fallen were released to plummet into the sea. Salutes were made as the 'Last Post' sounded before arms were returned rigidly to their sides.

Phyllis wondered at the lump she felt in her throat, as though the blackened bun she'd swallowed was stuck there, a sob that must not be heard. Despite a huge effort at self-control, a tear rolled from the corner of one eye and was dried by the breeze.

11

MAISIE

The first days of spring weather had truly arrived and there wasn't a sign of April showers.

There had been a number of air raids on Bristol since the beginning of the year and although nerves were frazzled, there remained an air of determination. People were being pushed to the limits of both their endurance and effort. Maisie Miles and Bridget Milligan were no exception.

Today was the final session for learning to drive an ambulance and Maisie was in her element. People smiled and waved when they espied a pert-faced girl behind the wheel. Not that it was any longer unusual to see women doing tasks that only men used to do. She'd even heard of some women flying planes, though not in combat, just collecting them from the aircraft factory out at Filton and delivering them to airfields all over the country. She wondered what that was like and imagined flying high above the clouds looking down on a midget earth below.

'Watch them gears.'

Fred was always telling her to watch the gears. When she'd first driven the ambulance, she hadn't been able to push the stick forward at the same time as depressing the clutch. She'd got the hang of it, but it wasn't easy.

Concentrating hard on getting it right so he wouldn't moan, she didn't really take much notice of the car that overtook the ambulance she was driving. Neither did she notice the piercing eyes regarding her or the fact that it turned off just before Bedminster Bridge, such was her determination to get things right.

*   *   *

Eddie Bridgeman had noticed her.

He leaned forward, his voice a low growl, his eyes hard with malice. 'Frank's girl. Did you see 'er? That was Frank's girl driving that bleedin' ambulance!'

Eddie's driver was wise enough not to mention the run-in with the Canadians when Eddie had been stuffed into the boot of his own car – this car.

Eyes narrowed and jaw clamped tight, the cogs of Eddie's brain mentally ground Maisie Miles into mincemeat.

A glint of gold flashed from a single side tooth as he picked at the gaps with a penknife. His voice was grim and his eyes dark slits in sharp features. He wore a double-breasted dark grey suit, white shirt, stiff-collared, silk tie of grey and burgundy. The folded-up handkerchief in his breast pocket was of the same shade. His trilby was black and so were the brogues he wore, which were polished to a high shine, though not by him. Eddie didn't deign to get shoe polish over his finely manicured nails. Didn't do anything much that required physical effort – unless fists were involved, though here too he preferred the beefy blokes who worked for him to do the dirty work. Brain beats brawn any time, he was fond of saying, though not to those who had the brawn, just in case they understood what he was getting at. A pound to a penny they wouldn't, but he didn't believe in taking hurdles unless he was sure of a soft landing. Only the women who worked for him or shared his bed got to hear it and they knew better than to open their mouths.

'Want to go after 'er, boss?' His driver was one of those who had the brawn but not the brain and was easily manipulated. He had a big square face and a prominent brow that overhung his eyes, plus a body that was so wide it spilled over from the driver's seat into the empty passenger seat beside him.

Eddie bristled at being bundled and bustled by a group of bone-headed servicemen – Canadians at that. They wouldn't have treated him like that if Maisie Miles, the little baggage, hadn't opened her mouth.

'No. I know where she works. I'll deal with that little slut in time.'

A grunt of agreement came from his driver.

'I fink I 'eard she ain't Frank's daughter,' he ventured.

'I don't care about that. It's all in the past.'

But not the other night, he thought to himself and rolled his shoulders as though shaking off the brawny hands that had bundled him out of the door. They'd made a fool of him, but it was all her fault.

Maisie's stepfather always brought the bile up from his stomach and soured his mouth. Frank Miles was the common, low-life thief who had got him a short prison sentence. Having the money and right connections had reduced that sentence, along with his promise to get involved with war work. Everybody was given that option, not that he'd had any intention of keeping that promise. To his mind, he was involved in war work, though not quite the sort the authorities accepted as bona fide assistance. He'd opened a night club in a cellar beneath a bombed-out building overlooking the river, where he offered everything a weary soldier could want in the way of refreshment, including girls who'd open their legs for a fiver. No less of course. That sort wandered the street, half a crown for a quickie in a dark doorway. There were plenty of those. He offered something a little more upmarket, nice-looking girls who got regular medicals and wore nice clothes.

There was more than one reason for ditching his old club. For a start, it was too far from the city centre. It was also known to the police. This one was well hidden, a totally new start-up. There was no bright light outside giving its name or attracting the notice of an air-raid warden. The Dungeon was word of mouth only.

Like most of the criminal fraternity, he had welcomed the blackout, readily accepting that so much could go on after dark – and to this end, the Dungeon didn't open until ten at night.

He had big plans to employ more girls. Young girls, the sort he liked. He'd liked Maisie Miles once, but wasn't so keen now. She'd grown up a lot. Besides she was Grace Wells's granddaughter. He'd never admit it, but he feared Grace Wells. She had property, she had money and knew too many bigger fish than him.

He dragged his mind back to his thoughts about girls – young girls. A lot of other blokes liked them too. Fresh meat with young faces. Mavis Thomas's daughter for a start – though only when he'd finished with her. He smiled at the thought of her. She tried to dress herself up as a woman, but he could see through all that. In that fleeting moment on the dance floor, he'd told her he'd give her anything she wanted. She'd looked terrified at first, but then had found her voice.

'Pearl earrings,' she'd said. It was odd the way she'd said it, as though he could easily get his hands on a pair.

'Anything you like, darlin'. Where do you spend yer time at night?'

Her eyes had widened. Her voice was nervous. 'In an alley off East Street when me mum's in a mood.'

There was something in that which made the hackles on the back of his neck stand up. She was nervous but also seemed to be getting one over on him. Cocky little mare, he reckoned. Still, soon knock that out of her.

Never mind about that. He knew where she was and that Mavis wouldn't object. How could she?

As for Maisie Miles, he'd get his own back on her one day, but could afford to bide his time.

12

MAISIE

There was an almighty scrunching sound of metal jarring on metal.

Maisie swore and so did Fred Partridge, the grizzled old former company driving inspector that W. D. &. H. O. Wills had brought back from retirement to train women chosen to drive ambulances to assist the city brigade.

'That is not a double declutch,' shouted Fred. 'It set me bloody teeth on edge.'

Maisie's jaw dropped when he promptly took out his two upper front teeth, as yellow as the rest of them.

'See? Germans blew me real ones out in the trenches so they made me these for nothing. They gotta last, you know. I ain't gonna be gettin' another pair. Now get back into first and change gear again, but this time make sure yer foot's pressing down hard on the clutch. Got it?'

Maisie wriggled in the seat and stretched her neck. Her legs were just too short to reach the pedals. 'I can barely see through the windscreen.'

Fred looked and growled beneath his breath. He'd taken on

this job but hadn't realised most of his pupils would be women. Twern't natural in his view.

'Look.' Maisie drew his attention to her diminutive position in the driver's seat. Her chin wasn't that far above the dashboard.

Maisie had christened the ambulance Big Bessie, and damn it all, she was going to do it no matter how often she would double declutch.

'I ain't high enough in this seat. Me legs won't reach. Where's that bit of wood you jammed under the seat last time?'

Moaning that enrolment of women should be confined to those with long legs, Fred got out his side of the ambulance and after making sure the brake was on, Maisie got out her side so he could adjust her seat as he had before.

With a bit of hefting and heaving, Fred pushed the driver seat forward and jammed the piece of wood as far forward as he could, grumbling all the time. Maisie thanked him and got back in. Fred continued to grumble. The only reason he'd thought to get away without the wood this time was pure laziness. Doing this job was a cushy number and the less he had to do made it even cushier.

Having had the same problem with reaching the pedals from her very first go at driving, Maisie had brought her own cushion, quite a pretty one of red and green tapestry that her grandmother had told her she'd stitched herself.

Her grandmother had been mightily impressed with her learning to drive, her fuzzy eyesight probing through the thick lenses of her spectacles, an expensive pair she'd bought with savings accumulated from less than legal opportunities over the years.

'So yer going to learn to drive an ambulance?' she'd said. It was never easy to gauge her grandmother's opinion on anything just by judging her expression. However, Maisie had sensed admiration on the wrinkled old face and in the tired old eyes.

'Yes, Gran. I am. Some people think it's unladylike. What do you think?' She'd asked her outright. She wanted praise that she'd done right. No matter her profession or background, Grace Wells was a wise old bird.

The strong, square hands that had aided fallen women to dispel their 'little problems', for a price of course, had made a loud whacking sound as she slapped her thighs. 'Women are as good as men at most things and can look after themselves if they're put to it – as I was.'

Maisie knew that her grandmother had been a widow for many years. Applying herself to what women wanted had made her quite well off. The proceeds of her businesses were kept in a biscuit tin, which in turn was kept behind a locked sideboard door.

'I'm taking yer advice, Gran,' Maisie had replied.

Grace Wells had nodded sagely, her already misted eyes misting over that much more, white, opaque and very close to blindness. 'You do that. I might be blind-sighted, but I can see into the future, you know. It enters my mind that one day there'll be a woman prime minister leading this country. So don't you go gettin' hitched to no loser like Frank Miles or anything close. Who knows? That prime minister might be you!'

They laughed at the absurdity of that ever happening. For the time being it was enough for Maisie that she was doing something for the war and her country by learning to drive an ambulance.

Maisie watched Fred's cap bob up and down at the end of the bonnet, where the cuss of a starting handle was being its cantankerous self, but refrained from looking amused. Every time they stopped it had to be restarted and the handle had a mind of its own. Fred would growl something fierce if he saw her smiling – or tell her to get out of the bloody cab and give a turn on the handle herself.

A picture of sobriety and serious intent, she kept her hands on the steering wheel and waited. All the time, Fred was heaving on the handle and using language that would make a vicar blush. Finally his efforts did the trick. The engine spluttered into life and then idled sweetly.

Face slick with sweat, Fred clambered into the passenger seat.

It was now that Maisie smiled at him. 'That was a job well done, Fred. Now where is that clutch?'

She stabbed at the clutch with the toe of her shoe and wrenched the gear change with her hand.

The ambulance inched forward and she selected another gear change as they got out onto East Street.

Fred begrudgingly told her it was much better. 'Listen to me and you'll get the 'ang of it all.'

She listened and did everything as he instructed and the gear stick slid noiselessly into place.

Maisie whooped with joy but wasn't letting Fred get away with such smugness so added, 'I'll only get the 'ang of it as long as I bring a cushion and you bring a bloody great big piece of wood!'

A slight movement drew her attention to the corded rope hanging between them and the windscreen. An impish smile curved her lips before saying what she knew would irritate him no end.

'Can I ring the bell now?'

Fred almost choked. 'No you bloody well can't.'

It was naughty, but in her opinion he needed a bit of needling. When they halted where roads crossed at Bedminster Bridge, her hand wavered in that direction, though stopped from actually doing it.

Fred almost burst a gut. 'I told you...'

His face was bright red and for a moment she thought he was going to choke, bending double as he tried to catch his breath.

She laughed all the way up Redcliffe Hill, glad the sky was blue and glad that she was learning to do something she'd never thought she would ever do. Things were looking up.

Behind her, glanced in the great prong of a mirror perched like a bird on the wing of the bonnet, was another ambulance and Bridget was driving it.

It was nearly mid-morning tea break. They'd catch up over a cup of tea. There might even be a couple of digestive biscuits if they were lucky and at lunchtime she'd seal the letter she'd written to Phyllis before popping it in the post. She'd crammed in as much news as possible. The one thing she hadn't mentioned was that night when two dead faces had shone like moons. Home was going to matter a lot to those serving with the forces. They had more onerous duties to perform than driving an ambulance and attending air raids. She needed to hear happy things, though reading about Robert having risen from the dead was going to knock her for six.

She drove her ambulance into a parking bay and turned off the ignition just as Bridget pulled in and parked beside her.

'Well that's it. You've passed. It's all over,' said Fred and looked pleased that it was.

Before Maisie could respond with a cheeky remark that she'd have passed without his help, she became aware of Bridget almost falling out of her vehicle and racing round to her.

'Maisie! Did you see him?'

Being short also posed problems for getting out of the ambulance. Maisie pointed her toe at where she thought the step was and finally made the ground.

'Did I see who?' she asked brightly until she registered the concerned expression on Bridget's face.

'Eddie Bridgeman. It was his car. I think I saw him looking out at you.'

Maisie frowned. 'Are you sure it was him?'

Bridget nodded. 'Pretty much so.'

Maisie was perturbed but still thought it might not necessarily be him and even if it was that didn't mean that he had been following her.

Bridget's chest heaved as she caught her breath, not because driving had tired her, but because Eddie Bridgeman worried her. 'I saw him turn round. Do you think he'll get his own back after you shamed him? You were certainly gutsy to do that.'

Maisie had no doubt. 'I wasn't going to let 'im 'ave 'is way. I 'ad a word with Carole afterwards. She pretended she hadn't needed help but was shaking like a leaf. I wondered about going round and warning 'er mother.'

'Do you think it will do much good?'

She shrugged. 'No idea. Perhaps not but that don't mean I shouldn't give it a try.'

* * *

The three new girls had learned quickly, but Maisie still kept an eye on them. She didn't bully or cuss them, but she did make sure that all was well on a day-by-day basis. It also pleased her that all three had got onto the first-aid course and that Jane and Carole had passed with flying colours. Pauline had backed out, her face pale as she admitted that she couldn't stand the sight of blood.

This morning, she congratulated Jane and Carole on passing their first-aid tests. 'All we gotta do now is toss a coin to see which of you joins which ambulance.'

She'd prefer Jane to be her new first-aid assistant, but if it was Carole, then so be it.

She still had it in mind to find out more about Carole's home life. She'd tried asking her about her mother and family, but didn't get much joy. In time she might gain a bit more of the girl's trust. On the surface Carole was full of confidence, but Maisie detected something else beneath the brassy surface.

Enlightenment came from an unexpected source. The baskets full of stripped leaves were being weighed before being tipped into the one of the trolleys. When she had started work, young men with cheeky grins and acne had pushed the trolleys, but that was before the war. Now it was just as likely in the midst of war to be a woman doing the job or young lads straight from school. Today the trolley pusher and weigher was Betty Knight, but she wasn't alone.

'This is Eric,' she said, introducing the lad with her who didn't look much older than the three girls. 'I 'eard you 'eard from Phyllis. Somebody said she's 'avin' a whale of a time.'

'Ain't she just!' Maisie exclaimed and didn't add that it had been received some time ago. Everyone liked reading about the sea and sunshine; it was like going on holiday abroad without leaving the factory floor.

Working in the tobacco factory had acclimatised Maisie to coping with more than one conversation at once whilst stripping leaves or keeping tabs on who was friends with who and who didn't look as healthy as they used to. During this conversation with Betty about Phyllis and her life in the sun, she observed the interaction between the three girls and Betty's new assistant.

Eric was a gawky lad, hair plastered to his head, with a long neck and an overly prominent Adam's apple. To top it all, he had a pudding-basin haircut. Once he'd matured, he might fill out, but for now he resembled a giraffe, all long limbs, a small head and bulging eyes.

She noticed Carole lean towards Pauline and whisper in her ear. Their eyes and giggles were fixed on the young lad. The poor chump realised the giggles and whispers were about him and in response his pale cheeks turned pink. His attention travelled to Jane, whose blush matched his when he returned her shy smile.

Carole's behaviour was far from shy. She held her head at a coquettishly high angle and there was cruelty in her eyes as she looked him up and down. To Maisie's mind, no girl of that age should look at anyone – certainly any man – in such a forthright manner. It was a disparaging look, the sort an older woman might use, but certainly not a young girl of Carole's age. She was barely fifteen yet acting like somebody more mature and experienced.

Betty was showing her the list of weights young Eric had just recorded. For his part, Eric stared at Carole in an odd way that she couldn't quite interpret and Carole fluttered her eyelashes and looked a bit pink in the face – as though she knew him.

On seeing Maisie watching her, Carole tossed her head and sneeringly said, 'Had yer eyeful or do you want yer penny back?'

'Knock it off, Carole,' Maisie warned. 'Nobody acts like this at Wills's. We're all friends together and yer too young to make enemies.'

The expression on Carole's face changed from femme fatale to a 'butter wouldn't melt in the mouth' kind of look. 'Why would I want to make an enemy of a spotty-faced boy?'

Maisie retaliated, her tone heavy with authority. 'This is a friendly place. We all get on with one another and I ain't letting the likes of you upset that. Got it?'

Carole's jaw dropped and for a moment it seemed she could respond either way, but it was Eric whose sudden outburst made all the difference.

'Oh come off it, Carole. We lives in the same street. I paid for us to go to the pictures the other night.'

'I don't recall,' said Carole, her nose set firmly in the air.

'You lives in Sally Lane. My mother's spoke about your mother. 'Er name's Mavis Thomas. My mum says she's no better than what she ought to be – all fur coat and no knickers.'

Pauline gasped, Jane blushed and Maisie's and Betty's jaw dropped.

'Well that's tellin' 'er,' said Betty, slinging the weighing record on top of the pile of leaves.

Eric hadn't finished. 'Says yer old lady's like a Boy Scout – always prepared, like a good man should be...' He frowned. 'No. I ain't got that right. It's not *like* a good man. What she said was that she's always ready *for* a good man – any man!'

'That's enough,' snapped Maisie and nodded at Betty, who read the look on her face and immediately got hold of Eric with one hand and the trolley with the other, shoving both on towards the next batch of leaves waiting to be collected.

'Come on, lad. We can't stand about 'ere. There's work to be done.'

Maisie could tell she was spluttering with laughter.

Carole was red-faced, her eyes round with fury, and she was muttering under her breath. 'Little shit! I'll 'ave 'im.'

'You ain't 'avin' anybody. I ain't deaf, you know, so knock it off – right now!'

An injured expression came to the heart-shaped face. 'Cheeky little sod. You 'eard 'im. Insulted my mother. I'm upset now.'

Maisie wasn't sure about her being upset – angry perhaps. Her face was flushed. Guiding her away from the others, she asked if she was all right.

Eyes downcast, Carole nodded. 'Yeah.'

'So you know Eric.'

Again the surly response. 'Yeah.'

Her lashes fluttered. Maisie fancied she wasn't wearing quite so much mascara as she usually did. The message about make-up might have hit home, but she doubted it. At no point did she thank Maisie for the Eddie incident at the dance. Not that Maisie wanted it. She'd done her bit and as long as she didn't run into him, that was good enough for her.

* * *

At teatime, Maisie collected a cup of tea and what resembled a scone but without the currants. She chose jam rather than margarine, which to her mind tasted like lard with salt added. The jam was watery but had some sweetness.

As usual, Carole and Pauline were sitting together. Just to ensure that nobody else took a chair nearby, they had placed their bags on the vacant ones, leaving Jane in no doubt that her company was not wanted.

'Wanna sit 'ere?' said Carole, smiling sweetly at Maisie whilst removing the bag from one of the chairs.

'No. Them chairs tend to be a bit greasy. The mechanics sit there.'

Maisie's insinuation about the stools was not lost on Carole. Her smile turned to a sneer when Maisie chose to sit with Jane.

Maisie smiled at her. 'Do you mind me sitting 'ere?'

'No. Course not.'

'So where do you live?' she asked brightly.

Jane looked down at her cup, her face reddening a bit more before she answered. 'Kent Street.'

'Not far to come to work then.' Kent Street went off West Street, which in turn fed into East Street where the factory was situated.

Jane shook her head.

Maisie would have asked more, but a worried-looking Aggie approached and asked if Maisie would come with her to the ladies' cloakroom.

'It's an emergency.'

Maisie left her tea and followed the indomitable stripping room supervisor.

'Is it Bridget? Is she all right?'

Aggie shook her head and carried on apace, Maisie with her shorter legs having difficulty keeping up.

'It's Judith.'

I don't know a Judith, thought Maisie. Before she could query it, they were in the white-tiled ladies' toilets. One of the cubicle doors was open and there was Miss Cayford sitting there with her head in her hands.

Aggie bent over her. 'Come on, love. You can't sit here all day and nothing's gonna change how things are.'

Maisie exchanged a questioning look with Aggie, who shook her head. She was none the wiser, though Miss Cayford had not been quite herself over the past few months.

Aggie took hold of Miss Cayford's hand. 'Now come on, Judith old love. At least you've still got a roof over yer 'ead. A lot of people lost the lot.'

Maisie now noted Miss Cayford's heaving shoulders and the sound of heart wrenching sobs.

'I wouldn't have gone to the shelter if I'd known. They took everything. All my mother's and grandmother's jewellery, including their wedding rings. Twenty-two carat – both of them – twenty -two carat,' she said again in case they didn't know just how pure gold could be.

Aggie sighed, straightened and looked at Maisie. 'It weren't only a bomb that hit the house, so did the thieves, ain't that right,

Judith?' She looked at Maisie and shook her head. 'She's been bottling it up all this time.'

Miss Cayford ran her hands over her face and through her hair. Maisie noticed she was no longer wearing the rings she usually wore. 'The house is damaged but still standing. A right state, mind you, but there, it's only a house. We're still alive – I should be grateful, fussing about valuables. But I just can't help it. When I went to look for the box where I kept all my jewellery, it was gone. If it was smashed in the blast, I could understand it, but the chest of drawers I kept it in was untouched. The box was gone.'

Maisie passed Miss Cayford her handkerchief, thinking how lacking in spirit she seemed in comparison to the woman who'd taken her on. She'd had such bounce, such pride in the firm she worked for. 'Looks as though you could do with a cup of tea,' she said with more confidence than she felt. Poor Miss Cayford wouldn't be cheered up that easily.

With shaking hands, Miss Cayford took the handkerchief and gave a trumpet of a blow. 'Sorry,' she said, squeezing the bridge of her nose with her fingers. 'I've coped with it well up until now, but once the clearing up was done and I wasn't so busy, I had time to think. I'm not usually one to come over like this. In time, I'll just be angry, but for now I feel defeated. Totally defeated...'

Aggie sighed and gave the hand she held the benefit of both of hers, her big grasp totally encompassing the birdlike hand of Judith Cayford. 'Can't blame you fer bein' angry, Judith, and defeated ain't a word you should use. There's some giving their all in this war, and there's some just taking.'

'You're right. I shouldn't even say the word, but I'm beside myself, out and out beside myself. I curse them, I do. I bloody well curse them!'

Cursing – something Maisie had never heard her do before –

seemed to do Judith Cayford the world of good. Her shoulders heaved halfway to her ears in an expressive sigh of resignation. 'I'm all right now,' she said, springing up from the closed toilet lid.

Throwing her shoulders back, she took hold of the hem of her jacket with both hands and pulled it tight. 'Well. Back to work. There's no point in crying over spilt milk is there.'

'Good for you.'

'Some rotten bastards around,' said Maisie, shaking her head as she walked back with Aggie, hands stuffed into her pockets.

It wasn't until they re-entered the stripping room when Aggie voiced what was on her mind. 'I've 'eard rumours about some of them that clears up after a raid.'

Maisie recalled her conversation with Carole. 'So I've 'eard.'

'It ain't just the likes of them that steal for a living. It's them that 'elp – only they ain't just 'elping to board up windows and suchlike, they're 'elpin' themselves!'

Once she had Aggie to herself, Maisie told her about Carole, the stolen valuables and Eddie Bridgeman.

'That figures,' said Aggie, nodding vigorously. 'That man don't give a damn about the living or the dead – 'e just cares about 'imself.'

13

MAISIE AND BRIDGET

The air in the canteen was always moist thanks to the steaming of suet pudding, available almost daily given its capacity to fill the hungriest stomach. Along with liver and onions, Somerset faggots or thick stews flavoured with a bit of scrag end or neck of mutton were the usual main course.

Maisie dunked the first digestive biscuit into her tea and sucked it whole into her mouth.

'That is so good,' she said, her eyes closing in ecstasy. 'Them canteen girls certainly know 'ow to brew a decent cuppa. What's their secret, do you think?'

Bridget, smiling fit to burst, broke into her thoughts. 'Lyndon's back. He took me quite by surprise last night.'

Maisie winked. 'Sounds like you enjoyed it.'

Bridget blushed. 'I'm going out with him tonight.'

'So what's he bin up to?'

'Well,' said Bridget taking a big breath, her eyes sparkling. 'He's involved in a survey about how ordinary people are coping with the war – you know – the shortages and air raids.'

She fell into sudden silence as she recalled the sight of him at the front door, him seeming to fill the living room, courteous as ever despite the querulous looks on her parents faces. Like him they were polite and recovered enough to offer tea. Her father had shaken his hand and asked what he was up to. Lyndon's enthusiastic explanation had aroused her father's interest, but only until Lyndon had asked her to go for a walk.

Hidden by the blackout they'd hugged and kissed until she felt he'd squeezed every breath out of her.

Maisie asking what this survey was all about burst the bubble of how those kisses and hugs had felt.

'It's for something called Mass Observation. We're doing it in this country and America has decided to do the same. He's been interviewing some people, but they were in London. His thinking is that this war isn't confined to the capital city; it's all over the country, including Bristol. I suggested he might like to interview Aggie and Curly about how they're coping with the war. He wanted diverse characters and, let's face it, Aggie's a big enough character all by herself.'

Maisie laughed. 'It could do 'er good. She's been looking a bit down in the dumps of late.'

Bridget agreed but didn't dwell on it. In her mind, she still thrilled at how it had been with Lyndon the night before. As they had stepped outside to go for the walk, Bridget had been ahead of Lyndon who light on his feet and in the midst of the blackout, had come up behind her unseen until his warm breath had fallen on her neck.

'Hey,' she'd said, laughingly. 'Has it ever occurred to you in this blackout that you might have your hands on the wrong woman?'

His hands had encompassed her waist, a small waist that he often remarked on. 'I'd know this waist anywhere.' His hands had travelled to her hips. 'Here too. And here,' he had added as his hands had cupped her breasts, his warm lips falling on her hair and ears before finally kissing her lips.

The lovely vision being replayed in her mind was interrupted by Maisie again, her expression quirky and nose slightly tilted. 'So 'ow are you gettin' on packing ciggies instead of stripping leaves?'

Bridget held up her hands and wiggled her fingers. 'Well, my fingertips look better now there are no leaves slicing into them. Shame there's no cigarette cards to collect nowadays, what with the shortage of paper. I used to like those.'

Maisie agreed with her. Before the war, you could have collected free cigarette cards on sports personalities, historical monuments, film stars or flowers. The war had stopped that.

'Hey, it ain't only Phyllis that's been writing letters. I got one from Sid. He sounds all right.'

She took the letter out and unfolded it, looking more pleased at a letter from Sid than Bridget could ever remember. Their relationship had been a bit fragile, to say the least, getting together in a queue outside the picture house where Maisie had made it clear she'd been far more interested in seeing the film than kisses and cuddles. But she'd been young then, not that long out of school.

'You can read it if you like,' Maisie added. Lots of girls in the factory were getting letters from sweethearts and it gratified Maisie to be able to say that she too had received one.

'You sure you don't mind?' Bridget eyed her querulously. It was part of her make-up that you didn't read other people's letters, but Maisie wasn't other people.

'Nah! He don't say anything lovey-dovey, just about 'ow it ain't 'alf 'ot and that there are monkeys swinging from the trees.'

In the few letters Maisie had received from him in the past, he'd drawn little triangles, which when she saw them Bridget had interpreted as pyramids, suggesting he was in Egypt. Mention of monkeys could put him anywhere and this time there were no drawings.

Although Maisie said there was nothing lovey-dovey in them, Bridget detected more than Maisie cared to admit. Back when they'd first got together, it had been noticeable that Sid had been smitten with Maisie. Unfortunately for him, Maisie had considered herself too young to have a boyfriend. She was older now. There was no excuse. One particular sentence jumped out at her.

'He's asking you to marry him.'

'No 'e ain't,' said Maisie, shaking her head emphatically. 'He's only on about gettin' engaged. That ain't the same, is it. That's only a might be, not a dead cert.'

Although Maisie's response amused Bridget, she curbed the urge to smile or disagree. Instead, she pronounced that he wrote a nice letter.

'Yeah,' said Maisie dreamily as she folded it away. 'Sid got a way with words. It seems only yesterday he was knocking around with Bert. 'Course I was only a kid back then.' A look verging on nostalgic affection came to her face. 'Cheeky bugger though weren't 'e.'

Her face glowed when she smiled and there was a dancing vibrancy to her delectably dark eyes.

The girl's growing into a woman, thought Bridget. She had come a long way from that skinny scruffy girl who'd bristled with attitude on her first day of work.

'I'm happy for you. It's nice to have someone who cares.'

As she said it her eyes fell on the BFPO details which were not fully obliterated by the censor. Singapore.

'There you are then,' said Maisie, slapping the table as she sat back in her chair. 'Sid will be all right. I just know 'e will.'

'Let's hope he did get away' said Bridget and felt an unaccountable surge of jealousy. There were no hurdles to Maisie marrying Sid – unlike her dealing with confusion and doubt about an unforeseen romance that she hadn't seen coming. Still, at least Lyndon was safe.

'I know I put 'im off at first, but I'm older now,' said Maisie, her happy voice breaking into Bridget's very private thoughts, dreams of what she'd like to happen between her and Lyndon. 'It's nice to 'ave a bloke talking about gettin' engaged and stuff.'

Bridget smiled as brightly as she could. 'You can leave off the decision until he gets back.'

'That's what I'm planning. In the meantime, I'm me own woman. Free as a bird.'

Bridget laughed and although her thoughts were with her own love, she heartily wished indeed that Sid did come home and that he hadn't ended up as a prisoner of war. She turned her thoughts to happier times. 'It seems such a long time ago now, you and Sid, me and Bert.'

'That day on the summer outing, standing on the pier, eating fish and chips...' Maisie laughed, but it was a nervous laugh.

It wasn't so long ago that the pixie-faced Maisie had descended on the stripping room and Bridget and Phyllis had taken her under their wings. Now here she was sounding as though she was thirty, not a bit shy of nineteen.

'What about Bert?' Maisie said suddenly. 'Remember how he used to ask you out at least once a week?'

Bridget blushed and pushed a silky strand of soft brown hair behind her ear. 'I remember all right. I wonder where he is now?' A sad expression came to her face. 'This is it with this war, people aren't just getting hurt, they're being scattered all over the place. All we can hope is that they come home safely.'

They fell silent for a moment as they considered old work-mates, like Bert, whom they hadn't heard from in ages.

Bridget did a lot of thinking throughout the day. Checking and packing was monotonous, something Bridget did without having to think about it. As she rolled the piles of cigarettes beneath her palms, she could afford for her thoughts to be elsewhere, with Lyndon or with her brothers and sisters who had been evacuated to South Molton. She missed them and thought about them a lot. At the same time, she blocked any thoughts about James, son and heir to the farm where her siblings were staying. Theirs had been a brief liaison, one she preferred not to think about. Bert was somebody she hadn't thought about in a long while. She hoped he was safe. There was only room in her heart and her head for Lyndon. He was the be-all and end-all of her existence, her past, her present and her future.

'Penny for 'em,' said Maisie. 'You got that faraway look in yer eyes.'

'Looking forward to our Sean coming home, though he wanted to stay there. Mum and Dad insisted he comes home and thinks about it before committing himself to working on a farm. To that end he'll need a job. I thought I might see if there's anything going here.'

Maisie didn't believe that's what Bridget had been thinking about, but went along with it anyway.

'They've been cutting down. You and I knows there ain't so many fags being made as there used to be.'

Bridget reluctantly agreed. 'I can but try. At least I could keep an eye on him – just like you're doing with this new lot. After what happened the other night at the dance, you've got your work cut out.

Maisie fixed her with a very direct look. 'Come on, Bridget. I grew up in one of the roughest areas in Bristol. I know Eddie Bridgeman. I know you 'ave to get one in first, show no fear –

though it ain't easy, mind you.' The last words were delivered with just the tiniest hint of a shiver.

'I suppose Carole is tough, but she is young. Do you think she might be a bit too fly for her own good?'

Maisie smiled thoughtfully. 'You seen 'er the other night. Eddie Bridgeman rattled 'er good and proper. I can't believe 'is nerve, walking in at the dance.' Her expression darkened. 'As I said, I tried to talk to 'er about it, but she clammed up.'

Bridget eyed Maisie warmly. 'Maisie Miles, you might be a pint-sized Venus, but you're nobody's fool.'

Maisie's eyes opened wide. 'Venus is it? Didn't you say she was a goddess?'

'The Greek goddess of beauty. You're just a smaller version.'

'Ta! Ta very much!'

Feeling as squashy as a marshmallow inside, Maisie concentrated on the remaining biscuit and what was left of the tea, stabbing it into the toffee-coloured surface until it was gooey enough to suck back in one.

She caught Bridget frowning.

'Somethin' wrong?'

Bridget's look was intense and full of worry. 'You know I said I suspected Phyllis was on her way to Gibraltar.'

'Yeah...'

'Also that it's only a stopping-off point and from what my dad had told me she will now be on the island of Malta.'

'What's that supposed to mean?' said Maisie, her frown matching Bridget's.

It was hard putting it into words without sounding terrified and Bridget gulped before it came out. 'The big battlefield out there is North Africa. Rommel is chasing our army backwards and forwards across the desert.'

Maisie gasped, eyes out on stalks. 'Do you fink she's goin' *there*?'

'No.' Bridget's voice was subdued, verging on awestruck, like whispering in church, the words getting lost in the rafters. 'Malta is a small island and according to the papers it's the main target for the enemy. If Malta falls, so does North Africa.' Her eyes rose to meet those of the younger woman. 'It would be another Dunkirk.'

'She didn't sound too worried in 'er last letter.'

Bridget's eyes met hers. 'You're right. She sounded light-hearted.' Just like Sid, she thought, but didn't say it out loud. Sid's letter was full of cheerful things, everyday things; references to home and past relationships figured large. Were they both hiding the truth so as not to upset anyone? Not to have anyone worry? If so, it was a very unselfish act on both their parts. Come to think of it, their replies to Phyllis had been pretty much the same, like a last grasp on civilisation.

'So this island...' Maisie began. 'What's so special about it?'

Bridget took a deep breath. 'I've read a bit of history about it. Three islands. They're a bit like the three bears. One big island, one medium and one small. They sit at the heart of the Mediterranean Sea, halfway between Gibraltar and Alexandria. If you're travelling across the Mediterranean, you can't help but get close. Its harbours are very deep and there's room for many ships. That's why it's being bombed so badly. It was on the news.'

If Maisie's eyes had been wide before, they were even wider now. 'My goodness. Poor old Phyllis migh' 'ave bitten off more than she can chew – and she's bitten off some big old pieces in 'er time!'

'She has indeed. But this...'

They ruminated on their own thoughts, the essence of which was that Phyllis had got herself in enough scrapes in the past –

some of them, like getting pregnant by one man and marrying another, were pretty serious. There was unspoken agreement between them that this was much worse.

'You were going to say that it could be the death of her.'

'I wouldn't say that,' murmured Bridget. 'Neither of us must ever say something like that. It's bad luck.'

She thought of her mother reading tea leaves, her belief in fortune telling a surprising adjunct to her faith in the Catholic Church. One of her tenets was that nobody should speak of deep-set fears just in case they became reality.

Maisie interrupted her thought pattern. 'I knows what you was thinkin', Bridge, but you didn't say it. I also knows you was thinkin' the same as me, that Phyllis would end up in some cushy little number repairing barrage balloons.'

Bridget didn't admit that she was right and that Phyllis had likely made a very rash decision. For a start, she'd volunteered to go abroad and one thing Bridget's father had once told her that no matter which branch of the armed forces it was, the accepted creed of the lowliest ranks was that nobody volunteered for anything. Serving abroad came top of that list because it usually turned out to be dangerous. He'd mentioned Gallipoli in the Great War. 'Thousands died trying to storm a position that couldn't be taken.' That's what he'd said. She wondered and worried what Phyllis had let herself in for and shivered.

For a moment they held their silence and mulled over their own thoughts, thinking back to how it had been when there had been three of them. Phyllis had been the glamorous one, tall, sleek and slender, whose lipstick was red and eyes a greyish green. To anyone meeting her for the first time, they would think her confident, full of bubbling personality and not at all the sort of person who could fall into and out of trouble at the drop of a hat. Unfortunately they would be wrong.

Maisie cupped her chin in her hand, elbow resting on the table and sighed. 'Makes you think mind, don't it. Us stuck 'ere, and 'er out there on a ship enjoying all that sunshine.'

'Enjoying the trip perhaps, but what about her final destination?' Bridget shivered.

Maisie sighed. 'Anyways, first as last it's 'er choice, innit?'

'I know it's her choice,' said Bridget in a determined manner, 'but it doesn't stop me worrying about what she's going to find. It's not as though it's a rainbow with a pot of gold at the end of it.' Her voice trailed away.

The remains of the original deep frown wrinkled her smooth brow. She thought about the history of Gibraltar, Phyllis's stopping off point, remembering what she had read about it: *Gibraltar was ceded to the British Crown in the Spanish War of Succession. In ancient times, it was called the Pillars of Hercules and was as important then as it is now, a vital link for vessels needing to traverse the Mediterranean and on to British India via the Suez Canal and the wide expanse of the Indian Ocean.*

She remembered it word for word pretty much as she'd read it. Reading had always been a great passion of hers. Now, in the midst of war, it was her way of escaping how things were. Though on this occasion the details of the past were too much allied to what was going on in the present.

When she shivered again, Maisie noticed. 'You goin' down with a cold?'

'No.' Bridget shrugged the shiver away and glanced over her shoulder at the canteen doors. 'Someone's left one of the doors open.'

Bridget didn't meet Maisie's stalwart gaze until she said, 'Knowing our Phyllis she'll be 'avin' a right knees-up when she gets to wherever she's goin'; on the way there too, if I know 'er at all.' Maisie grinned. 'So don't worry yerself, Bridget. And don't tell me you ain't worrying. I know you.'

'Then I won't tell you I'm not worrying,' declared Bridget as they made their way back to their respective jobs.

She failed to see Maisie watching her progress to her new workstation. Neither did she see the downturned corners of her mouth. They were both worried about Phyllis, though neither admitted it to the other. What would her reaction be when she heard about Robert, whenever the mail caught up with her?

Bridget tried not to dwell on her concerns and keeping busy helped. The cigarettes began to fly through her fingers, the fine white sticks now in prime condition and ready for packing in batches ready to go through the machine and into packets of five or ten. They'd been checked for flaws, those rejected gone back to have the tobacco removed and sent through the system again. Even the bits that fell onto the floor were swept up and put back through the system. Supplies of fresh tobacco were down. Rumours were rife that horsehair was being used to add bulk to the cheaper cigarette ranges. It could be true, if the smell was anything to go by, though nobody wanted to believe such a thing; but everybody realised that nothing could be wasted.

She'd settled well enough into her new job, though at first the other girls in the packing room had not been sure what to make of her. Gossip was rife about her relationship with a very rich American who owned a tobacco plantation. They became friendlier once they realised that she was as down-to-earth as they were.

'You looks as though you've got the weight of the world on yer shoulders, Bridget.'

The speaker was Annie Hicks, a married woman with a vulgar laugh, a matching sense of humour and the habit of opening her mouth before thinking what she was saying. She'd been brought in to replace a single girl who had opted to join the forces.

'A friend of mine's serving abroad. I'm a bit worried,' Bridget explained.

Annie looked at her in surprise. 'Before the call-up?'

'Yes. She wanted to see a bit of the world.' It seemed a good enough explanation.

'Oh well. I expect she 'ad 'er reasons to jump before she was pushed. They reckon it'll be ages eighteen to sixty,' stated Annie, a sliver of wood hanging by a lick of spit to the corner of her mouth. Smoking was banned in the workplace so those who couldn't wait until their break used a substitute. Although she was only a moderate smoker, Bridget supposed that just the feel of something hanging there – a sliver of wood even a matchstick – helped satisfy her craving.

Annie had been a housewife home alone for too long, which perhaps explained why she talked twenty to the dozen, catching up for lost time. Her voice carried round the room.

'That's the ages when they call up us women – well, the single ones anyway, though not them in the family way. You ain't in the family way, are ya?'

Taken off guard by the bluntness of Annie's question, Bridget blushed profusely and just about kept up the momentum of packing without crushing any or failing to feed the machine the cigarettes it expected. Sometimes at night she imagined herself and Lyndon naked in bed, the vision remaining in her mind when they were out on a date, her body burning with a deep desire to make that scene come true. Only one thing stopped her and that was getting in the family way.

'No,' she said, once she'd regained her self-control, and shook her head so vehemently that one of her turban ties flopped onto her forehead. 'No. Just worrying about the war and my mate serving abroad.'

Annie almost whooped her response. 'Don't worry, love. She'll do 'er duty and 'ave experiences she'll remember for a lifetime. Stuff to tell her grandchildren. Or some fings she might be better off keeping to 'erself,' she added with a wicked chuckle.

'No doubt,' said Bridget, and sincerely hoped she was right, that she would have grandchildren, but most of all that she would come back.

14

BRIDGET

It was a bad day. Right from early morning, Bridget had felt sick with apprehension. Lyndon was flying back to America, travelling across from Scotland to Ireland and then boarding a US military flight across the Atlantic. On top of that, the Germans had decided to pay a flying visit.

There hadn't been a really heavy raid since the end of March. In its aftermath, Mr Churchill had visited and, despite the devastation, there'd been a lot of cheering and waving of flags. Since then, the raids had become lighter and more intermittent, almost as though Hitler's attention had turned elsewhere.

Bridget and Maisie, clad in navy blue siren suits, their white helmets wobbling like upturned pie dishes on their heads, ran, then climbed into their ambulances.

Jane, her face as white as a sheet, ran behind Bridget, one hand holding onto her helmet.

Fred ticked their names off his list with gruff precision. Although he didn't say, he sincerely hoped that they got back safely.

'Hope you've 'ad yer supper, girls. Looks like being a long night.'

Bridget, her hands hanging onto the steering wheel as though she'd drown without it, drove the ambulance out through the double gates at the back of the factory where the light from half a dozen torches darted like overlarge fireflies.

It was gone eight and the air raid was in full swing, an arc of copper-coloured brilliance painting the sky. The thunder of anti-aircraft guns was accompanied by flashes of shells fired at the incoming raiders.

Of necessity, Bridget followed the feeble light falling onto the road from the restricted headlights, flashes of the white-painted kerb helping her to see her way.

Jane jumped. 'What was that?'

The girl was terrified and perhaps might have been less so if she'd gone with Maisie. But Maisie had insisted Bridget take Jane.

'I need to keep me peepers on Carole and if I lose me rag, I can box her ears. You take Jane. She'll be better with somebody like you.'

Bridget smiled as she recalled her reply, that Maisie was half hoping for a chance to box Carole's ears.

Jane was nervous. Bridget could tell that by her silence and the occasional little gasp when they went over a pothole or spotted the beam of a torchlight swung by a policeman or some other ancillary personnel. But then, it was Jane's first night. She was bound to be scared.

Dark streets bounded on either side, but ahead of them was a curtain of light thanks to the dropping of incendiary bombs. Pillars of flame shot up from dark roofs and painted flickering patterns over elegant facades and windowpanes.

A fire engine came up behind them, ringing its bells, nudging past at a higher speed than might be considered safe.

Bridget pulled over to let it past.

Now I'm nervous, she thought, aware of the sweat plastering her hair to her head beneath the tin hat.

On hearing Jane cough, she took a quick glance, saw that she'd opened the window and was throwing up whatever it was she'd had for supper earlier that evening.

'You OK, Jane?'

The girl pulled back in and nodded weakly. Despite the amber brightness from the incendiaries, Jane's face was still a white mask.

A policeman signalled Bridget to open the window on her side.

His face was red with sweat and it seemed as though his chin-strap was cutting into his throat.

'You OK?' she asked, presuming he wanted attention for himself.

'I'm fine, little lady. There's a few got burned trying to put the incendiaries out. We'll sort out them that need to go to hospital if you can spare the time to hang around a minute.'

'I'll get my bandages and give you a hand.'

Her hands groped for the first-aid kit, found it and tugged it forward.

'Come on, Jane. We've got work to do.'

Jane, sat there like a stone statue, didn't respond, unmoving, eyes fixed at the scene on the other side of the windscreen.

'Jane?'

Still no response.

'JANE!' One hand still holding the handle of the first-aid bag, with the other Bridget gave Jane a good shake. 'Come on, Jane. I need your help.'

Sheer terror was written on the face that turned and stared at her. The girl was petrified and it was down to Bridget to do something about it, not that it was in Bridget's nature to be violent, but this, she decided, was one of those times when it was necessary.

One slap landed on one cheek, one on the other.

Jane's first reaction was a jaw-dropping gasp. After that, she cupped her face and eyed Bridget in disbelief, seeing somebody new and not Bridget of the calm, sensible disposition who never lost her temper and was the epitome of everything nice.

Bridget shouted at her again which resulted in a series of rapid blinks.

'Do you hear me?'

Jane's bottom lip trembled and she replied, yes, she had heard her.

They tumbled out from the ambulance which used to be green but had been painted white, to which had been stuck a St John Ambulance cross.

Sulphur blew in puffs of yellow from the incendiary devices. The blackout was fighting a losing battle. The area round where they'd been dropped was almost as bright as day.

'Over here.'

Keeping low and moving swiftly, they followed the policeman behind a tumbledown wall, where a number of firefighters were sheltering, nursing burns received from trying to put out the fires caused by the incendiary bombs.

Bridget smiled at Jane and told her none of them warranted going to hospital.

Reassured that things were not as bad as she'd expected, Jane helped her apply iodine and bandages to the worst of the wounds.

They were making their way back to the ambulance, Bridget advising as to what their next task might be, when the low drone of an aircraft sounded from overhead.

'Take cover,' somebody shouted.

They looked up and perceived the long shape of an aircraft, coming in low, its insignia leaving nobody in any doubt that it was an enemy.

'Let's go,' murmured Bridget, her eyes wide with surprise.

Her intention had been to get back to the ambulance, but an ARP warden pushed them towards a pile of sandbags.

'Keep down,' he shouted.

They kept down, but their eyes stayed looking upwards. With grim fascination, they stared at the silvery grey of the enemy aircraft, so low they could just about discern the pilot lit by the flames he'd laid down himself.

'Bastard,' growled the man who'd pushed them behind the sandbags. 'He dropped the incendiaries and come back to take a look. Then he'll report back.' There was hatred in his eyes and also fear. 'The explosives will be next.'

Hearing a little intake of breath from Jane, Bridget placed a reassuring hand on her arm.

'It's all right, Jane. You'll be all right.'

She felt the trembling of Jane's arm.

The low throbbing of the aircraft subsided, then rose again. Somebody shouted that it was coming back.

In the meantime, a number of people who'd sheltered in the cellars came up for air.

At first, they stared up at the sky in grim fascination. Then suddenly there was screaming. The enemy aircraft had turned and was heading back, even lower this time.

The ARP warden shouted at somebody across the road who was hanging out of a ground-floor window, the light from within flooding into the street. Not that it mattered much. Its light was punitive compared to the fires started by the incendiary bombs.

'Put that light out...'

Suddenly a burst of machine gun fire came from the aircraft.

There were screams, bits of tarmac spitting up from the road in response to the bullets.

Bridget cowered, aware that Jane was doing the same. She'd thought the warden was too, until he slumped backwards, head falling forward and blood spurting from his chest.

Jane looked on, horrified. Bridget felt nauseous, but with trembling hands she undid her bag. It seemed to take an age and during that time she realised the man was dead.

'Too late,' she said.

Jane sprang to her feet and ran from behind the sandbags, out into the street, screaming as she joined other civilians, some carrying children, all of them running down the hill in some crazy search for a safe place to hide.

Bridget shouted, 'Jane. Come back.'

The sound of screaming and running feet was loud enough to drown out her cries, but nothing prepared her for what happened next; more short bursts of machine gun fire, people's terror, their tumbling one on top of the other.

As the low-flying plane wheeled, the dreaded bombs began to fall. Incendiaries were designed to light up targets. The job of the ones dropping now was to destroy buildings.

One after another, the shrill sound of bombs dropping was followed by the crashing of masonry and clouds of dust.

The smell and the dust were choking, the sound of explosions deafening.

Dust caught in her throat as she shouted Jane's name. The dust was thick and even though she tried to get out from behind the piles of sandbags, it proved impossible. Her legs were pinioned to the ground by the legs of the man who had been the first to be hit by machine gun fire.

Struggling against the heavy weight that prevented her from getting up, Bridget wouldn't have been able to see much once she did. Besides that, she could no longer hear the running feet and the screaming that had accompanied it.

'Stay put,' somebody said. 'There ain't nothin' you can do.'

The dust from flying debris cleared. The sound of the planes diminished somewhat but was still there, at a distance, still bombing but further up the hill and perhaps a mile away. She didn't know for sure. All she did know was that there were people out there who needed an ambulance.

'I have to go now. I'm needed.'

She struggled to get out from beneath the weight that pinned her down. Two or three pairs of hands pulled her. She recognised a man with a dirt-encrusted face as being one of those she'd tended earlier.

There was barely a moment to thank him when somebody else broke into their sad little group. The man reminded her of her father, of his age, creases of dirt-filled wrinkles framing his red-rimmed eyes.

'Miss.' We need you over the road. There's a woman buried in the cellar and the men are too big to get through the small opening we've managed to make.'

She didn't wait for more explanation. This was her job and whoever needed her, she was here to help out.

The top three floors of the building had impacted and a bit like her with the man's body, the weight of it was pressing down on the cellar.

One of the rescuers showed her the narrow aperture in the debris, no more than a large rabbit hole sloping downwards.

Bridget immediately thought of Maisie, who was far smaller than she was, but most likely already caught up in ferrying the injured to the hospital. Jane was slender too, but there was no sign of her either. She swallowed the dryness in her mouth and tried not to think of what might have happened to her. A clear mind was needed if she was to do what she had to do.

It was suggested she wear a harness and a rope, but probing the narrow passageway, the rescue torches alighted on broken pipes, stonework and jagged pieces of wood. It also seemed as though the way in stayed straight for only a while before twisting off to the left.

'Better not.'

Nobody argued, resigned to taking the chance. Like her, they were unsure of what she would find. What she did do was to slide a piece of rope through the handle of the first-aid bag and tie it round her waist.

Initially, she crawled on her hands and knees, but as she eased in further, she flattened herself against the ground. The surface was a mixture of stone, wood and even glass. She grimaced when sharp edges of what she couldn't see cut at her hands.

Just as she'd guessed, the opening did curve away to the left and also dropped downwards.

Like a rabbit hole, she thought, *though it certainly doesn't lead to Wonderland and I'm not Alice!*

A nail attached to a rough piece of wood caught her shoulder and made her cry out.

A weak and frightened voice called, 'Help... help...'

She focused her torch to where the corridor narrowed. The light bounced back at her off a series of smooth bricks – the chimney breast, she thought, and immediately felt a little relief. A chimney breast was the strongest part of any building. It wouldn't fall on her, or at least, she hoped it would not.

On her belly now, the roof above her bearing down, she edged forward, wriggled round the corner and gave grateful thanks that her siren suit was made of good stuff.

It was hard at first to see the person she could hear whimpering for help. Except for the weak torchlight, everything was black and it wasn't easy to discern the half-buried woman.

With great effort, she raised her head. 'It's coming,' she said soulfully.

Bridget wondered what she was referring to and whether she was delirious.

On gaining a little height, Bridget took the torch from her mouth and shone it ahead. The scene was confusing but she assessed as best she could that the woman's left arm was pinned beneath a pile of fallen masonry.

'You can get your arm out,' said Bridget, assuming that was what she meant.

'No.' The woman groaned, then shrieked. 'It's coming. The baby's coming.' She raised her right arm and rested her hand on her belly.

'Oh my God,' whispered Bridget.

Given the choice, she would have retreated, but she couldn't do that. As Maisie had said, they had a duty to the injured. It was true, they did, and she was ready to help wherever she could, but this was different.

She took a deep breath, forced herself to be calm. It was important to properly assess the situation.

The woman continued to groan, then cry out, her belly convulsing as she arched her back.

'Do you mean...' The words stuck in Bridget's throat, along with the grit and dust she was breathing. She tried again. 'Are you in labour?'

There was an almighty scream before the woman replied that she was.

Bridget gulped. Of all the things to happen. The last birth she'd attended had been her mother's miscarriage when she'd been so traumatised by what she'd seen her mother endure that she'd vowed never to go through it herself. Now here she was faced with a situation that she would prefer to avoid.

Taking a deep breath, she eased her way forward. The nurses from the medical unit at the factory had run a first-aid class but hadn't touched on what to do if faced with a woman about to give birth in a building that was in danger of crashing down on them.

'Right. Let me examine you. Just hang on. I have to move very slowly.'

There was no answer, just a low groaning interspersed by occasional screams.

Bridget managed to get forward enough to feel the woman's heaving belly, the contractions that would bring another human being into the world.

Suddenly she was overcome by fear. What do I know?

Grit entered her mouth and filled her nostrils with each breath she took. On top of that, the air smelled foul. Her courage weakened. She just couldn't do this.

'You need a doctor.'

'No.' The woman grabbed her hand with the one that had been rubbing her belly. 'Don't leave me. Please! Don't leave me.'

The light from the torch picked out the woman's dirty, sweaty features. It was hard to see the colour of her hair or even the shape of her face.

Her fingernails dug fiercely into Bridget's hand. 'Please don't leave me.'

It had occurred to Bridget that the woman needed morphine to dull the pain in her injured arm. If she hadn't been clinging onto her hand so forcibly, she might have gone to get some, a doctor too.

She blinked the dirt from her eyes. This poor woman was in pain and very frightened. She had no choice but to stay.

'I'm here to help you.'

Even to her own ears, Bridget thought she sounded unconvincing.

A rumbling sound came from overhead, but she forced herself to ignore it, to concentrate on the woman and the child waiting to be born.

It was coming quickly. That was her impression as she forced herself to think back to how it had been with her mother, with the miscarriage and the times before that when healthy babies had been born.

The woman coughed, held her head to one side and cleared her throat.

Bridget began to do the same as her hands became warm and sticky from blood and birth liquid.

She heard the sound of shovels digging away the debris behind her in a bid to make the escape route wider. Every so often, they stopped and she knew they were looking through the rest of the building for signs of life.

In that moment of silence, she heard a hissing sound.

Gas! Her heart raced with the knowledge that it was a fractured gas main that was making her cough and gradually causing a tightness in her chest.

You mustn't panic!

Bridget took a roll of bandage from her first-aid bag.

'This will help stop you coughing,' she said, tying it round the woman's face.

Spots of light wobbled round her. She was getting dizzy, so swiftly wrapped another bandage round her own mouth. She had to carry on. She had to help this woman in any way that she could.

Stronger contractions warped the woman's belly. Bridget knew the baby was close to being born and noticed the woman's cries were less vocal, though her pain could not have lessened. Bridget realised it was likely caused by the gas the woman was breathing in.

With the memories of her mother's still birth and desperate to get this over with, Bridget spoke soothingly encouraging the mother-to-be to push and was rewarded with the top of the baby's head gradually coming out, then the whole head, then the shoulders. Absorbed in the natural process of birth, she pushed the possibility of a gas explosion to the back of her mind.

It struck her that she mustn't let the woman drift off completely. They were almost there, just turn the shoulders – she knew that much at least, then it would be over. The rest of the body, smaller, narrower and slippery, would slide out.

'What's your name?'

The woman didn't answer at first, so Bridget repeated the question more loudly.

'What's your name?'

'Daisy.'

'Is that what you'll call your baby? If it's a girl that is.'

'I don't know.'

The sound of shovelling echoed along the narrow tunnel behind her. She couldn't tell for sure whether it was coming closer, but hoped it was.

Dirty as it was, there was nothing for it but to return the torch to her mouth. She needed both hands to deal with the baby. Before she could do what she knew had to be done, it slithered out all by itself and burst into loud cries. Holding her head to one side, she managed to angle the beam of the torch so she could tell whether Daisy had delivered a girl or a boy.

'A girl,' she exclaimed with a great gasp of relief as the beam flickered over the child's body; there was no blanket, no sheet, nothing lying around. All she had was the scarf round her neck, the lovely silky one that Lyndon had given her for good luck. She whipped it quickly from round her neck and, wrapping the mewling baby in it handed her to her mother.

'There you are.'

The air seemed thick with gas one minute, then less so the next.

'Hey, miss.' The voice came from not too far behind her. 'How's things goin'?'

Bridget felt a fresh blast of air and, even though it was the dead of night, knew the gap through which she'd climbed had got bigger.

'It's a girl.' Her voice sounded as though she was close to breaking down, yet she felt relieved and strangely happy.

She was ordered to back out so the rescuers, burly men with purpose, could take her place and release Daisy.

Tired out and filthy dirty, she took great gasps of air once she was outside, her hand grasping at her throat. There was something she wanted to say, something very important. Staggering forward, she finally spouted one single word. 'Gas!'

A man took hold of her gently and assured her that the gas and water had been turned off.

'First rule. Don't want anybody gettin' gassed or drownin', do we now.'

Bridget looked at them blankly, her thoughts all over the place, and so was her gaze, searching, though she couldn't quite work out what or who she was seeking.

Suddenly she saw Maisie wrapping a bandage round someone's head. Alongside her was Carole, rolling up fresh bandages as she chattered away to the men working there as though she was attending a dance, not the likely scene of a tragedy.

'Maisie!'

On hearing her shout, Maisie turned and saw her, face streaked with dirt, eyes looking red and sore.

'My God!' She ran over, reached out and gripped her by the shoulders. Her round-eyed look was all-seeing yet also questioning.

In response, all Bridget could do was raise hands that were sticky with blood and body fluids. Her bottom lip quivered and although she tried to speak, words would not come, but the tears did. Great big globules running unabated down her face, trickling off her chin and mixing with the snot from her nose.

'Bloody hell, you look awful,' said Maisie, looking disgusted. ''Ere's me 'anky. Give yer nose a good blow.'

Bridget's hands shook as she took the handkerchief, gripping it tightly as though expecting it to fly away if she didn't.

Maisie looked over her shoulder and shouted at Carole to fetch Bridget a cup of tea. 'With plenty of sugar!'

Carole hesitated, much preferring to chat and pose as though a tin hat and a siren suit made her look glamorous.

Bridget was glassy-eyed but jumped when Maisie shouted at the top of her voice.

'Get on with it, you stupid cow, or I'll slap you both sides of yer face!'

In other circumstances, Bridget would have smiled at the huge voice coming from such a fairy-like person, but she was too tired and too torn. She wanted to go to bed. Attending a birth in such horrendous conditions was debilitating.

The tea was hot and as sweet as it could be; emergency workers tended to have a little bit more sugar than other people. Sugar helped shock, so she'd heard.

'There. That better?' A worried-looking Maisie searched for signs that she was recovering.

Actually, she was, and as she returned to normal, Bridget began to look about her for one familiar face that was absent.

She remembered the brightness of the incendiaries and the loud bangs of the explosions, people shouting, screaming and running downhill.

'Where's Jane?' she asked, cupping the warm mug with both hands.

Maisie swallowed and lowered her eyes. 'I don't know. Fancy another cup of tea?'

Bridget was immediately suspicious and very afraid.

'Ambulance! Can you take mother and baby to hospital?'

Maisie sprang instantly into action, grabbing her first-aid box, bundling in what bandages she had left.

'Course we can.' She shouted at Carole. 'Looks like our shout. Get the stretcher.'

Carole did as she was told. The stretcher was awkward and heavy. Carole being Carole, she managed to get a young man to give her a hand.

Maisie grabbed hold of Carole and the stretcher, dragging both to where mother and baby were being carried across the rubble.

Baby nestled against her breast, Daisy was sitting on a plank of wood being carried between two strong men. Another behind her, hands against her back to prevent her falling off.

Their progress was slow and they picked their way carefully. Bricks and debris tumbled beneath their feet. In some places, steam rose from the bricks and concrete of what was left of the building. The steam was a result of the fact that a vast amount of water had been directed onto it.

Daisy and her cordon of volunteers finally made level ground, where she asked for them to stop. She looked directly at Bridget.

'What did you say your name was?'

'Bridget. Bridget Katherine Milligan.'

'Bridget Katherine,' said Daisy, looking down with a loving smile into her new-born's face.

Bridget touched the baby's hand and her finger wandered to the baby's screwed up face. She wanted to laugh. She wanted to cry. Instead, she said, 'That's nice. I like that.'

Mother and baby were loaded into Maisie's ambulance.

Too exhausted to do anything else, Bridget sank down onto a low wall. Her eyes felt sore and she would prefer to go home, but the sugary tea had done its work.

She heard the jangling of the ambulance bell as Maisie drove off. At least they would be all right.

'You all right, love?'

The shadow of an ARP warden fell over her. She looked up into kind eyes. Dust choked her throat, though not as much as the fear she was feeling. She asked him about Jane. He asked when was the last time she'd seen her.

'She was running down the hill... The enemy plane opened fire... She was frightened.'

The nausea of outright fear gripped her stomach when she saw the look in his hooded eyes and the slackening of his jowls.

'They're over there,' he said, straightening up at the same time as jerking his head to some point further down the hill. 'St Michael's Church Hall.'

Apprehension gripped her stomach as she got to her feet.

The man reached out to stop her. 'Spare yourself, love. Most of them were shot by that...' He chewed at his lips rather than swear in front of a lady. 'It's not a pretty sight, love.'

She looked up at him in disbelief and shook her head. 'I've got to see her.'

He nodded silently and turned away.

It wasn't as she'd expected. The dead had been laid out in

rows, their bodies covered with a piece of tarpaulin. Only their feet were on view and quite a few were women, their stockings shredded, shoes missing – feet missing – legs missing.

She saw Jane's feet, still wearing the court shoes she'd specifically told her not to wear.

'Flat shoes. They make more sense. You can run quicker in flat shoes.'

'These are me dancin' shoes,' Jane had said. 'I can dance fast and run fast.'

A sob caught in her throat. Poor Jane would never dance again.

15

BRIDGET

Every night after that raid, Bridget sat in bed reading. It helped her blot out that she'd been in danger, that she'd delivered a baby in the direst circumstances. The crumbling building could have fallen on her at any time; if the gas hadn't been turned off the whole building would have gone up. And poor Jane was gone and it was all down to one ruthless rogue flyer.

She'd been too shattered to explain anything to her family following the shift. Feigning extreme tiredness – which was pretty much the truth – she'd headed for her bed and had fallen asleep fully clothed.

Three nights had passed. She'd been in the factory when the Prime Minister Winston Churchill had visited yet again, waving his hat and giving his famous V for Victory salute.

The rumours remained that he'd only really come to inspect the new cigar-making machine down at Number Two factory in Raleigh Road.

People had cheered. She'd clapped, her mouth too dry to cheer as tears ran down her face.

Maisie had asked her if she wanted to go for a drink or to the pictures. She'd said she was too tired. Maisie, shrewd as ever to the truth, told her that either activity would help her cope.

'The war goes on regardless.'

Yes, it did, but having a drink or watching a movie didn't take her into another world, somewhere far away and long ago. She had a whole pile of books beside her bed: *Little Women* by Louisa M Alcott, *Tales of the Arabian Nights, Ivanhoe* and *Lorna Doone.* It was different times she needed and if she had the chance to fly away on a magic carpet, she'd do that too. There was only one thing likely to lift her spirits as no book could do.

On the following morning, a telegraph arrived from Lyndon stating that he hadn't gone to America after all, was back from London and would pick her up this evening. No asking, but seemingly taken it for granted that she would be available. And she would! She most definitely would.

That night, she stood in the dying evening light by the garden gate hugging herself, her eyes searching for the sight of his little car coming along the road.

He was one of the few people who could get hold of petrol for his car, though he had swapped the Daimler for an Austin Seven, which he'd said to her laughingly resembled an orange box on wheels.

'A second-class ride is better than a first-class walk,' he said as Bridget slid into the seat beside him.

For at least ten minutes they clung to each other as though to let go, one or both of them would vanish.

Bridget felt the beat of his heart against hers, the hardness of his arms round her, the feeling that their lips were melting together.

'I've missed you so much,' he said to her, his breath warm upon her face, his fingers stroking her hair.

'I bet you say that to all the girls,' she said laughingly and instantly regretted it. Sometimes it was hard to believe that a man like him could claim to love a girl like her. As her mother never failed to remind her, they were from different worlds.

'*Don't trust too much. Nothing lasts forever.*' Her mother had said.

She hadn't responded except to say that she was enjoying herself. That he was good company. That they lived in desperate times and each moment was precious.

He stiffened at her words, then pulled back. 'There's not a girl in London or even the whole world who could hold a candle to you.'

It was too dark to see his expression. She only hoped it matched the sincerity in his voice.

'I'm sorry, but it's just that—'

'Yeah, yeah. You're from here and I'm from somewhere totally different.'

He didn't mention wealth and neither did she.

'Do you fancy a drink?'

'Do I! My throat's as dry as Arizona, but nothing that a warm pint of British beer couldn't deal with.'

The engine of the little car hummed like a large bee as he crashed the gear and pulled away from the kerb, which made Bridget laugh.

'I have that trouble driving the ambulance.'

'It's not the smoothest gear change I've come across.' He laughed with her.

After a slow journey through the darkness, he pulled onto the tarmac apron at the front of the Engineers' Arms.

Over the warm beer he'd expected and half a cider for her, they talked at a table in a tight corner. He spoke a little about the work he was doing, of gathering information on public morale, on how society was being affected by the war.

'It's important work, more important than it sounds.'

'Ordinary people are important.'

'You bet they are. I'm using less petrol and driving myself about. Had to anyway. The company chauffeur left me to it. Decided he wanted a bit of adventure. The chance to get shot at, but I take my hat off to him. He's a brave man, though a bit crazy.'

She laughed and felt comforted by his closeness, the warmth of his thigh close to hers – not naked as in her vision, but still intoxicating.

'Of course, I know what you mean. Let me remind you that I work in production so being driven round in a company car doesn't happen often, so I'm not privy to what the company's chauffeur gets up to.'

His smile tightened and she replied perhaps a little too sharply.

'Stop doing that, Bridget.'

She sighed. 'Lyndon, I'm a girl that catches a bus. I don't jump into a car. My family can't afford one and that makes me feel uncomfortable.'

'I'm sorry. I don't mean to do that. I guess I should just think a bit more before opening my big mouth.'

'And putting your foot in it.'

'Yeah. Sure, though I have to say, right here and now, that I know what you are. Despite the British class system selling you short on education, your intelligence shines through. I love you for everything you are, and I mean everything.'

His words and his closeness brought the night-time vision bursting into her consciousness. Her body felt too warm and her heart hammered with expectation. She forced herself to change the subject, even though she didn't want to change the subject, even though he was the subject, one who meant more to her with the advent of time.

'So how's your interviewing going?'

He nodded slowly. 'It's going good. Apparently they appraise reports on public morale with a view to working out how it affects policy – you know – to help them work out what's best to do next.'

'So now it's Aggie and Curly at the Llandoger.'

'You're sure they're OK about this?'

Lyndon had sent her a note asking for suggestions and she'd mentioned it to Aggie and what a good idea it might be to interview her and her husband, Curly, a pub landlord. Curly loved his pub, but Aggie preferred to go out to work – at least by day. By night, she was there beside him, giving the customers the benefit of her wisdom and strength of purpose as they supped their pints.

Aggie was thrilled to be asked and beamed from ear to ear. '*Love to take part. Tell 'im I keep the blokes in order. I says to them, any nonsense and you can pick a window for me to throw you through.*'

'Positive. You'd have thought Aggie was being asked to take a screen test. She asked if she needed to wear her Sunday best. Said she was thinking of spending five ration coupons on a new hat.'

Lyndon laughed. 'I don't have a camera.'

* * *

Bridget had agreed to accompany Lyndon to the interview with Aggie and Curly. Two days later and they were on their way to the Llandoger Trow.

The darkness was all-consuming. Restricted by tape and thus rather feeble, there was something reassuring when the narrow beam from the headlights picked up the white paint on pavements and lamp posts.

'Am I going the right way?' Lyndon asked.

Bridget leaned forward, doing her best to work out where they were. In her head, she ticked off the clues: first, there was the delicious smell coming from the faggot and pea shop; added to that was the fact that they were going uphill, but the shopfronts were indistinct blocks of black, if seen at all. It wasn't until they could see the unmistakeable spire of St Mary Redcliffe Church pointing skywards like a huge black dot, that Bridget was confident. 'I know where we are now. Left into Queens Square and then right.'

Nothing was quite as recognisable as when the car began bumping across the cobbles of King Street, to where the ancient inn, the Llandoger Trow, dominated the riverside quay they called The Welsh Back.

'What did you say that name means?' asked Lyndon as he turned off the engine.

Bridget was happy to oblige. Lyndon certainly respected her interest in all things historical. 'A trow is a kind of sailing barge used to transport goods, mostly tree trunks when they come down river from the Forest of Dean. Llandoger means it came down from a village over there on the Welsh side of the River Severn called Llandogo. It's just along the road from Tintern and its famous abbey.'

'Really? A famous abbey?' He leaned across and kissed the side of her head. 'Well, it can't be that famous. I've never heard of it.'

She slapped his arm playfully. 'You're pulling my leg, Lyndon O'Neill.'

'Scout's honour, I am not,' he said, raising his hands above his head. Even in the depth of blackout, she could see the amusement playing round his lips. 'Anyway. What would I know about an abbey? I'm not a monk.'

'We'd better get inside. Aggie insisted laying on sandwiches

and told me not to be late or they'd be curling at the edges –
either that or her old man, as she put it, would scoff the lot.'

'So it's Aggie and Curly,' said Lyndon.

Bridget giggled. 'Yes. Curly's the one with no hair.'

'Really?'

Lyndon laughed all the way up the steps before pushing open
the door, the noise and chatter falling out, along with a sliver of
light before the curtain was tugged firmly across.

Bridget was right about the sandwiches. Aggie had pushed
the boat out.

'Some are cheese, and some a nice bit of ham.' She tapped the
side of her nose. 'Don't ask questions about where it came from
and you won't be told any lies!'

Lyndon took off his hat. 'Wouldn't dream of asking that
particular question, ma'am.'

They followed her through the odd sequence of higgledy-
piggledy interconnecting rooms.

'There. We got some privacy in 'ere,' Aggie said and patted
her hair as she showed them into a final room and shut the door
behind them.

Aggie was wearing her best dress and had her hair pinned up
in a chic manner Bridget had never seen before. Curly, his bald
head shining, was wearing what looked like his best suit, a white
shirt and a tie. Both beamed enthusiastically.

Lyndon thanked them for the beer and sandwiches. 'You
needn't have gone to so much trouble.'

'You've come from a long way. Seemed only proper,' said
Curly. When he smiled, a gap showed in his teeth. He got out a
packet of small cigars. Bridget recognised them as Whiffs, yet
another product produced by W. D. &. H. O. Wills. She declined
and sat down on one of the well-worn but highly polished
wooden chairs.

Lyndon took one of the small cigars at the same time as setting out his notebook and pen.

Aggie insisted on everyone having a sandwich and a sup of beer first.

Curly raised his glass. 'Good health to us all and a vile death to Adolf Hitler.'

Aggie raised hers and followed his lead with her own more vivid insult. 'Too right. 'Ere's 'oping 'is crown jewels drop off!'

Although looking a little perplexed, Lyndon raised his own glass and exchanged a smile with Bridget. She was used to Aggie being a bit risqué at times, but didn't bother to warn Lyndon. As expected, he was amused rather than shocked.

Once they'd eaten and drank to Aggie and Curly's satisfaction, he picked up his pen.

'Right then. I've been asked to get the low-down from the people of this island about how they really feel about this war. The American people have seen the newsreels at the movies telling them that you're going through hell, but I've been sent to ask ordinary people what it's really like. So tell me. How is it?'

Curly and Aggie looked tongue-tied.

Lyndon waited. The fixed smile wilted when time went on and still they said nothing.

'Is something wrong?' he asked.

Bridget looked from him to them and back again, then gave him a sharp nudge in the ribs.

'What?' Lyndon met her direct gaze.

'Just relax and tell him all about it, Aggie. It's vital that the US and our own government know how its people are managing. They can't plan for what's needed if they don't know your needs.'

Aggie sniffed and clasped her hands in front of her. 'But they ain't in the war.'

Lyndon smiled the slow smile that Bridget had come to love.

'Not sending in the troops, no, but we are helping out – in the background; giving you what support we can. And in time, who knows what might happen.'

There was love and understanding in the shared look between Aggie and her husband. Aggie always said that she went out to work to stop the pair of them getting on each other's nerves., but it didn't mean they weren't close. Theirs was a long lasting and tolerant marriage.

'All right,' said Aggie with a resigned shrugging of her shoulders. 'Ask us a question.'

'OK. Let's keep it basic. Is there anything in particular you'd like more of?'

'Beer,' said Curly without a moment's hesitation. 'Spirits are hard enough to come by, but what most working men want at the end of a long day is beer. Too busy on a weekend and we're down to the dregs of the barrel by Wednesday.'

Lyndon wrote it down. 'A pub with no beer. That's pretty gruesome.'

'You're not wrong there, son,' said Curly as he reached for the rest of his drink.

'What do you think about Churchill's speeches?'

'I thinks them stirring. The man speaks like a general not a town clerk. Now, that Chamberlain put me in mind of a town clerk, the sort with inky fingers who don't see no further than an accounts book. That's what I think,' declared Curly, banging the table with his hand.

Lyndon grabbed his beer and Bridget the plates as they rattled across the table with the force of the blow.

'Cheers,' said Curly, lifting his glass and seemingly oblivious to the force of his action.

'Cheers,' Lyndon echoed.

Other questions followed, and what with the food and the beer, the evening was becoming jollier.

The moment was interrupted by the thick plank door banging back against the wall. The candles stuck into wall sconces flickered as a figure passed between them and the solitary group sitting at the table.

The new arrival wore a green satin blouse that strained over her breasts, a skirt that was so tight it bordered on indecent. Finely lacquered fingernails tapped the curved hip and a tight belt accentuated the small waist. There was haughtiness in the mascaraed look that flashed over them.

'Looks like a tea party and very nice too, I must say, though nobody thought to invite me. Care to pass me a sandwich, ma?'

The corners of Aggie's mouth turned downwards. Two meaty hands pressed down on the table as she got to her feet.

'Angie,' she said with a grim set of her lips. 'Our daughter comes and she goes, and that's what she should be doing now,' she added grimly.

The good-looking but blousy young woman struck a pose. It was one Bridget had seen in a film, one where Bette Davis played a gangster's moll and was too sassy for her own good.

'Well, that's a nice way to welcome yer daughter 'ome, I must say.' Her voice bounced off the low ceiling and lumpy walls.

Curly rose from his chair, his voice heavy with contempt. ''Ome? What do you mean 'ome? This ain't yer 'ome. Ain't bin yer 'ome since you shacked up with Eddie Bridgeman.'

'Kept 'im off yer back,' she said. 'As long as I was on my back, 'e didn't come round 'ere demandin' 'is due.'

The slap Curly landed on his daughter's heavily made-up face was swift and unexpected.

Bridget gasped as Angie's head snapped to one side. She

chewed her jaw at the same time as placing her palm on the growing redness.

'Little tart. You ain't no daughter of mine!'

Then Curly was gone.

Not that his daughter took much notice. Eyes shrouded in makeup settled on Lyndon. She took out a cigarette, leaned into him and asked for a light.

Lyndon glanced at Bridget before he obliged. He'd noticed the peroxide blonde hair, the low-cut satin blouse and the ostentatious earrings. He'd seen the like of her before in plenty of places, though not so close up as this.

'Sure,' he said, both his voice and manner casual.

Her bright red lips pouted over the end of her cigarette and her hand brushed the fingers that held up the lighter. Her eyes bore into his.

'Ain't seen you 'ere before. Should I know you?'

Lyndon shook his head. 'No. This is my first time here – in this pub, that is. I have been to Bristol before.'

'You're an American!' Her face lit up with interest.

'I sure am.'

Angie glanced at Bridget. 'This your girl?'

'You could say that.'

'Hmm,' she exclaimed, tossing her head. 'Lucky girl.'

'Angie, I think you should go,' said Aggie. She moved towards her daughter step by step, closer and closer, so Angie had no option but to take backward steps towards the door.

'I'm curious about the Yank. What's 'e doin' yer?'

Aggie's expression was resolute. Bridget had always known Aggie Hill as a woman of strength who lay down the law when she had to. But that was at the tobacco factory. This was in her own home towards a member of her own family.

'If you must know, he's here to ask us some questions about how we're coping with the war.'

Curly suddenly appeared at the door. He looked directly at his wife and averted his eyes from his daughter. 'Let me know when she's gone,' he said, his mouth an angry snarl.

It was only fleeting, but Bridget was sure she saw a slight wince crease Angie's face. Aggie's daughter was acting hard, but in that moment Bridget had detected vulnerability. Then it was gone and her attention and wide-lipped smile was back again and directed at Lyndon.

Angie perched herself on the edge of the table, her thigh close to Lyndon's elbow. She gave only a cursory glance at Bridget.

'Get any time off to 'ave a bit of fun?' she asked, yellow teeth showing through red lips.

'Getting time off is a bit of a scarcity these days. I've got a lot of work to do. War work, you could call it.'

'Is that so?' She leaned in closer. 'All work and no play makes Jack a dull boy.'

'My name's not Jack.'

She laughed a long throaty laugh. 'Don't matter what yer name is, bet you could do with 'avin' a good time. I could show you a good time,' she said, a length of hair caressing his face as she leaned in some more.

Curly's swift slapping of Angie's face had been sudden enough. It was now her mother's turn. Aggie dragged her daughter from her seated position on the table.

'Get out, Angie. Yer dad don't want you 'ere and neither do I.'

Bracing her hands on her hips, the two women, both of equal height, faced each other with eyes blazing.

Angie recovered quickly and her words were scathing. 'Well, thur's gratitude! Me own mum and dad don't want to see me! Fat thanks fer all that I've done fer them.'

'You ain't welcome 'ere as long as yer livin' in sin with that Eddie Bridgeman. Like you just said yerself, lying on yer back fer 'im.'

'I did it fer you. I told you that. Otherwise 'e'd 'ave put the screws on you and dad good and proper.'

'You're a tart. That's what you are. Nothing but a cheap tart. Not my daughter. Not now and never again.'

A deep flush came to Angie's face and her lips set in a stern straight line.

Angie sniffed and pouted before saying, 'I ain't livin with Eddie no more. I've moved out. Me case is out on the doorstep. I wants to come 'ome, Ma.'

Hidden beneath the table, Lyndon gave Bridget's hand a little squeeze of reassurance. She continued to watch with wide-eyed surprised.

Aggie shook her head. 'You ain't left 'im, 'ave you. Not really.'

'I just told you so, ain't I?'

If Bridget didn't know Aggie better, she'd say that it was a cruel sneer on her face. Aggie had always been a big presence, but this evening she detected hurt in those soft brown eyes, totally at odds with the twisted lips. It was as though her daughter was a book, though not as closed as she might like to be. Aggie knew her. Understood her. Could read her mind.

'Got a new tart in 'is life 'as 'e?'

Angie winced; looked as though she'd been found out. From the moment she'd swaggered in, all brassy bravado and woman of the world, Angie had brimmed with confidence. Mention of Eddie Bridgeman having a new girlfriend had now broken through to the vulnerable woman beneath the brassy façade.

Her look of abject defeat did not last. She recovered quickly. Her jaw stiffened, the eyes that for a moment had pleaded, hardened.

'Little tramp! It won't last. She's just a kid.'

'Like you were,' said Aggie.

Her tone was not just hard, it was brittle, as though deep regret swam beneath the surface.

Lyndon gave Bridget's hand another squeeze and whispered in her ear: 'Honey, I reckon we should leave.'

Bridget gathered up her things and got to her feet. Like Lyndon, she was uncomfortable with the telling exchange between mother and daughter.

'Aggie, I think we should go,' Bridget said to her.

Aggie looked at them both as though she'd forgotten they were there. She nodded. There was embarrassment on her face, but also anger and confusion.

'See you in the morning, chicken.'

They passed back through the series of rooms into the main bar, where a single solitary log, the size of a small tree trunk, smouldered in the huge inglenook fireplace.

Curly had discarded his tie and jacket and his shirtsleeves were rolled up to his elbows, forearms resting on the bar. What looked suspiciously like a double – or perhaps even a triple – whisky sat on the bar in front of him. Two men she took to be dockers; labourers of some kind with beefy shoulders, stood at the bar leaning towards him, three heads together. Whatever they'd been discussing stopped. Dark, shadowed eyes glanced at them but briefly.

Curly held up his glass. 'Come in again when you can. You'll always be welcome.'

Even before the door had closed behind them, the three heads had come together again and Bridget wondered what they were up to.

Outside, the night was dark, but the air was fresh. Bridget didn't quite know what to say, but once they were in the car and heading for home, she gave Lyndon a brief resumé about Eddie Bridgeman.

'Maisie and I went to a dance. Eddie turned up there. Was pawing young Carole until Maisie announced what he was doing to everyone there.'

He laughed when she told him about how the Canadians had bundled him out and into the boot of his car.

'After he left, Carole blurted out that she'd seen him dealing in stolen jewellery looted from bombsites.' Her voice faltered. 'Even from dead bodies.' She shook her head. 'I can't believe people could do that.'

Lyndon's arm was gentle round her, his warm palm caressing her shoulder. 'Sounds like a guy best avoided.'

She turned her face to the window, unwilling to tell him about the night she'd been dragged into Eddie's car, where he'd demanded to know Maisie's whereabouts. She'd been so scared she'd blanked that moment out, and anyway, it had no bearing on the present.

There was only blackness outside the window, buildings and people smudges of dark grey movement against impenetrable blackness. There was not much to be seen out through the windscreen either, except for the dots of light thrown onto the road ahead by the reduced beams of the headlights.

'Still, I'm sorry you had to see that. Aggie doesn't deserve it.'

'Honey, you don't have to apologise. It was me who wanted to come here tonight.'

'Aggie's a really nice person. I don't know much about her daughter. Aggie never mentioned her much. I didn't know she was involved with Eddie, but it's no surprise that he's ditched her.' *He'd prefer Carole*, she thought and shuddered.

'Home,' Lyndon said to her as the car pulled to a stop outside the cramped council house in Marksbury Road.

He lit a cigarette in complete silence which gave her time to study him, to try to guess what he was thinking, to guess at what he would say next.

A tingle of excitement caught in her throat at the sight of his face softly illuminated by his cigarette lighter: shadows, highlights, the angle of his jaw, the nobility of his forehead. He was everything of the romantic lead she'd read in books, far more so than the likes of Clark Gable or Errol Flynn; because he's real, she told herself.

What he said next was unexpected. 'War upsets a lot of things. It parts people when they want to be together.'

Her laughter died. There was no getting away from it. She knew that at some point Lyndon would be required to return home. 'I thought you might be saying that your job's done and you're off home shortly.' Her voice dropped to a whisper. 'I don't want you to go back.'

He drew slowly on his cigarette. 'And I don't want to go back.'

Lyndon hadn't expected to like this country so much. One visit had been all it took – and meeting Bridget of course. They both knew the day would come, though he didn't want to leave. To him it was as if he was deserting this country. England was like a second home. He'd got used to its quirky ways. He'd also got used to Bridget – in a big way.

It wasn't just the fact that she held his eyes with her fresh-faced beauty. Beauty, as they say, is only skin-deep. With Bridget it went deeper than that. He appreciated her intelligence, the way her complexion glowed and her eyes sparkled when she was imparting an interesting piece of historical information, the way she laughed, the honesty of her dealings with others – especially with him

He sighed. 'We have to accept that I will be called back. Can't say when, but it can't be far off. If it was my choice alone, I wouldn't go back. But,' he shrugged, 'I have to.'

Bridget felt an immediate tightness in her chest. He wasn't giving her any specific date. It scared her.

'When will you know?'

Despite the darkness, she felt the intensity of his eyes.

For his part, Lyndon was desperate to remember every little detail, to consign it to memory in the empty days to come – whenever they might be. The feeble glow of his cigarette was just about enough to pick out the outline of her chin when she nodded. My, but he loved the shape of her chin. Everything about her in fact. It brought him to a sudden course of action over which he had no control.

He kissed her. It wasn't the first time, but so much deeper and demanding. A kiss that conveyed everything that was in his heart.

'Marry me.'

Her breath caught in her throat. So did the prospect of any answer.

Playing careful attention to the lighted cigarette so the tip wouldn't connect with that very soft skin, he cupped her face with his hands.

'Did you hear what I said?'

It was reassuring to feel her nod into his hands. 'Yes.'

Her voice was small. His chest felt tight. 'So, what does yes mean? Yes, you heard or yes, you'll marry me?'

The vision of them finally lying together was like a flame burning inside.

'Yes,' she said again. 'Yes. I mean... I will.'

He enfolded her in his arms, breathed in her scent, felt a familiar stirring in his loins. He'd had other women, but none of them had meant as much to him as Bridget did.

'We can get married here before we go to the States. I'll send a telegram to my folks, and then...' He suddenly felt her stiffen. 'What is it? What's the matter?'

'Go back with you to America?'

'Of course.' He sounded surprised that she sounded so surprised.

Bridget knew that she did love him and wanted to go to bed with him for the rest of her life. What she hadn't considered was leaving her family: her mum, dad and her brothers and sisters. To marry and make a home in her own city or even her own country was one thing, but to leave everything she knew?

'Bridget. You do love me, don't you?'

'Yes,' she said. 'Of course I do, but just don't tell anyone, not yet. Not until we've got everything planned.'

He readily agreed.

* * *

Just for once, she was glad that she was new to the packing room and that the girls working there, though friendly enough, didn't question why she didn't speak much or even sing along to the popular songs being played on the wireless.

At teatime in the canteen, Maisie asked her if she was feeling all right.

'Just a bad period this month,' she said.

Maisie took in her pale expression and told her to get some beef tea. 'Aggie recommends it to all the girls.'

Bridget smiled and said that Aggie was usually right. 'I'll feel better tomorrow.'

Maisie accepted her excuse and Bridget was glad she wasn't pressed into explaining what was really worrying her. Neither did she say anything about Aggie's daughter. For the moment at least, she didn't want to convey anything about last night, especially the fact that Lyndon had asked her to marry him. Her thoughts were in turmoil. Speaking to someone would help, but not face to face, so how could she get it off her chest?

The answer came to her when one of the girls she worked with sobbed over a letter she'd just received from her beau. He was stationed in a Scottish loch overseeing communications with submarines. Members of the Women's Royal Navy were also stationed there. He'd fallen into a relationship with one of the Wrens and was now telling her that their romance was all over and that his new love was expecting a baby.

'I loved 'im. 'Ow could 'e do that?'

Scotland wasn't so far away. America was a lot further, thought Bridget. The choice to stay or go was hers and hers alone.

16

CAROLE

Carole knew the moment she saw the glow of a cigarette splitting the darkness that Eric was waiting for her at the end of the street.

'Turns up like a bad penny,' she muttered to herself.

She sensed his presence darker than a shadow, the ember of a cigarette tip facing her now.

'You again?'

She said it tersely. Eric had taken to waiting for her every night. She couldn't quite make out why. He said little to her at work, though Pauline had said that he couldn't take his eyes off her. Well, what was that to her? Lots of blokes gave her the eye.

The cigarette was thrown to the ground and stubbed underfoot.

'I thought you might fancy goin' for a walk.'

'Why would you think that?'

'Don't know. Unless you got anything else planned.'

He sounded cocky. *Well*, she thought, *if you're that keen...*

'You could take me to the pictures.'

She heard him suck in his breath, which was followed by an arm movement that suggested he was delving into his pockets.

'Yeah. All right then.'

Relying on instinct and the familiarity of streets during the day, they made their way to the picture house and easily got in on the second house. Eric's willingness to pay a bit extra for seats in the balcony also helped them get in quicker.

Carole knew he was trying to impress her. Well, if he was hoping for a kiss and a cuddle he was going to be disappointed. She'd already made her mind up on that score.

She took off her coat before settling back into her seat, folding it over her lap and resting her hands on it.

'Let's get one thing straight,' she said in a low voice. 'No hanky-panky. All right?'

He looked surprised, as though such a thing was miles from his mind. She fancied a blush.

'I ain't that sort,' he replied in just as low a voice.

Funnily enough she believed him, settled back in her seat and watched the film.

It might not have been the best of films, but Carole found herself getting absorbed in the storyline – a romance between a flashy saloon girl and a cowboy. She'd always liked cowboys. Always liked romantic films, for that matter.

Just as hero and heroine were about to get into a hot clinch, the projector shut down and a message flashed up onto the screen for everyone to go down into the air-raid shelter.

There were hisses and boos, a few people exclaiming that they'd chance their luck and stay to watch the film.

It wasn't an option. As one of the usherettes said, the projectionist isn't going to keep going with a load of bombs dropping round him.

Carole was surprised but didn't object when Eric grabbed her hand and led her along through the seats to the aisle and down the stairs.

Just as they got to the entrance to the shelter, the all-clear sounded.

'False alarm, folks, false alarm,' cried the cashier, his eyes, head and then his whole body appearing behind the glass of his kiosk.

Carole decided she'd had enough. 'I ain't goin' back in. Just in case they change their minds and tell us it's for real.'

'Please yourself,' said Eric.

'I always do,' Carole trilled.

They weren't the only people to traipse out into the darkness, where trails of searchlight still criss-crossed the sky.

'Fancy a drink?'

'Port and lemon.'

'Crikey!'

'You can afford to take a girl out, can't you?'

'Course I can.' Eric sounded very affronted. 'Think I might 'ave one meself.'

'It's a girl's drink.'

'Oh. Yeah. I suppose it is.'

Inside the nearest pub, she pointed him towards the bar whilst she promised to get them a table.

A black bloke in uniform was hammering out a tune that was fast and full of energy. It wasn't the usual kind of music much heard in suburban Bedminster, or even in provincial Bristol for that matter.

His friend, of a rich chestnut in colour, came across and asked her to dance. His teeth flashed white and his eyes were full of fun.

'Yeah. Why not?'

So there she was doing some kind of dance she'd never done before with a man called Chip, who told her he was from Jamaica.

In the midst of laughter and spinning, she was jerked away to crash into a broad chest and a man who smelt of cologne.

The face that looked down at her was black-eyed and stern of jowl. Eddie Bridgeman had stopped her fun.

'Carole. I bin lookin' for you everywhere.'

Her blood seemed to drain down into her shoes. She briefly glanced over to where Eric was sitting at the table looking shocked and also scared.

'You all right, girl?'

It was Chip asking. His friend was still playing piano, the laughter and singing going on all around.

'I'm fine,' she said, nodding stiffly, her gaze fixed on Eddie Bridgeman's face.

'I'm going to ask yer old lady about you coming to work for me. Right?'

She nodded. Whether it was right or wrong was neither here nor there. All she did know was that Eddie Bridgeman wasn't giving her a choice. Her mother had once told her that what Eddie wanted he got and he wanted her, Carole Thomas.

17

BRIDGET

> *I'm sharing a room here with two other girls in a very grand*
> *building, one of many in a place they call Whitehall Mansions.*
> *Two of the buildings are occupied by female staff only. You*
> *won't believe how many soldiers, sailors and airmen we see*
> *strolling by looking up and shouting invitations if we happen to*
> *be sitting outside on the balcony.*
>
> *If I can't sleep at night, I imagine myself back in the*
> *stripping room or sitting with you lot in the pub, chatting our*
> *heads off over three halves of Somerset cider.*
> *Love Phyllis.*

The letter had arrived at the Milligan household. 'At last,'
breathed Bridget when it popped through the letterbox.

Her mother hovered expectantly at the same time as wiping a
pudding basin with a tea towel. 'Good news, is it?'

Bridget put on a happy face. 'It's from Phyllis.' The truth was
she would have been much happier if it had been from Lyndon,
but she excused him not writing because his first task was to
report to the US state department. It all sounded very grand,

which in turn made her feel rather diminished. Self-doubt set in easily. The fact that there was no mention of Robert in Phyllis's letter added to her concern. 'She sounds cheerful enough but doesn't mention Robert, so I suppose she hasn't received the news just yet.' She sighed. 'We've been waiting for ages for a letter to get through.'

She caught the look in her father's eyes. He followed everything in the newspaper that was war-orientated. She waited for her mother to leave the room before she asked him how it was in Malta.

'I'm certain that's where she is, but that's about it. She makes it sound all sea and sunshine. I don't think she wants us to worry about her.'

Her father's face clouded. 'It's bad. What's she saying?'

'That she's helping out with relief at a church. She makes it sound as though she's having fun. She mentions nothing about air raids. I wonder whether things are really as bad as they say.'

There was something bordering on despair in her father's eyes and also pity. 'How long have you been waiting for that letter?'

Bridget answered. 'A long time.' She frowned. 'I suppose the letters crossed in the post. Do you suppose so?'

It concerned her that Phyllis hadn't been in touch that much. She liked to think that she was out enjoying herself, but the look in her father's eyes said otherwise.

Her father sighed and laid down his newspaper. It seemed only a short time ago that he'd been inundated with watches and clocks to mend. Now he was inundated with voluntary work and scouring the newspaper from cover to cover. The more he read, the more concerned he got and the more his joints ached. Shame really. He enjoyed mending clocks but lately bits of clocks were sometimes scattered over the table, where he would sit with a faraway look in his eyes. He just couldn't seem to concentrate on the job in hand as he used to. The war was taking its toll and in more ways than one.

'What does your mate Maisie think about it?'

Bridget passed the letter from one hand to the other, her face downcast. 'I'll show it to her in the morning at work.'

'Not tonight? I thought you two might be out somewhere for a drink.'

It grieved him when he saw a sad expression come to his daughter's face as she explained why she and Maisie wouldn't be off out tonight.

'Maisie's going with Aggie Hill to see the father of the girl that was killed.'

Patrick Milligan clasped his hands together as though in prayer. Unlike his wife, he wasn't one for churchgoing and praying, but there were occasions when there seemed there was nobody who could help, except some intangible being more powerful than man or government. 'God bless the poor child.' He let his hands rest in his lap. 'And God bless young Maisie. 'Tis not a job I would favour doing.'

18

PHYLLIS

The very air trembled in response to explosion, after explosion, after explosion. Dug out from the rock, the normal work of the Ops Room carried on. Calm voices, steady and precise, reported height, direction and strength of enemy planes as their gentle hands – young women's hands – moved the magnetic tipped wands across the map. Radio operators received and sent messages, their voices and general demeanour oddly calm in the midst of the madness of war.

Phyllis rattled off messages that in turn were passed to the officers in charge of charting movements and organising battle plans.

Nobody lost their temper. Nobody ran screaming under the stairs their morale ripped to shreds as the enemy hoped it would be.

Being bombed was becoming the norm, the short intervals of peace in between more nerve-racking than the actual event. Waiting for it to happen was far worse.

A short lull occurred between messages coming in and the

rattling of the teleprinter. It was a long enough lull for Phyllis to rip open the letter from her dearest friends. Reading a letter from home made her feel for a moment that she was there, back in the old routine, back with her old workmates.

She read it avidly and quickly.

Dear Phyllis,

Bridget and I have decided to take it in turns to write to you. Excuse the small writing, but I wanted to cram in as much as possible. The factory sponsored a couple of ambulances to help in the raids. Bridget and I volunteered to learn to drive. They're a bit old and got gearboxes that make a crunching noise when you push the stick forward and my feet barely reach the pedals, but I manage.

There's precious little time to go out and enjoy ourselves, what with work and ambulance driving.

You'll laugh – or perhaps you won't, but me and Bridget arranged to have a big night out back in January. We were off to the Stoll – the old Bedminster Hippodrome. Just our luck that Gerry decided to go out that night too. We didn't have time to get there. The siren went off and we did a mad dash into the factory cellar.

It was late when we got out, not that it made a scrap of difference. The Stoll was hit. It's still standing, though I can't see it ever showing a picture again or have Gracie Fields singing about her aspidistra.

Had a few raids since, though not too big. Expecting a really big one though. The Gerries don't give up easily. It's just a case of when they fancy flying over here again. That will be when me and Bridget will be there to deal with the wounded. We've been told we'll have somebody with us to help out once

they're trained up to do first aid like me and Bridget did at first.
With a bit of luck, they might be able to do bandaging better
than me.

Now this next bit is going to come as a bit of a shock...

Phyllis felt a scalding sensation behind her eyes as she read the rest of the missive. Her jaw dropped, her hands shook and just for once it was nothing to do with the fact that Malta was being heavily bombed.

Robert was alive! It felt to her as though a ghost had come back from the dead. A shiver ran down her spine. He was no ghost, but a living, breathing man.

'Come on, Harvey! The war is not gonna wait for you to finish that letter!' The order was sharply delivered with a Yorkshire accent.

Phyllis dashed off the awaiting report of enemy action and passed it to a radio operator, who swiftly relayed it to every airfield and military installation on the island, plus the ships and submarines currently in the Grand Harbour.

Although everyone was well trained in their specific jobs, there were times when it was necessary to step in and help out. Just of late, Phyllis had also been trained to use the radio. In the present dire situation. it was a case of every man and woman to the pumps.

'Cocoa?'

'Yes please.' She took the proffered enamel mug with shaking hands, her eyes stung by dust, her throat too dry to respond to even taste the rather weak and sugarless beverage. She'd taken one hell of a knock from Maisie's letter.

As was the norm nowadays, the bombing went on for hours. Phyllis did her job in a clockwork fashion, her eyes and hands working independently of her mind. In her mind, there was

Robert and ragged memories of how it had been when he'd been there, how it had been when he'd marched off to war and she was left living with his parents. Then losing the baby.

Her life would have been so different if she hadn't lost the baby – at least she thought it would. For a start, she wouldn't be here but back there, though she wasn't quite sure where. If there'd been no war, everything might have been different. They might have been just an ordinary young married couple leading a humdrum life, years of the same stretching out before them. All this went through her brain whilst she worked. All this past and now searing questions about the future which she'd thought all cut and dried. But it wasn't. Robert had come home.

It was dawn before she was finally stood down and she was unaware of how much work she had done or how tired she was.

It was the loud voice of Warrant Officer Harrison, the gruff Yorkshireman who'd shouted at her earlier. 'Go home and get some rest, lass.'

Shocked by the news, she was slow responding, slow to see him and when she did, she saw that, like most of them, his uniform was plastered in dust.

Whitehall Mansions where she was billeted in a room with two other girls overlooked a wide esplanade and the sea in a place called Ta'Xbiex, which was pronounced Tashbeesh. The buildings were grand and had green shutters and a flat roof suitable for sunbathing – if it hadn't already been occupied with a lookout post and an ack-ack gun round which sandbags were piled.

Dawn was painting the sky in shades of violet that were brushed with blue at the edges. A new day was about to begin. There would be blue skies and bright sunshine, perhaps a fluffy pillow of cloud here and there. Those were the best points. In no more than an hour, another wave of enemy aircraft would batter the island.

The other girls were on early shift so already had the kettle on when she got there. Breakfast was tomatoes on toast; sometimes a freshly laid egg would be added, but not today. Eggs were getting scarcer because chickens were getting scarcer, and the more the island was starved of supplies, the more the people – both service personnel and civilians – would starve too.

Although tired out, Phyllis forced herself to eat breakfast, at the same time vowing that once this war was over she would never eat another tomato in her life.

The tea was weak and sweetened with honey rather than sugar. Like tomatoes and rabbits, bees were fairly plentiful, though diminishing as supplies from the outside world became infrequent thanks to the incessant attacks of enemy aircraft and submarines.

When she'd finished, Phyllis rubbed her face with both hands, then sat on her bed with her head in her hands. Reading the first paragraphs of the letter from Maisie had made her spirits soar, but they'd crashed to earth once she'd read the last paragraph. Robert was alive, which meant she was no longer a widow.

Usually the life and soul of the room she shared with the other two girls, her mood was noticed.

'Is that just fatigue on your face, Harvey, or have you had bad news from home?' Beryl Jarman was an aircraft plotter, one of the girls who moved little blocks of magnets across the huge chart table on long poles.

They were terrible times and the girls' friendship was very much one of mutual support. Homesickness was felt and shared by all. Malta was the most bombed place in the whole world, yet still their thoughts were of those suffering at home. Photographs of families and sweethearts were everywhere they could find the smallest space. Pictures cut from magazines and newspapers. There were none of bombed cities, but happier things: members of the royal family, a thatched cottage in bright colours that had once been the cardboard lid of a chocolate box – the chocolates long gone. It was the picture that mattered, an idealised English scene that touched their deepest feelings of what England was, though each admitted never having lived in or even close to such a pretty home.

Brow puckered with concern, Beryl came and sat beside Phyllis on her bed, placed an arm round her shoulder and gave her a hug.

There was a reassuring strength to that hug which made Phyllis think of Aggie back at the tobacco factory. She was built like a bear and hugged as she imagined a bear would hug too.

She managed to stage a smile. 'My two best friends at the tobacco factory have learned to drive ambulances. They're sounding very proud of themselves...'

Beryl laughed, a deep throaty laugh fed by too much smoking, too much nicotine. 'And you wish you were with them. Well, dear, you're not. You're here with us lot and we're all you've got.' She gave another hug and grinned. 'Don't suppose there's any chance of them sending us some fags? The rations are almost non-existent; fancy putting spare parts for Spitfires above fags for us girls!'

It was said laughingly, but Phyllis was in no mood for merriment. Homesickness had gripped her as she imagined the old days. Overcome with emotion, she tried to explain it to Beryl.

'We were like sisters. In fact, everyone at the tobacco factory is like that, all girls together. I don't mind saying I miss it lots. I might have still been there if it hadn't been for this war.'

Beryl was a few years older than most of the girls. Her husband had drowned at sea, and her little terraced house in

Liverpool had been flattened. 'Didn't have a rag to me name, like.' She'd told them how much she'd loved her husband, how empty her life felt when he was gone. 'Nobody to spoil,' she'd said. 'Have to spoil you lot instead.' Beryl was like a mother hen – another thing she had in common with Aggie Hill. She took care of the others, listened to their fears and worries and gave them useful advice, principally about their love life and what to look for in a possible husband.

She patted her shoulder. 'Look, love, this war won't go on forever and when it's over, you can rejoin your mates making fags and stuff for the rest of us. Where would we be without you, eh?'

Phyllis smiled. 'Thanks Beryl. I can always count on you to make me feel better.' Normally it would be true, but not now. Not after reading that letter.

Although she sensed something else going on here, Beryl didn't let it get in the way of giving reassurance. 'We're all home-sick. All in the same boat.'

Wendy, the other girl they shared the room with, reminded Beryl that it was their watch. 'The boys who fly the kites await our input,' she said gravely. Wendy, the daughter of a vicar, did every-thing in a sombre voice and with a serious countenance – almost as though she was giving a sermon.

'Can't do without us,' retorted the effervescent Beryl, who was always upbeat, always the one who looked on the bright side. Grabbing her tin hat, she sprang to her feet. 'Come on then, Wendy my girl. Let's be off.'

Even once the door had closed behind them and the room echoed with silence, Phyllis didn't move but sat contemplating the rest of that letter, the bit she had kept to herself.

Everyone talked of home and their wish that the war would end so they could pick up where they left off. Being posted abroad was an experience she would never forget, but she too had yearned to go home, to see her old mates. In fact, she dreamed of the day. The letter had dimmed the brightness of that particular hope. The very thought of going back to her marriage to Robert filled her with dread. Whatever happened, she had no wish to return and live again with his parents, or even with him for that matter.

19

BRIDGET AND MAISIE

The houses in Kent Street in Bedminster were two up, two down, the front door opening directly out from its flat facade onto the pavement.

Some weeks before, a number of people from the factory, including Bridget, Maisie and Aggie, had gone to Jane Goode's funeral. Carole had been there too. Condolences had been expressed and Bert Goode, Jane's father, had shaken many hands between mopping at his tear-stained face.

Maisie and Aggie were in Kent Street with a few items Jane had left behind in the cloakroom before she'd clambered enthusiastically up into the ambulance. They also had wages and a bonus owed to her, plus her free issue of cigarettes for the period before her death.

The knocker was made of cast iron. The front door was a dull brown in colour, a solid barrier between the interior of the house and the world outside. Aggie took hold of the knocker and was just about to thud it firmly against the tired paintwork when the door swung open.

The most notable thing about Bert Goode was the heavy bags

beneath his eyes. No doubt he'd been having trouble sleeping since the death of his daughter, but Maisie was of the opinion that they'd been part of him for most of his life. He wore no collar with his shirt and the top button was undone, but he was not scruffy. On the contrary, his shirt was very white, he was clean-shaven and vaguely smelt of coal tar soap. In effect, his appearance was both acceptable and unsurprising. It was the person who stood with him in the doorway looking as though they were about to leave that was most surprising.

'Carole!'

Maisie locked eyes with Aggie before going back to Carole, who was dressed in black, her face devoid of make-up. A knitted black beret almost covered her bright white curls and matched a clutch bag she held with both hands.

'Oh. Hello.' Carole seemed hesitant and nervous. 'I didn't expect to see you here. I came to give Mr Goode my condolences and a necklace Jane left behind. I think it was hers anyway.'

Maisie knew nothing of any necklace but made the right noises. 'That's very kind of you, Carole.'

Carole shrugged rather prettily. 'It was the least I could do. Still. Better be off. Nice to see you again, Mr Goode.'

His eyes full of sadness, Bert Goode thanked her. 'It was very kind of you, me love. Very kind indeed.'

Carole nodded a swift goodbye to Aggie and Maisie before trotting off in the direction of North Street.

After they'd given their names and explained why they'd come, Mr Goode invited them in.

The house was as spotless as he was and there was a certain pride in his voice as he pointed out sepia photographs of his late wife, Jane as a child, Jane at various ages.

Both Aggie and Maisie declined tea when it was offered but

handed over what was due and declared Jane a credit to both him and the factory.

A half-light appeared in his eyes. 'She loved that job. Told me how kind you were to her and how friendly the girls were. I didn't expect one of them to call that's for sure, but having this necklace...' He held up a single pearl on a silver chain. It was delicate and exquisitely made. 'At least she earned enough to buy herself something nice. I'm glad of that.'

Aggie was as surprised as Maisie. Jane wasn't the sort to buy a necklace so ornate and expensive-looking.

'I expect you are,' said Aggie, then turned to Maisie, who also had questions whirling in her mind. 'Better be off then. We'll leave you in peace,' she said to Bert Goode.

Their goodbyes were polite enough and Maisie gave no sign of her consternation until they were outside.

As they walked out of Kent Street, Maisie mentioned her misgivings to Aggie.

'That necklace. I don't believe it ever belonged to Jane. She didn't wear jewellery. She weren't that sort. Come to that, I never knew 'er to go out shopping.'

'So Carole's lying, but why?'

Maisie shrugged. 'Not a bloody clue. But I aim to find out.'

Out on North Street, she was surprised for the second time that night. Carole was standing at the tram stop and it was obvious from her stance that she was waiting for them.

Totally disbelieving Carole's claim about the necklace, Maisie determined to know the truth.

'Waiting fer us are yah?'

Carole nodded. 'Yeah.'

She wasn't exactly her exuberant self, but neither was she subdued in any way.

'Right,' said Maisie in her no-nonsense manner. 'You've got

some explaining to do.'

The last thing she'd expected was for Carole to burst into tears. 'I had to give it away. I had to.'

Maisie and Aggie frowned at each other.

'Three halves at the London Inn, I think,' said Aggie. 'It's startin' to rain.'

Carole shook her head vigorously. 'No. I don't want to go in there. I know people...' Her sobs shook her whole body.

Maisie gestured to the quiet doorway of a shop with a closed sign hanging on the door. 'That'll do.'

The doorway was just about big enough to shelter all three of them from the rain.

After she'd blown her nose a few times, Carole explained about the necklace.

'One of my mum's men friends gave it to me. Said it was for services rendered, though not by my mother. Said she was too old fer 'im.' Her eyelashes flickered. 'Said 'e liked 'em young – like me.'

Maisie turned cold. She'd remained silent, but the name in her head fell like bitter almonds onto her tongue. 'Eddie Bridgeman? The same bloke who tried to pick you up at the dance.'

'Yeah. Me mum was supposed to 'ave sold it for 'im, but it was a bit 'ot – if you know what I mean,' she said, her lashes fluttering between Maisie and Aggie.

Maisie understood all this, but it didn't explain everything.

'Why did you give it to Jane's Dad?'

Tears hung like pearl drops on Carole's lashes. She sniffed and dabbed a few more times at her nose. 'I was rotten to 'er. I needed somebody to pick on and I picked on 'er. Then she died.' A fresh spate of sobbing wracked her body. 'I did think of throwing it into her grave, but there were too many people there, so I thought 'er dad might like it as a keepsake.'

Maisie was shocked but also touched. It did seem indeed that Carole wasn't such a bad person inside.

'But it wasn't her necklace was it. That was a lie,' said Maisie.

'I know! But don't you see? That poor dad of 'ers needs a bit of comfort. That's why I told 'im it belonged to 'er. A little reminder of 'er, even though it weren't 'ers.'

'Does your mother know Eddie gave you the necklace?'

Carole nodded. 'She reckoned a few years down the line and it'll be worth holding onto. Could make my fortune with it; that's what she said. And so could Eddie.' She studied the handkerchief she was twisting round and round in her hands. 'Said she wished she was young again. She'd be into bed with 'im like a shot and 'e'd be straight into bed with 'er.'

'Sounds a right nice woman, your mother,' said Aggie grimly. 'Mark my words. Don't get involved with Eddie Bridgeman. Once you're in yer twenties, you'll be out on yer ear.'

At first, Maisie thought it was defiance in Carole's eyes and that Aggie was going to be reprimanded for daring to insult her. As it happened, she was very wrong.

'Do you know 'ow many nights as a kid I've walked the streets because Ma was doing business. Not one bloke a night, but sometimes six. Couldn't 'ave a kid around, could she, so she flung me out and told me not to come back until the morning.'

'Even in the winter?' Aggie couldn't help herself.

Carole nodded. 'Not when Eddie calls though. She shows me off when 'e comes round. He comes over to me all gushy, stroking my face in front of 'er and all that.' An uncharacteristic flush came to her face. The things that went on obviously embarrassed her. 'I don't like 'im. 'E gives me the creeps.'

Maisie's blood turned cold. Was it possible that her mother would sell her own daughter?

20

MAISIE AND BRIDGET

Tea break mid-morning in the canteen was far from being an island of calm. There were no machines making a racket, no trundling of trolleys piled high with tobacco leaves, but there was still chatter and the odd bit of singing along with the wireless. The outstanding difference was the depth of silence likely when the latest news was announced. In a way, the machines were missed in such an instance, a clattering accompaniment that helped negate the seriousness of the grim news.

'London again last night, but at least it wasn't Bristol,' somebody remarked.

Worried eyes exchanged worried looks.

'I hear they've only just found the legs of a bloke killed in the last raid. Deep into the ground they went, beneath the weight of the bomb. Bloody awful.'

One of the girls who'd heard the comment turned green with fear, left her cup of tea and ran for the ladies' lavatories.

Aggie, Bridget and Maisie noted what had happened but made no comment. Aggie lit up a cigarette after offering one to the others, who both declined.

Aggie addressed Bridget. 'Sorry about Angie when you came to the pub with your Lyndon. Trust 'er upsetting the apple cart. In and gone, she was. Blew in and out like a storm. Typical of 'er ever since she shacked up with that Eddie Bridgeman. Seems 'e's got another piece on the go – a younger model knowing 'im!'

'Or after another,' said Maisie grimly, her look straying to where Carole was chatting amiably enough between biting nails, something she'd never seen her do before.

'So where's she gone?' asked Bridget.

Aggie shrugged. 'I don't know for sure, but wouldn't be surprised if she's gone back to 'im.' She shook her head and her eyes darkened. 'I would 'ave let 'er stay, but Curly...' She shook her head some more. 'Said she was no longer a daughter of 'is. Said some other pretty 'orrible things that I won't go into.' She sighed and her whole, big body, as plump as a barrage balloon one minute was deflated the next. 'I wish Curly would be a bit more understanding. The girl's 'ead was turned when she was young. After all,' she added, tears glistening in her eyes, 'she is my daughter.'

'If there's anything I can do,' offered Bridget at the same time giving Aggie a reassuring pat on the shoulder.

'Thanks for offering, love,' said Aggie with a grateful smile.

'That man...' muttered Maisie. The very thought of him sickened her and she felt for Aggie, but also for Angie. How old had she been when Eddie had approached her, showered her with praise, given her expensive presents? The question burned and finally spilt out from her tongue. 'How old was she when she went off with 'im?'

Aggie looked down at the cup she was twisting round and round on the saucer. 'Fifteen. Curly went after 'er, faced Eddie off and told 'im to leave 'er alone. Eddie said he'd not forced 'er and it was down to 'er to stay or go. Angie told 'er dad to sod off, that she was in love with Eddie and that 'e was goin' to marry 'er.'

Maisie almost choked on her tea. 'What the 'ell made 'er think that?'

A warning look from Bridget made her apologise.

'Sorry, Aggie. That came out all wrong? What I meant to say was—'

Aggie shook her head and puffed smoke into the air. 'It didn't come out wrong, Maisie. My Angie ain't like you. Yer feet's firmly on the ground. Always 'ad 'er 'ead in the clouds did my Angie, reading romance stories and mooning over soppy songs. Thought Eddie with 'is flash ways and flash car was bloody Prince Charming.'

'I read a fairy tale about a princess kissing a frog who turned into a prince. Seems to be that in Eddie's case it's the other way round. He's a frog and never going to turn into a prince.'

It pleased Maisie to see Aggie smile, even though it was fleeting and touched with sadness.

Aggie looked down into her tea. 'Can't 'elp thinking that I'll never see 'er again.'

It was difficult to find the right words to say, but the sudden crackle of the wireless grabbed their attention. It had been turned up to its loudest, a sign that something important was about to be announced.

Here is the news. Enemy planes bombed London again last night. The RAF sustained only light losses and a number of the enemy bombers were shot down.

'We already 'eard that,' Maisie grumbled. 'Tell us somethin' new.'

Bridget's tea was halfway to her lips when the radio obliged.

General Allenby has confirmed that the supply line to the enemy forces in North Africa is being greatly impeded by the Royal Navy and the RAF from their bases in Malta, which as a consequence is experiencing heavy bombardment.

Even Aggie fell to silence.

'We're hoping that Phyllis is still in Gibraltar,' Bridget declared with confidence.

Maisie's expression was doubtful. 'Let's hope she is.' Her brow furrowed a bit more as a thought occurred to her. 'I wonder if she's got our letter yet.'

A blank look passed between them. If Phyllis was still in Gibraltar then the letter they'd sent should have caught up with her by now.

21

MAISIE

Maisie made the effort to trot along to Sally Lane and see where Carole lived. 'Just to get the lay of the land. Might even 'ave a word with 'er mother.'

Bridget was sceptical. 'I wouldn't think she was the sort to invite you in for tea and cakes.'

'I'll play it by ear.'

The house Carole lived in was one of a terrace of flat-fronted houses dating back over a century and a half. Its sash windows looked out over what might once have been a pretty cottage-style garden of hollyhocks, lupins, foxgloves and roses. At present, it was difficult to tell flowers from weeds and brambles.

A man came out of the door on the other side of the road to where Maisie was standing pulling the brim of his hat down over his face in a furtive fashion. Obviously he didn't want to be recognised.

Right, she thought. *Now's yer chance, Maisie Miles.*

'Want a cauliflower, love? I've got loads.'

The sudden address startled her. The man standing in his

front garden close by was holding out a very fine cauliflower, big enough to feed a family.

'How much?' she asked.

'Free,' he said. 'I like the look of you.' His attention seemed suddenly to wander as the sound of a car drifted their way. 'Blimey. She is doin' all right today.'

One glance over her shoulder and she knew whose car it was. Eddie Bridgeman was paying a visit.

'Those are lovely,' said Maisie, going into his garden and slipping behind a dark green bush while pointing at what looked like a row of carrots. The bush was her height at least so hid her from Eddie's view.

The old man insisted she took carrots too, pulling up a bright orange handful. 'They ain't as big as they'll be later on in the year, but sweet as you like.'

What am I doing 'ere talking about carrots and cauliflowers, I need to help Carole but can't do much while 'es in the 'ouse.'

While she waited and the old man was distracted by some weeds amongst his vegetables, Maisie's' thoughts were doing somersaults. It seemed Mavis Thomas welcomed Eddie to her house. The girl had mentioned about the looting of valuables in the aftermath of air raids. Eddie was ripe for that kind of trade, and it was more than likely that her mother was involved.

Coming from across the road the sound of a front gate opening was the signal that Eddie was leaving. Maisie ducked a little further behind the hedge and waited for him to depart.

* * *

Eddie sang and whistled as he made his way to the rotten front gate held to the wall by a single broken hinge. He'd stayed long enough to get another look at Mavis's pretty little daughter.

He'd considered giving the girl a present but decided not to do so when her mother was around. He didn't want any suspicions or jealousies either. He'd get Carole all in good time.

* * *

Maisie heard the car start up and drive away.

'Thanks a lot for these,' she said, cauliflower in one hand, carrots in the other. 'Me gran will be grateful.'

He insisted she call him Len and that it was no bother. 'You come and see me any time you like when you're in need of a bit of greens an' whatever.'

As she edged towards the gate, she said that she would. At the gate she paused.

'Do you know the woman across the road?' she asked, jerking her head in the general direction of the house Eddie had gone into.

Len's expression hardened. 'Only as a neighbour who 'appens to live opposite me. Not in the Biblical sense.'

'I didn't think—'

'Just so's you know,' he went on. 'I'm broad-minded, but that woman pushes things a bit too far. I know she's no bloke so 'as to earn a livin', but it's the way she treats that girl of 'ers that I don't like.'

'You've seen things?'

'I know 'er of old. Know that bloke that arrives in the flash car too. Reckon I remember them when they were younger. In fact I'm sure I do. Eddie and Mavis. Sweethearts they were.'

'Are you sure?'

He wagged a dirt-encrusted finger in front of her face. 'I might be gettin' on in years, but I've got a good memory. They were sweethearts. I know damn well they were.'

* * *

Over their usual two halves of cider in a pub close to the factory, Maisie told Bridget all that she'd found out.

'Can you believe that? Eddie and 'er being sweethearts when they were younger?'

Bridget shook her head. 'Will you mention to Carole that you went to where she lived?'

Maisie pushed a stray dark curl back from her face. When she shook her head, it fell forward again. 'I don't want Carole to think that I'm prying.' She blew listlessly on the stray curl, but her efforts came to nothing. It remained in the same place.

'It's for her own good.' Bridget paused. She considered herself lucky she had such a good family and couldn't imagine what it would be like otherwise.

Maisie shook her head and emitted a heartfelt sigh. 'I chickened out when I saw his car, and let's face it, he wouldn't be well pleased to see me. Still,' she said, beaming from ear to ear, 'I did get a cauli and a bunch of carrots from it.'

They both laughed before Bridget's expression turned serious. 'I was thinking of Miss Cayford having her jewellery stolen. Poor woman. That's bad enough but to hear about looting from bombed out buildings where people died. Loads of people died in that hotel ballroom a while back. There was a piece in the newspaper about how they'd been seen going in dressed to the nines and wearing jewellery that wasn't there when their bodies came out.'

Maisie stared silently into space before saying quietly, 'It wouldn't surprise me in the least that Eddie Bridgeman's got a hand in it.' Her expression darkened. 'He's evil. Downright evil.'

Bridget was thoughtful. 'We should tell the police.'

'Yeah. If they're inclined to listen.'

'Why shouldn't they... I think I know the reason we don't see enough about it in the newspapers. It undermines public morale, in which case...'

Lyndon sprang to mind. He sprang to her mind a lot during the long hours of staring at the packing machine that helped her get the right amount in the box that was slid through the machine that packed into fives, tens and twenties. Perhaps if she mentioned it, he might be able to use it in his reports, then it couldn't be ignored.

Maisie was gazing round the canteen. As usual, Carole was sitting with Pauline, laughing and smiling prettily in response to admiring glances from what males were left in the factory.

The canteen was nowhere near as busy as it used to be. Now tobacco was in short supply and there was less available to make the products W. D. & H. O. Wills was famous for fewer staff were needed. Food was the main cargo on merchant ships to fill British bellies. However, tobacco was considered important for morale just the same as beer and spirits, but getting hold of it was difficult. Britain did not grow tobacco, though Bridget had informed Maisie that it hadn't always been the case.

She'd told Maisie that back in the seventeenth century it had been grown in South Gloucestershire – not far from Bristol. On the orders of King James, the First – an avid opponent of smoking – mounted dragoons were sent in to burn it down. Public outrage from confirmed smokers and producers followed, leading him to relent, though only partially. He refused to allow it to be home-grown again, but issued a royal decree subjecting it to an import tax and only allowing importation through certain ports – Bristol being one of them.

So the very best tobacco was shipped in from North America, but not all of it was getting through. U-boat attacks in the Atlantic had devastated shipping; thousands of tons and good seagoing vessels blown to bits. Tobacco supplies were reduced compared to pre-war, thus less tobacco products were being manufactured.

Along with the supply problem, there was also the problem of men and women being called up to serve their country. The workforce was thinning, women taking over male roles and young people who had only worked there for a few years promoted and trained to do other jobs. All this was on top of their war work, whether it was a few hours fire watching, serving tea with the women's voluntary service or, after a short and fast training, donning the uniform of an auxiliary nurse. Surviving on reduced rations, their hours added up to at least twelve hours a day, six days a week and sometimes more.

Bridget expressed a need to visit the ladies' cloakroom and passed Miss Cayford, who was coming into the canteen. On seeing Maisie, she came trotting across to ask how everyone was getting on.

'Fine. They're getting on with their jobs and are ready and willing to come out on the ambulances – should we have another raid.'

An awkward silence suddenly descended as they thought about Jane – such a young life taken in the blink of an eye.

Like everyone else, Miss Cayford looked to have lost a bit of weight. The dark turquoise woollen costume she wore hung loosely on her frame, her bosoms no longer straining against the tight-fitting jacket. Her cheekbones were more prominent and tiredness mapped the skin round her eyes.

'That's good,' Miss Cayford said at last. 'And you yourself?'

'I'm walking in big footsteps,' said Maisie. 'Got to get it right. Bridget and Phyllis did a good job on me, didn't they, so I gotta measure up, ain't I?'

'And you do,' returned Miss Cayford and was about to go

when Maisie, figuring she looked as though she needed cheering up, spoke to her.

'Talking about Phyllis,' Maisie said brightly. 'Me and Bridget got a letter from her. Care to read it? I don't mind and neither will Bridget.'

'Oh,' said Miss Cayford her eyes brightening. 'How wonderful. If you're sure neither of you mind?'

'Course not,' said Maisie.

Maisie let her read the letter.

'My,' said Miss Cayford. 'The writing's very small.'

'That way she gets more words onto the paper,' Maisie informed her.

With a certain amount of ceremony, the spectacles Miss Cayford wore suspended on a chain round her neck were brought up to perch halfway down her nose. Her smile broadened as she read. 'My, but it makes you wish you were there too, doesn't it,' she said.

It gave Maisie great pleasure to see the tiredness lifting from her face and was pleased that she'd made the offer.

Miss Cayford beamed as she handed back the letter. 'Thank you for letting me read it, Maisie. It certainly helped take my mind off things.'

Peace and calm seemed to come to Miss Cayford's face, until yet again it creased with concern, though Maisie fancied the furrows on her brow weren't quite so deep.

On Bridget's return, Maisie told her what she had done and Miss Cayford's reaction. 'She looked so tired and run-down beforehand, then whoosh! Phyllis's letter certainly perked her up.' She didn't add that the worried brow returned afterwards; all that mattered was that the letter had for a brief moment made Miss Cayford look her old self.

Bridget thought a moment. 'I never would have guessed that Phyllis could write such a good letter. I wonder...'

Maisie eyed the dreamily blue eyes and guessed their thoughts were heading in the same direction. 'What she writes sounds lovely. I bet there's a few 'ere that would like to read it. It ain't much, but reading about faraway places takes yer mind off things. Don't you think?'

With Maisie humming 'The Road to Mandalay' in the background, they passed the letter round for others to read. There followed squeals, sighs and heartfelt comments that they could all do with a bit of sunshine and sea. Nobody touched on any drawbacks because Phyllis hadn't mentioned any.

'Sunshine and sea. Who could ask for anythin' more,' exclaimed Aggie. Her sighs of delight were heavier and she also expressed the equally heartfelt wish that she was young enough to get called up. 'And she's being fed. The services get that bit extra anyways. Not much, but it's bound to make a difference. Oh, but I do like me food. This rationing could be the bloody death of me!'

'Still, I bet you're 'avin' some fun living in a pub,' somebody said. 'I ain't never seen a skinny landlord! You do all right you publicans!'

Aggie's brows beetled, she glared at the person who'd dared voiced the comment. 'The pub trade ain't what it used to be.'

'Looked busy enough when I popped in for a drink with my soldier boy,' said Joan Parker, a young widow who had once looked downtrodden but now seemed to be living life to the full. Rumour had it that she was out with a different bloke every night or at least every week. Not that anybody criticised her for that. Rumour also had it that her late husband had been a bit too carefree with his fists. So what if she wanted to have some fun? She was free to do as she pleased, and anyway, who was to say when a bomb with your name on might drop on you at the height of your fun. Living for today was definitely becoming the mantra for many people.

'That's about it,' said Maisie, who had seen Aggie's response and instantly leapt to her defence. 'If you want a bit of fun and a decent drink, Aggie's place is where you'll find it.'

'It's getting the drink that's the problem,' Aggie added in a lower voice.

Joan Parker had picked up on what Aggie had said about having trouble getting beer. 'Is that so? Can't say I noticed,' she said sniffily. 'I had a small port and my soldier, Douglas, had a whisky. He reckons he can always get a whisky at your place.'

Aggie's glare was fierce enough to start a bonfire. 'Bet that's nothing to what 'e can get at your place – and I don't mean a cup of cocoa!' Down went her teacup; down went the stub of her cigarette into an ashtray and off she stalked, her footsteps heavy and her fists clenched in readiness to give somebody a damn big punch.

'Well!' exclaimed Joan, her face red as a beetroot. 'I've never bin so insulted in all me life, I'm sure.'

Maisie pushed the letter from Phyllis into her overall pocket. She exchanged a lopsided grin with Bridget.

'She'll get more than insults if she upsets Aggie Hill,' murmured Bridget.

Maisie frowned in the direction where Aggie had disappeared.

'Blimey! She went out of 'ere as though 'er drawers were on fire.'

Bridget shook her head in a disconsolate fashion. 'You've got a rare way with words, Maisie Miles.'

Maisie made a grunting sound. All manner of thoughts were in her head but one in particular floated uppermost. Beer was getting weaker and just like tobacco supplies were dwindling. Yeast and sugar were needed to make beer. What with that and the horrible bread: in pre-war years it had been white, but it was now full of the whole grains and of a light brown in colour. Some people liked it. Most did not, but it was beer and Aggie's furtive look and hasty exit that sat at the front of her mind. She voiced her fears to Bridget.

Bridget listened. Finally she admitted sharing Maisie's suspicion. 'I feel for her, but it's her business.'

Maisie shushed her. 'Listen to Mrs Know-All,' she said quietly, nodding to where Joan was complaining about the cost of booze to a workmate.

'Some boozers are gettin' it on the black market. Must cost 'em a packet, mind. Spivs and worse they are, them blokes that flog all that stuff. Still, they got to be making a bundle from it, ain't they? Ever met a pub landlord who was short of a few bob?'

The conversation went on about how it was all about thieving and there were more thieves about in this city in a war than there had been in peacetime.

'Criminal organisations 'cordin' to the newspapers. Read it, didn't I.'

'Blimey, Joan Parker. Didn't know you could read.'

'Well, you cheeky cow!' Joan Parker looked fit to burst.

On seeing Maisie about to open her mouth, Bridget hissed at her to let it be.

'All right, all right. I'm off back to work.'

Maisie flounced off, leaving Bridget trailing behind her.

'Maisie. Wait for me.'

When she got level with Maisie, Bridget spotted the worried frown on Maisie's face. 'Something wrong?'

Maisie shook her head, but Bridget wasn't fooled.

'Tell me.'

'I fancy going out tonight, but ain't got nobody to go with.'

Bridget wasn't sure whether to believe her, but went along with it anyway. 'Lyndon's in London. I can go out with you.'

Maisie pulled a face and tossed her head. 'That's just it. You've got Lyndon and I ain't got nobody.'

'What about Sid?'

Maisie nodded. 'Well he was writing to me, at least once every fortnight but I haven't heard from him lately – not since we figured out he was in Singapore. They're nice letters.'

Bridget eyed her accusingly. 'And how often did you write back? Once in a blue moon if I remember rightly.'

Maisie thrust her chin forward in her usual pugnacious manner. 'That's just it. I likes 'is letters and I did write back to each one.

Bridget spotted the pinkness that suddenly appeared on Maisie's cheeks. 'Glad to hear it. Sid thought the world of you. It takes lot of effort for a serving soldier to find time to write. You're a lucky girl.'

Maisie knew she was blushing, but wouldn't come out and tell Bridget exactly why she was suddenly so enthusiastic about writing to Sid. At times, it was difficult to remember very much about him at all. Their liaison had been brief and at the time she hadn't cared one way or another if he wrote to her.

Bridget's eyes sparkled and she too felt her cheeks warming. 'There's nothing like being in love,' she said. Loving Lyndon had made her very happy and the fears she'd attached to being a wife and mother had diminished from what they had been. Her only fear now was that he would shortly return to America. She consistently pushed the fear to the back of her mind. It wasn't wise to dwell on anything in the midst of war. Live each moment as it if were your last; that was the mantra everyone was adopting.

Maisie eyed Bridget with something bordering on disapproval. 'I didn't say I was in love. I just said that I liked 'is letters.'

'Better get back,' said Bridget turning away so Maisie couldn't see the smile of disbelief on her face.

Once they'd agreed a time to meet, they both went in the direction of their relevant workstations.

As she made her way back to the packing room, Bridget thought of Maisie and her changed attitude towards Sid's letters. In the past, she'd been very casual about both his letters and his interest in her. Listening to the other girls and their moony looks and sighs of longing had a lot to do with it. Maisie was becoming curious. Sid was likely at last to have a chance to enter her life.

It might have surprised Bridget to know that romance and Sid serving overseas was not the only thing crowding Maisie's mind. Every so often that afternoon, she glanced along the room to where Aggie sat concentrating on the job in hand, checking her 'chicks' were all doing their job properly, but also a bit quieter than she usually was.

There was no point in asking Aggie outright whether she was buying booze on the black market. She'd probably tell her to mind her own bloody business. The fact was that Maisie considered it her business. If Aggie was obtaining supplies of booze and tobacco on the black market, then it was a pound to a penny that Eddie Bridgeman's mucky fingers would be in there somewhere and Eddie Bridgeman was best left alone.

Aggie took charge of everything, always organising something towards the war effort or things to make her fellow workers' lives more enjoyable. For a start, she collected for the Spitfire Fund, the running totals of which were displayed on a huge hoarding on the far end of the building. On top of that, she collected for anyone bombed out and in need of funds to buy a few second-hand bits and bobs to tide them over. She also collected when anyone was leaving or for a birthday, a night out, or even a birth, marriage or death. She was also in charge of the weekly collection for the record club so they could buy a new record or two for the wind-up gramophone kept for emergencies down in the shelter. The shelter was actually the huge basement area beneath the factory and when the air raid sounded that was where they all went. There was tea and chairs down there, the gramophone and a pile of records. Along with a bit of knitting and reading, listening to music whilst the building shook in response to an explosion kept them sane.

The money for the record fund was collected once a week – only sixpence or so – but Aggie was a stickler for everyone paying their due. So far today there had been no collection. Maisie was in no doubt that something was very wrong and she couldn't shake off the feeling that the Llandoger Trow was at the centre of it.

There was a moment of laughter from Aggie's end of the room. Drawn by the familiar sound and hoping her suspicions were just that – suspicions – Maisie looked that way. Their eyes met and, in an instant, Maisie read that look and knew beyond doubt that not only had she guessed right about where Aggie and Curly were getting their beer from, but that Aggie knew she had. But who could blame them? Everyone was doing what they could to survive.

22

CAROLE

In the aftermath of the raid when Jane had been killed, Carole couldn't stop telling her mother all that had happened, how she'd been credited with doing a good job and also about what happened to Jane.

She should have known better. Back before then, when she'd just passed the first-aid course, she'd also told her mother about that. Carole had awaited her mother's reaction on that occasion too.

'I don't suppose they're paying you any extra, are they?' Mavis had sniffed, totally unimpressed by anything that didn't concern money or men. 'You don't do any extra for nothing. Ain't I always told you that?'

Unperturbed, Carole had tried again. 'When the ambulance next goes out after an air raid, I'll be goin' with it again. Can't wait.'

No matter how loudly she trumpeted her success, Mavis, who sat in front of a mirror in her petticoat, continued to concentrate on the careful application of bright red lipstick.

Carole crossed her arms and leaned against the door jamb.

Her mother was as blonde as she was, though mostly from the effects of peroxide. When she didn't dye it, the grey hairline showed through.

She didn't bother to say any more about her work. Instead, she asked, 'Are you going out?'

'Course I bleedin' am.' The red lips pouted in and out. 'That's what you should be doin',' she said, eyeing her daughter up and down and seeing herself as she used to be. 'Get yerself a bloke.' She turned abruptly back to the mirror. 'I ain't lookin' after you forever. Now get on out. I got work to do.'

Carole turned away. When she'd been little, her mother had locked her in the coal cellar with just a blanket to cover her and a one-eyed teddy bear. Then later she sent her out no matter what the weather. As she'd got older and prettier, she'd used her as an enticement for her customers to give her that bit more money. Carole had been a pretty child. She now looked mature for her age, as well as blonde, pretty and curvaceous – and the punters had noticed.

It was a bit warm for wearing her new fur coat, but Mavis put it on anyway. It had cost a few bob on the black market. Eddie had stashed a bit of gear with her and paid her to look after it so she could afford it.

She smiled as old memories surfaced. He'd been a handsome bloke back then and she'd been a very pretty sixteen-year-old. Oh yes. She and him went back a long way.

It had come as something of a surprise for him to visit her and she'd told him so. 'So what you got this time?'

She kept a straight face. This was just business. There was nothing else between them now and hadn't been for a long time.

'Nice bit of gear,' she'd said to him. 'Not pinched from 'round 'ere. A bit of quality that is.' She'd fingered a particularly pretty necklace that looked like diamonds. There was no chance of him making her a present

of it and she didn't expect it. She knew Eddie very well – just as well as he knew her. Few knew him better.

He'd strolled about the room, hat in hand, touched a photograph of her with Carole in her arms. She snatched it from him, threw it into a sideboard drawer and slammed it shut.

She'd been wary, knowing that Eddie did nothing without reason. He'd wanted something from her. His excuse was that he wanted her to store stolen goods for him – such as the flashy jewels. That was OK by her. It was no big deal to do that, and besides, he'd pay well, well enough to have a couple of nights' break from lying on her back beneath some sweaty, heaving bloke who didn't own a bath.

'That girl of yours looks a lot like you when you was younger,' he'd said to her then.

She'd eyed him warily. 'Yeah. I seen you looking at 'er.'

At first her expression was hesitant until he said, 'Just as pretty. You always was the prettiest in the street, Mavis.'

His sweet words and the way he stroked her cheek was reassuring. It almost made her feel that they could be what they were to each other all over again. Only if that happened could she tell him more about Carole and why she hadn't had her adopted at birth.

23

BRIDGET

It was a fresh and breezy Sunday morning. Bridget's mother insisted on washing up. She slid her a sidelong look as she took the dishcloth from her hand.

'What time did you say he was picking you up?'

'Ten o'clock. We're going for a walk through Leigh Woods. He's bringing a picnic.'

Her mother's smile was warm though reserved. 'That'll be nice. I suppose you'll be driving over the bridge.'

'Yes. It'll be a nice view from up there.'

The bridge her mother was referring to was Clifton Suspension Bridge, a marvel of Victorian engineering spanning the Avon Gorge from the Leigh Woods to the Clifton side.

Her mother bowed her head over the sink and poured on a kettle of hot water. The steam rising from it failed to hide her frown.

Bridget loitered by the draining board, not sure what to say. What she did know was that her mother didn't entirely approve of her relationship with Lyndon.

'Mum, I love him.' It came out before she had chance to think.

Her mother carried on with the washing up, all her attention fixed on erasing the tiniest sliver of grease from a breakfast plate.

'And I suppose he's told you that he loves you.'

'Yes. Of course he has.'

'And he's mentioned marriage.'

'Well... yes, as a matter of fact he has...'

Her mother rounded on her, eyes blazing with warning. 'Has it not occurred to you that he's only saying that until he gets what he wants? Think, Bridie. The man is rich as well as good-looking. He can have his pick of any girl he likes, posh girls who play tennis and keep a stable of horses and have bank accounts and backgrounds similar to his own.'

Bridget smarted at the verbal assault. She'd long known of her mother's reservations about her relationship with Lyndon, but never had it been expressed so forcefully. She took a step back, feeling both surprised and hurt – but undaunted.

Reining in her self-control, she held her head high. 'I love him and I will marry him.'

She didn't add the stipulation that it would mean her moving with him to America. She couldn't bear to cross that particular bridge until their plans were fully formed.

Determined as she was, her mother's parting words followed her out of the front door.

'And what do you think his parents will say to that?'

The fresh breeze stroking her face helped her calm down as she waited by the front gate for Lyndon to arrive. She was ten minutes early, but she'd just had to leave the house, though her mother's words still rang in her head.

Face turned to the direction he would come from, she stepped from one foot to another. She was angry with her mother. Didn't she know that love conquers all?

Her father's limping footsteps coming down the front garden path sounded behind her before he stood with her at the gate.

'You mustn't blame your mother for her strong words,' her father said quietly, his pipe clenched at the corner of his mouth.

'She doesn't understand,' said Bridget, tears pricking at the corners of her eyes. She turned to face her father. 'I love him, Dad. I really do. And he loves me.'

Her father's eyes narrowed. He seemed to be scrutinising the yellow climbing rose tangled round the drainpipe. It was the only plant in the whole garden to whom he gave any nurturing at all. 'I don't doubt it.'

'You don't?'

He wasn't to know it, but those few words made a difference – or perhaps he did know.

'It'll run its course one way or another, but for now you can only live in the moment as we all must do.'

'But Mum doesn't agree with me being with him.' She placed her hand on the warm tweed of his old jacket. 'Can you have a talk with her? Can you tell her it's for real?'

There was sadness in his eyes when he looked at her. 'Don't be so hard on your mother. She has her reasons.' He patted the hand that rested on his arm. 'Live in the moment, Bridie. That's the only advice I can give you, mainly because you'll follow your heart anyway and neither of us can condemn you for that.'

* * *

His words stayed with her as she sat with Lyndon near a gorse-covered hump in Leigh Woods that Bridget knew to be an Iron Age fort. She nattered on about its history until Lyndon grabbed her shoulders and pushed her down onto the grass.

'Enough of your lecturing, Bridget Milligan. Sunday is a day of rest, even for schoolmarms.'

'Unless you go to Sunday School,' she responded laughingly.

He smiled down into her face and she smiled back, loving his features, the well-shaped eyebrows, the laughter lines at the sides of his eyes and his mouth, the single dimple that punctuated his chin like a full stop.

His laughter stopped. His expression became one of pure affection, nothing more; nothing less.

'I've made arrangements for us to spend a night away.'

Bridget felt a sudden draining through her system. 'You mean before you go home.'

He looked a little embarrassed. 'Before I go home.'

She didn't want him to go home. She dreaded the moment. Spending one single night in close intimacy would be so wonderful, but it wouldn't be easy.

'I'd have to lie. I don't lie easily.'

He nodded. 'I realise that.' His look turned serious. 'I can't eat, I can't sleep, I can't do anything without you creeping into it. Even the observations on civilian life are suffering.'

'In what way?' she asked softly as she drank in the look in his eyes and the way his hair flopped over his forehead.

'They'd prefer me to observe Londoners, but I much prefer to observe Bristolians.' The smile returned to his face. 'One Bristolian in particular.'

His kiss was pure pleasure, the sort of kiss that could easily make them forget that they were in a public space. It was lucky that they were and it couldn't go any further. That would only happen on this weekend away. A believable excuse was needed and it would help if she had an ally.

Bridget caught Maisie on her way to the canteen. 'I need to talk to you.'

'Can't it wait until I've got my tea?'

'No.'

Bridget dragged her along to the ladies' cloakroom, where Bridget checked all the cubicles before turning to her looking breathless and pink-faced.

'I've got something to tell you.' Eyes shining, her lips widened into a happy smile. 'This is a secret between us. Lyndon's asked me to marry him. I've said yes.'

'Of course you have. I wouldn't 'ave expected anythin' else.'

'You wouldn't?' Bridget was taken aback that Maisie showed no surprise.

Maisie tilted her head to one side and grinned. 'Come on, Bridge. The moment you met the Yank, that was it. Bowled over.'

It was rare for Bridget to blush, but just thinking of Lyndon made her do so. Her whole body warmed the moment he was close, so what did a blush matter?

'He wants me to go away with him for one night – before he goes back to America. I'm not sure...'

She felt Maisie's eyes cutting into her, the look that made her feel as though every thought and emotion was laid bare.

'My, but I could do with a cup of tea.'

She tugged the brass handle and hurried out with Maisie following in her wake.

'Yes,' she said, before Maisie had chance to ask. 'I want to.' She leaned towards her, her eyes sparkling and features intensely earnest. 'I love him, Maisie. I never thought I'd say this about any man, but I love him to distraction.'

Maisie took a thoughtful sip of her tea. 'So you love 'im.'

Bridget nodded. 'Yes. I do.' She paused, the quickening of her pulse undeniable, so much so that the truth couldn't help but slide out. 'I want to go away with him. I want to go to bed with him, to feel him...' Her blush intensified as she dropped her gaze, not wanting Maisie to read her more personal thoughts. 'The thing is,' she continued when Maisie didn't say anything. 'I don't know how to tell my parents. I mean, they're a bit old-fashioned and so, to some extent, am I... you know... going to bed with someone before you're married...'

'Do you know that for sure?'

Bridget blinked. 'Do I know what for sure?'

'That your parents won't approve of you going away with 'im for the weekend. 'Ave you asked them?'

Flustered, Bridget shook her head emphatically. 'I couldn't! I just couldn't!'

Maisie took on one of her forthright looks. 'There's only one thing for it then ain't there?'

Bridget waited, hoping that Maisie did indeed have a solution.

'Lie. It's all you can do.'

It was hardly the answer she'd either expected or wanted.

Lying was something you spoke of in confession and so far she couldn't remember ever doing it – or at least confessing to having done it. Consequently, Bridget was more confused than ever. And dumbstruck. She just didn't know what to say.

On noticing Aggie on her way to their table, tea in one hand and toast in the other, Bridget hissed at Maisie. 'Promise you won't say a word.'

'Cross me 'eart,' said Maisie, and made a swift movement over her breasts which had been almost non-existent but she could now describe as pert.

'Just sold me bicycle,' said Aggie as she pulled out a chair and sat down. 'I ain't rode it for years, so when young Carole offered, I let 'er 'ave it.'

Bridget noticed the dark rings under her eyes.

Maisie frowned. 'What do she want with a bike?'

'It's got a basket, which means she can do the shopping. Her mum's too busy sleeping in the day 'cause she works nights.' Aggie frowned.

'Helping with the war effort?' quizzed Bridget.

Aggie almost choked on her crust, the margarine greasing her chin. 'Depends on what you mean by 'elpin' with the war effort. I've 'eard rumours about what she does, so I'll say no more.'

It wasn't Aggie's habit to speak ill of anyone, so neither Bridget nor Maisie pressed the point.

'So when's your Sean comin' 'ome? Bet he's gonna miss that farm. It was nice down there, weren't it?'

Bridget raised her eyes and met those of Aggie. 'Next weekend.'

She pretended to sip tea from her cup, though there was nothing left in it, and purposely avoided the look Maisie was giving her.

'Will you be going down there again?' Aggie asked, totally

innocent of the fact that Winter's Leap, the farm where her siblings were staying in South Molton, was also the scene of a brief night of passion for Bridget with the farmer's son, James, an RAF officer who spread his wings just a bit too far. Even when he'd damaged his legs in a flying skirmish, he'd still been playing the field. Bridget blamed herself for getting carried away. Lyndon had reappeared shortly afterwards. That was when she'd realised that James had never mattered.

Bridget shook her head. 'No. I won't be. We're keeping an eye on air raids. If we don't get any more, the kids will be coming home. But our Sean does need a job. I was going to ask if there was anything going here.'

'Leave it to me,' said Aggie. Her smile was weak on warmth but strong on apology. 'I owe you one.'

Determined the conversation wouldn't go back to the farm, Bridget asked Aggie if she was friends now with Joan Parker.

Aggie's mantelshelf breasts rose and fell before she answered. 'There's money to be made in this war and some are making more than others. Fact is,' she said, her voice lowering so only they could hear, 'Eddie's got us over a barrel – a barrel of bleedin' beer! Spirits too.'

'Stolen?' asked Bridget.

Aggie's jowls quivered vigorously when she shook her head. 'There's ways and means of doin' things legally – buying in bulk gets the likes of Eddie a good deal, one the likes of me and Charlie just buying a few barrels or a few bottles can't do. But Eddie can. He buys loads of cases of spirits – beer isn't so much of a problem – then he sells us a bottle or two at a time – six bottles at the most – but for top dollar.' She shrugged. 'We ain't got no choice but to pass on the cost or we wouldn't be making a living. We'd close the doors and not bother.'

Bridget didn't have any great understanding of business, but it didn't matter. All that mattered was that Aggie was worried. It wasn't like her to be down in the mouth. Her presence was as big as her voice, which resembled a very loud trumpet sounding reveille.

'Still,' said Aggie, slapping the table with her big hands. 'Can't grumble. We've got plenty to put up with, but at least there's no Germans marching in our streets and telling us all what to do.'

'Nah,' said Maisie in the kind of drawl she'd heard at the pictures. ''Earing about Aggie Hill's put 'em off. Invasion's no fun with the likes of 'er around.'

They all laughed, then Maisie sloped off to the ladies' loo and whilst she was gone, Bridget took the opportunity to return to the events of the night when she and Lyndon had visited the Llandoger.

'How are things going? I mean with Angie.'

Aggie shook her head. 'Not so good. She wanted money. Eddie's opening up a new club down by the river. Even though she's still living with him, he's got a new tart on his arm, younger than my Angie.'

Bridget flinched at the word she'd used to describe her own daughter. Tart to most people was another word for prostitute.

Aggie carried on. 'Thing is, she wanted new clothes. Reckons if she bought a new frock he couldn't resist 'er.' She tossed her head dismissively. 'Fat chance. You can buy a new frock, but you can't buy back the lost years.'

Bridget felt numb when Aggie rested her chin on her hand and lowered her eyes. She sensed that Aggie had tears unshed and could only guess at the pain she was feeling inside.

25

BRIDGET

Sean had filled out since being evacuated to South Molton. Not only was he taller but there was a deeper colour to his face and the boy had returned almost a man.

His mother was so happy to have him back that she threw her arms round him and burst into tears.

Sean was embarrassed. 'Ma, come off it. I'm not a baby.'

No matter his protest, his mother couldn't restrain from showering him with kisses and failed to desist until his father came to the rescue gently admonishing. 'Now, now. Listen to what the lad is saying.'

Despite rising from his favourite armchair to welcome his son home, Patrick Milligan's newspaper had not left his hand. It hung there, flapping at his side awaiting his return and scrutiny of the latest war news. His pipe was jammed firmly into the corner of his mouth, unlit at present. He was being careful with his tobacco allowance, free issue by virtue of the fact that his daughter worked in the tobacco factory.

Overwhelmed with emotion, a touch of the old way of

speaking fell casually from his tongue. 'Sean, me son, tis glad I am to see you home.'

He shook his son's hand with great deliberation as one man to another, though as yet Sean was going through that gangly phase. It would be some time before he was as fully formed a man as his father.

Bridget also shook his hand but couldn't resist hugging him just the once.

Sean began unpacking his rucksack. 'And see what I've brought with me.'

Gasps of thanks ensued on seeing the pat of butter and large wedge of cheese, both wrapped in greaseproof paper, followed by a bowl of eggs, each one double-wrapped in old newspaper and packed round with straw.

It was Sunday and Bridget had drawn ambulance duty that night.

Her mother was not pleased about it and mentioned it over the midday meal.

'Our Bridie's got ambulance duty tonight,' she said to Sean. She cast a halfway critical glance at her daughter. 'Shame she couldn't get out of it, what with you coming home.'

Bridget didn't want to go into details about why she couldn't get tonight off so deliberately moved the conversation along.

'Potato Pete is generous this week,' she said brightly on plating up the steaming food.

'Potato Pete is always generous,' her mother declared, referring to the mascot used by the Ministry of Food to promote the eating of potatoes which were home-grown and relatively plentiful. 'He's funny with his little round body and smiley face. Good job we all like our spuds!'

Sunday roast dinner was pretty much the same as it had been

before the war, though there was less meat and more vegetables, especially potatoes.

Keeping her thoughts to herself, Bridget concentrated on placing everyone's meals in front of them whilst noting with some amusement that her father's newspaper was folded up on his lap. It went everywhere with him – including the lavatory.

Sean was uncaring about Bridget's plan. 'That ain't a problem,' he said between mouthfuls of roast potatoes and slivers of breast of lamb. 'I'm going out to see me mates at six outside the park gates. They always gather there. Might 'ear some word about work. Outside work would be best. I likes working outside. Got used to it on the farm.'

Bridget saw her mother blanch. Her father also noticed his wife's reaction and patted her shoulder.

'Our Sean's growing up, lass.' He winked at Bridget. 'All our children are growing up, me darling.'

Sean's brothers and sisters had each sent postcards on which they'd written about what they were up to. Adding that they missed their parents seemed a bit of an afterthought and Bridget wondered whether Sean had had a hand in that.

Mary Milligan's eyes filled with tears. 'My poor darlings. I do miss them,' she said, hugging the cards to her bosom. 'Me and your dad are going down in two weeks' time.'

'Ain't you going, our Bridget?' Sean asked his sister.

'No,' said Bridget, immediately seeing her chance. 'I'm being sent on a course. All about ambulances and first aid. We all have to do our bit, you know.'

Her mother looked disappointed. 'Do you have to?'

Bridget nodded vigorously. The opportunity had come and she'd jumped on it. 'Yes. It's better than joining the forces, then I'd never be home.'

'That's a fact,' declared her mother. 'I'd prefer you even half here than worrying myself sick if you ended up in a uniform.' She turned back to Sean. 'And you're sure they're all happy and well fed?'

'They're as good as when you'd last seen them at Christmas, but longing for the summer. Doing good at school too. The girls want to know how old they have to be when they can go to the village hall dances.'

Mary Milligan shook her head and a smile played round her full and generous lips – the same lips that Bridget possessed. 'My girls. I can't imagine them grown up, though thank the Lord that won't be for some time to come. Still,' she added with a chuckle, 'I can't help thinking they'll be belles of the ball when they do – all four of them.'

Bridget caught her father's eyes on her. 'Our Bridie could do with a bit of dancing and romancing.'

Her mother's eyes caught him. 'Romancing is it?'

A slow smile spread across Patrick Milligan's face as his eyes met those of his wife. 'Yes, me love. And don't pretend you disapprove of the word or have never experienced it, because I know you have.'

Now his very pronounced and cheeky wink was for his wife Mary. Her cheeks flushed like a maid in May.

Bridget smiled down into her food.

Sean, whose mind appeared to have been elsewhere, jerked very upright, shoulders well sloped back. 'So when are you taking me for my first pint?' he asked his father.

'Plenty of time for that, lad. Plenty of time. And yer only fourteen.'

'My mates go in the pub – they did down at the farm and I had a few drinks of cider during the harvesting.'

His father's eyebrows arched. 'But did you go into the pub?'

A mischievous smile came to Sean's face. 'I'm not supposed to tell you I did. But it's different in the country, Dad. They do things different. Boys and girls do things different.'

There was a moment when Patrick Milligan's brow furrowed in consternation. It only lasted until Bridget's mother started taking the empty plates and dishes to the kitchen. Then that wink again. 'You're a lad after me own heart, Sean. Definitely a lad after me own heart. Not a word,' he whispered as the boy's mother returned from the kitchen.

Bridget shook her head at him in mock disapproval. 'Naughty,' she whispered but went no further. She was contemplating – no – determined to go away with Lyndon and had told the first lie. It seemed her reference to going away on the same weekend as they were going down to South Molton had been believed. There would be more lies to come. Maisie was right. Though it was out of character, she couldn't help herself. She was in love and dared to follow her heart.

* * *

Monday evening and Bridget was finding it hard to concentrate. Following yet another trip to London, Lyndon was coming back to Bristol that evening.

She'd told her parents that she was meeting up with Maisie straight after work, which was only partially true. There was no need to mention Lyndon at all – or at least she didn't think there was.

Maisie walked with her as far as the station for the simple reason it was on her way home. Normally she would have carried on up the hill on the other side of the road to the station. At Bridget's request, she had the good grace to stay a while, joining Bridget in a cup of tea in the frigid and dull surroundings of the platform cafeteria.

The lighting was dim, the station grimly filled with steam and the windows crisscrossed with sticky tape. It had rained all the way and the warmth of the interior smelled of wet wool as well as stewed tea. What looked like Easter biscuits were also on offer.

'One biscuit between two. They are big. There is a war on, you know.'

Of course, there was and didn't they just know it!

Over a cup of tea and sharing a biscuit, which, although devoid of currants, did taste of cinnamon, Bridget asked for Maisie's help.

'Ah yes. You want me to lie for you,' declared Maisie in that very matter-of-fact manner Bridget had become used to.

Taken aback at first, Bridget recovered quickly. Maisie had insight, not the kind of intuition that was read in tea leaves, but a natural way of sizing people up and guessing what was on their minds. 'How did you know that?'

Maisie grinned, took a sip of tea and, not liking the taste, pulled a face. She put the cup down. 'We did discuss it, I suggested you lied, and you've been thinking about it.'

Bridget nodded. Inside she felt a mix of fear, excitement and sheer determination, but the nervousness showed in the way she fidgeted, tapped the table, fiddled with the clasp of her handbag. Her eyes intermittently strayed to the large wall clock. The spidery black minute hand jerked stealthily towards seven o'clock when his train would arrive from Paddington Station in London. No amount of licking seemed to alleviate the dryness of her lips. Neither could she help glancing round as though to check if anyone was listening. 'What I thought was...'

She paused. There was nobody around, but it proved hard declaring how she felt, words seeming to stick to her tongue. It wasn't as though she was a virgin, but what had happened with James had been a spur-of-the-moment kind of thing; reaffirmation of being alive, of fearing what tomorrow might bring. With Lyndon it was different. In peace or war, she believed she would still feel this passion for him.

'I love him, Maisie,' she blurted.

Maisie made a so-so toss of her head. 'I know that. You know that. I ain't judging you, Bridge. Just get it out. Tell me what you want me to do?'

Bridget made the effort to pull herself together, to put into words what she'd planned in her mind. 'He's managed to rent an apartment in Bath during the time my parents are going down to Devon to see the kids. Sean's going down with them.'

'I'm no map reader, but Bath ain't too far to travel.'

Bridget felt her face warming as her eyes flashed between her handbag, the clock and Maisie's face. 'It's far enough away for nobody to recognise us, yet close enough to travel without it taking too long.'

'Right,' said Maisie, slapping the tabletop with an act of finality that made the cups bounce in their saucers. 'I get it. You're not really going away with Lyndon; you're going away with me. Where are we supposed to be going and what's the excuse?'

Bridget stared at Maisie open-mouthed. 'Well. Yes,' she said hesitantly. Yet again Maisie had stated all that had been on her mind. 'I thought at first that it could be something connected with your family – that we were going to stay with some aged aunt or something, or...'

'No.' Maisie's voice was soft, but her tone adamant. 'Number one, I don't have any relatives except for my grandmother and Alf – who's floating around dangerous waters somewhere. I don't think your parents would wear that.'

'Then I thought of another idea...'

'We're going away on a medical training course.'

'Oh. Yes. How clever of you to guess?'

One side of Maisie's mouth curled up in a querulous smile. 'I 'ad to be devious where I was growing up. I'd probably 'ave starved if I 'adn't been.' Although that familiar cheeky grin lit her face, Bridget detected a deep-seated darkness of the soul in Maisie's equally dark eyes. She knew a certain amount of what Maisie had put up with, but had not been privy to everything, secrets that Maisie preferred to keep hidden.

'It'll be nice to have a look round Bath. It's full of history. There's even Roman baths and loads of lovely buildings. Jane Austen lived there.'

'That ain't what yer goin' there for,' said Maisie, wearing a quirky grin. 'Is it?'

Bridget blushed. 'No.'

* * *

Carole decided she liked Pauline because she could tell her anything and she'd believe it.

'That Eric was waiting for me on the corner again. I told 'im I wouldn't go out with 'im if 'e was the last man on earth. He's besotted. That's what 'e is, besotted.'

'I wouldn't go out with 'im either,' said Pauline who still hung on every word Carole said.

'I shouldn't think so! You can do better than walk out with the likes of 'im.'

She told herself she wasn't fussed about it but it wasn't entirely true. She'd liked the feeling of power it had given her to put him down, pretend she couldn't stand him chasing after her. Rumour had it that he was taking somebody else to the pictures and she was jealous. The one thing she didn't want was for Pauline to go out with him and learn she was lying.

Carole insisted they go for a drink.

Pauline was hesitant. 'What if the landlord asks us how old we are?'

'He won't, but if he does, just say you're eighteen and add four years onto your proper birth date. 'E won't know any different.'

The nearest pub was the Barley Mow. Its main doors were on a corner, so fairly easy to find in the blackout.

Carole went first, tugging on the brass handle that opened the door before pulling back the blackout curtain.

As with any public bar, the air was rank with tobacco smoke, the smell of bodies, malt and cider. Customers jostled for room between them at the door and the crowded bar. It was a case of standing room only.

'Come on,' said Carole, turning aside to the glazed door to her left. 'Let's see if there's any seats in the saloon.'

The saloon was smaller and quieter than the public bar, a place of more comfortable seating and a smaller server, where the barmaid only attended when somebody shouted for another round. It was more usually frequented by couples who wanted to be alone, some of whom were married, though not to each other, or people who just wanted to hear themselves speak, which was impossible in the public bar.

Just as Carole had guessed, it was nowhere near as busy as the public bar. It was gloomily lit, as though somebody had dragged the blackout inside. Indistinct faces clouded with shadow looked their way.

The air in here smelt different too, refreshing even. She detected a hint of cologne, of somebody who could afford to splash it on generously, and the smell of cheap suits and work wear was replaced by good clean wool.

Her satisfaction turned to concern as one figure straightened and looked right at her.

'Well, this is a lovely surprise. 'Ow's you Carole? Mother all right is she?'

Carole froze, took a step backwards and stepped on Pauline's foot.

Eddie Bridgeman got to his feet. 'Come on, girls. No need to be shy. Take a seat and I'll get you a drink. I just bin 'round to yer mother's,' he said to Carole as, with a firm hand, he guided her onto the banquette seating that was fixed to the wall.

'Oh! That's nice,' she said, trying her best not to let Pauline see how nervous she was.

'Yeah.' His smile was all teeth and tough intensity. She didn't like the look in his eyes. Didn't like how he'd singled her out the last time she'd seen him.

'This is my mate, Pauline,' she blurted suddenly.

Eddie's gaze settled on Pauline and for a while lingered. 'Blimey. You two could almost be twins.'

Carole wanted to kick Pauline when she blushed and smiled, her fluttering eyelashes a sure sign she was a pushover.

She hardly heard what Eddie was saying as she and Pauline sipped their drinks. Not half a cider each as they would have bought, but port and lemon. Did he just say something about taking her out one night?

'Yer mate can come along too. I'm sure she'd enjoy it.'

Pauline was all gushing enthusiasm. 'I would that!'

Carole stared at his hand, which was presently fondling her knee. Up until this moment, she hadn't taken much notice of the other men he was with. One of them seemed as wide as a double wardrobe. The other looked familiar. She wouldn't have guessed where she'd seen him before if he hadn't opened his mouth.

'I'd better be going now, Eddie,' said the man, getting to his feet and placing a tin hat onto his head. 'I'll be in touch when I've got something you might be interested in.'

'Sure.' Eddie's attention immediately returned to Carole. 'At present, I've got something else to be interested in. Shame I gotta go now too, but I'll be in touch. We've got a date, darlin,' he said, one square-edge finger stroking her face, then lifting her chin. 'I'll be in touch sweetheart. Soon. Real soon.'

The smell of the cologne wafted over her as he closed in and kissed her lips. He tasted of pricey cigars and the cloth of his jacket smelt expensive.

Pauline watched open-mouthed and said nothing until he was gone.

'That's the man who was at the dance isn't it? Who is he?'

Carole frowned at the closed door through which Eddie and the others had gone, wishing she hadn't come in here. Wishing that her mother wasn't doing business with him – hiding stolen gear. That alone wouldn't have mattered. It was where those goods came from that mattered; looted after an air raid and some from the dead.

When she didn't answer, Pauline asked her the same question again.

'Come on. Who is he?'

Carole shivered but did her best to put a brave face on it. 'Somebody best avoided.'

26

Maisie had headed for home by the time the train from Paddington pulled into the station. Whilst waiting, Bridget gazed round at the gothic-style buildings across the way from the platform she was standing on. A Victorian engineer named Isambard Kingdom Brunel was responsible for building that old section and the main Great Western Railway from the West Country to London. Normally she loved spouting information on local history, but this evening her mind was only half concentrating. Inside, she was bubbling with excitement, her nerves on edge, her heart skipping against her ribs and goose pimples seemed to be erupting all over her body.

There was an announcement over the tannoy which was garbled and indistinct. Bridget had taken the precaution of asking a railway employee what time the train from London was coming in and at what platform. It didn't matter that the announcement was indistinct, she knew this had to be the train from London. She was in the right place.

Steam belching from its stack and beneath its wheels, the

majestic monster bulldozed its way into the station. She glimpsed
the blackened face of the driver in the cab as it passed and
slowed. Railway employees with whistles, flags and luggage trolleys stood back until the great beast had come to a standstill.

There followed a clattering and banging of doors as they
slammed against the main body of the carriage. Civilians, servicemen, men, women and children were disgorged, some almost
tumbling out in their haste to once more place a foot on firm
ground.

Third, second and first class; she knew Lyndon would be in
first.

There were not so many coming out of the first-class carriage.
Civilian or military, male or female, those that had been in first
class were well-dressed, professional people, the gentlemen
wearing bowler hats and carrying rolled-up umbrellas. Members
of the military sported the insignia of serving officers. Ladies
wore expensive-looking coats and smart-looking hats with
feathers and net veils over the top half of their faces. Head in the
air, one woman brushed past her, the unmistakeable smell of
powder and perfume trailing in her wake.

Night was drawing in and the platform was unlit, figures no
more than grey shades in the all-encompassing gloom. The
wartime lighting of the station consisted of blue lights which
were difficult to see by – even more difficult, so she'd heard, for
enemy bombers.

Like ghosts, the figures in the crowd marched across the platform towards the steps that would take them to other platforms
and destinations or straight ahead to the concourse and the
way out.

Her eyes searched the grey mass of figures, but to no avail.
Where was he? Panic set in and sore thoughts assaulted her mind.

Had he missed the train? If he had, would he be on the next one and how would she know what time it would get in?

Panic clouding her mind almost as much as the steam fogging the station, she turned back to the first-class carriage. She saw a railway guard get on, but nobody got off. The railway guard who had just got on now alighted. She could hear him laughing, and then saying in a loud voice, 'You wouldn't be the first passenger to fall asleep and wake up to find 'imself in Plymouth!'

'Lyndon!'

Without needing to see his features, Bridget knew it was him. Her body collided with his and his arms were round her, holding her close. Like the railway guard, he was laughing, a deep gurgling sound in his chest.

'Can you believe it, honey? I fell asleep. I've never been to Plymouth and, from what I've heard, would prefer things to stay that way.'

She breathed in his smell, the warmth of his body, the tiredness that oozed from him.

'Plymouth's being bombed.'

'So I heard. Any chance of a drink round here?'

* * *

In the public bar of a dimly lit pub close to the station, she saw the rings of tiredness beneath his eyes.

'I'll get these,' she said, rising to go to the bar.

He stayed her hand. 'No. I'm tired but still a gentleman.'

Over half a cider and a double whisky – given over reluctantly by the woman behind the bar, but more readily when he handed her a ten-shilling note and told her to keep the change – they talked.

He half drained his glass before beginning to tell her what had transpired in London. 'It seems my reports have made a few people in Washington sit up and take notice. Some had been under the impression that Britain was close to caving in, that morale was low.'

'Who told them that?'

Lyndon grinned. 'The Germans. It's all part of the plan to keep America out of the war. Yes, the US are aiding and abetting behind the scenes, but that's nothing compared to what could happen if they join in. Some guy at the embassy reckoned the US could produce seven tanks a day, compared to one for the Germans. Planes too.' He shook his head and the rings of tiredness beneath his eyes seemed to become deeper.

Bridget had a nasty feeling that there was something more he wanted to tell her, something she wouldn't like.

Lies did not roll easily off her tongue and she'd little practice at deception, but looking at his face, feeling the longing inside, everything she shouldn't do was displaced by those things she wanted to do. Sleeping with Lyndon was top of her list, especially now when she sensed he had something to say that she wouldn't like.

'I think we should do as you say and go away to this place your friend's willing to loan us.'

The tiredness didn't entirely drop from his face, but it did diminish. 'You think you can swing it?' He looked hopeful and also in love. The palm of the hand that covered hers was warm and a smile lit his face.

She nodded. No, it wasn't easy to lie, but it was what she was going to do. She couldn't help herself. These were dark days. Who knows what tomorrow might bring?

She outlined the plan Maisie had devised. 'Maisie will back me up and say that we're both going. My parents will believe me then.' Overlong eyelashes brushed her cheeks as she lowered her lids, knowing she was blushing and that he was looking at her with the same desire that she felt for him.

The pub table was the only thing keeping them apart, no boundary at all to the feelings that had sprung up between them on the day they'd spent together touring the sites of Bristol not long after they'd first met when he'd visited the factory. It was hard not to suggest there and then that they should go to the hotel in which he was staying. The thought thrilled her, but the old Bridget, the one who feared childbirth, held her back. Besides, good girls didn't do that, but was she a good girl?

She pushed away the memory of James and that night down at South Molton. It didn't count, she told herself. She'd been missing Lyndon and now he'd come back. Lyndon was all that mattered.

A slow smile creased his lips and she felt like she was drowning in his eyes. 'To tell you the truth, honey, I'm too tired tonight otherwise I'd whip you off without a second thought – except that I'd hate to get on the wrong side of your father. But a weekend away sounds like a real great deal. I'll drive. It'll be just the two of us. I'm up for it if you are.'

Relief and tremendous happiness surged through her. 'I'm up for it.'

For a moment there was nothing but their eyes fixed on each other before he said, 'You're the only girl who's ever meant anything to me. I love you, Bridget. Don't ever doubt it.'

Her heart took wings. She could barely breathe. 'I love you too, Lyndon.'

They had another drink before they left the pub, Lyndon for his hotel and Bridget for home. A private taxi sent by the company was waiting outside.

'I'm giving you a lift.'

'You don't have to.'

'I'm tired but not so much as to not be up to a bit of canoodling in the back of the car. A taste of things to come.' The blackout had descended in its entirety, though the lengthening daylight hours of spring did go some way to holding some of the darkness back. There was just enough light to see his smile.

The kisses and closeness in the back of the car might have gone a lot further if it hadn't been for the fact that they were being chauffeur-driven.

She asked him to drop her at the end of the street so as not to disturb her parents.

'They go to bed early and it's Dad's night off from air-raid warden duty.'

On arriving home, she didn't mention to her parents that Lyndon was back. When they asked, she merely said that she'd been for a drink with Maisie.

'We were talking about the course we're going on when you're down at South Molton. Hotel and everything – near an air base, mind. A bit more first-aid training and how to drive an ambulance even faster than we do now. I'm looking forward to it.'

'Sounds dangerous,' said her mother. 'You make sure you take care.'

'Of course I will.' Bridget swallowed hard. Lying to her parents was far from easy. Going to confession crossed her mind, something she'd only done when younger because her mother insisted. To do so of her own volition might lead to questions she was unwilling to answer.

Once her mother was damping down the fire for the night, she sensed her father's attention fixed on her rather than his newspaper.

'Goodnight, Pa.'

Her smile was weak and there was something in his look that made her think that there was something unsaid.

Finally he spoke. 'Just be careful.'

She headed for her bedroom so he couldn't see the look in her eyes, couldn't read any more of the guilt he'd already seen.

27

BRIDGET AND MAISIE

When the wireless crackled into life, the air in the stripping room also crackled expectantly, sudden silence fuelled by apprehension.

Aggie requested one of the younger women to climb up onto a table and turn the sound up.

'*This is the news... The island of Malta sustained heavy air raids, but its defences brought down a number of enemy bombers...*'

The news bulletin had barely come to an end when Maisie became aware that Carole had got up from her stool.

'Come on, Pauline. Time for tea.'

'Oi!' Maisie was on her feet. 'It ain't time to go yet!'

The heads of those who'd heard looked bemused.

Carole sniffed, placed her fist on her hip and stared defiantly. 'It's only five minutes early. That ain't gonna matter.'

Maisie controlled her temper. She wanted to slap the lofty sneer from the peaches and cream complexion, but it wasn't necessary. She had a far better weapon than that at her disposal. 'That's fine, long as you two don't mind yer wages being docked.

Five minutes late gettin' 'ere or five minutes early going to break and you get fifteen minutes' pay docked.'

Her action bore fruit. Like fallen apples, Carole's face scrunched and her eyes glittered with fury as the two girls returned and slumped unceremoniously back onto their stools.

Being in charge of other people had turned out to be more of a challenge than Maisie had imagined. Carole made her grind her teeth. She always had something to say and disliked being told what to do.

'You were like that at first,' Bridget said to her that night when she mentioned it

They'd arranged to have a night out, one without ambulances or being dragged in to cover for incendiary lookout up on the roof. Tonight they were away from everything and out to enjoy themselves.

It was always something close to wonderful bowling through the doors of one of the old pubs in the city centre and leaving the blackout behind them.

Bridget pushed her way to the bar whilst Maisie bagged a table.

As usual, there were cheeky remarks, offers to buy drinks made to both of them.

'Never mind an ambulance, I reckon I should learn to drive a tank just to get through this lot,' stated Bridget as she set the drinks down on the table and took a seat. 'Cheers to us.'

Maisie touched her half of cider against that of Bridget's. 'To the three musketeers.'

Getting out was becoming rarer nowadays and they'd both agreed to make the best of it.

Their first subject was Phyllis. Still no letter; they did their best not to worry, but the news from the Mediterranean was dire.

Perhaps it was the Lyndon effect, but Bridget tried to stay light-hearted. 'I think we can expect a letter any day now. Here's to you, Phyllis.'

They both raised their glasses. 'Cheers, Phyl.'

'Still, she is in a nice warm place,' said Maisie. 'Wouldn't mind being there meself and away from that little cow Carole.'

There was something about Carole that bugged her, held her back from grabbing hold of her and slapping the pout from her face. Not that she dared do that really. W. D. &. H. O. Wills didn't hold with that sort of thing.

'She's one of those that will keep on coming. The thing is...' She frowned. 'I can't help thinking that what's on the surface ain't the same as what's underneath and after seeing Eddie Bridgeman paying her mother a visit, I think I'm getting closer to what it is. Seems OK with the girls close to her age, but older women and them she thinks are telling her what to do – like me – she's like that bloke in that story, the one you told me about. Two people in the same body.'

'Jekyll and Hyde?'

'That's them. Or 'im. Or 'er in this case.' Maisie shrugged. Out of the corner of her eye, she could see a bloke in uniform leering in their direction, winking and grinning every time he thought she was looking his way. 'What about your lot? 'Ow's young Sean? Settlin' in is 'e?'

Bridget's face dropped. 'He told my parents he's got no intention of working in a factory. He's applied for a gardening apprenticeship with the Parks Department at the Council. They want to see him.'

'That's nice.'

'I think so. My parents though...' Bridget grimaced.

Maisie leaned forward, curiosity lighting up her face. 'Talkin' of yer parents, 'ave you told them about next Saturday?'

Bridget had the creamiest complexion, perfect skin, slender eyebrows and ripe, full lips. Dots of pink erupted on her cheeks and slowly spread over her face. 'As we agreed, I've told them we're going on a course. You and me.'

'That's fine.' Dimples appeared at the sides of Maisie's mouth. 'I can lie as though I'm telling the truth.'

'I can't wait.'

Maisie noticed the softening of her voice. Bridget had changed since Lyndon's return. She'd always seemed totally immersed in her family. OK, she'd had a few dates, but nothing that had lasted. But Lyndon had blown in like a hurricane. She only hoped he didn't blow just as quickly out again – once Bridget had gone to bed with him.

Maisie swigged back the last of her drink. 'Long as yer sure. Fancy another drink?'

Over their second round, they skirted around any further mention of Lyndon. For her part, Bridget feared talking about it might bring some unseen flaw to the surface. Maisie had more or less the same reservations. If going to bed made Bridget happy, who was she to burst the happy bubble?

'How's your gran? Knitting like crazy, I suppose. All grandmothers seem to be knitting socks and scarves and such like for the war.'

Maisie nearly choked on her drink at the thought of her grandmother – Grace Wells – even being considered the sort of grandmother who sat knitting. If only Bridget knew, but there was no way she was ever going to tell her that her grandmother owned properties, lent money and that in the past her main profession had been backstreet abortionist.

'Her eyes are too bad for that,' said Maisie. It was true, though she could still see well enough with the aid of a pair of spectacles to read the entries in her accounts book. She knew who owed rent, who'd borrowed what and the due date for repayment. Maisie had vowed not to get involved with her grandmother's business but did believe that at some time she would be expected to take a more hands-on approach. After all she was the sole beneficiary; her grandmother had told her so. However, she had no wish to dwell on the subject and, as she couldn't think of anything else to say, turned their conversation back to where it had been before.

'You mentioned Lyndon asked you to marry 'im. Is that still on, I mean, once you give in, will it still be on?'

Bridget felt herself blushing to the roots of her hair. 'I love him, Maisie, and I'm going to have this weekend with him.' She turned and looked intently into Maisie's chocolate brown eyes. Despite her outspoken bravado, Maisie was a warm and caring person. 'Who knows where either of us might be tomorrow, next week or next year. People think the bombing raids are over, but that isn't necessarily so. I can't wait. I just can't.' She looked down into her half-finished drink.

'Bridge, I can read what yer thinking.'

There was no escaping it; she was forced to meet her friend's inquiring look.

Maisie knew what Bridget was going to say even before she said it – or at least the general gist of the words.

'It might be all I have, Maisie. I can't consider marrying him and going to America, not yet anyway. I can't leave my parents at a time like this, at least until the war's over.'

Maisie frowned. She knew very well that Bridget was committed to her family. They were all very close, but still, what price happiness and the prospect of starting her own family?

'Won't they be 'appy about you marryin' 'im? I mean 'e's a nice bloke, good-looking and got enough money to buy Bristol – well, Bedminster p'raps.'

Bridget concentrated on turning the glass around on the table, her coat cuff trailing in drinks spilt by previous customers who appeared to have spilled more than they'd drank. 'I love him, but I also love my family. It would be better if he stayed here, but... he's got commitments.'

Maisie read between the lines. 'And a family over there, parents who ain't keen on 'im marrying somebody from over yer or settling down over yer.'

'Oh, Maisie,' said Bridget, sounding as though her heart was breaking, her eyes brimming with tears. 'I love him so much and although part of me wants to go with him, part of me wants to stay. Is that such a bad thing?'

Maisie shook her head. Bridget's declaration of love was so intense it sent shivers down her spine. She'd also a modicum of envy, that she had nobody to love her or to love. Sid was sweet, but was she ever likely to marry him? Could she ever state with all honesty that he was the love of her life and would he even come back from this war?

'I think you should marry 'im regardless. You loves each other. I mean,' she said, resting her chin on her hand whilst carefully avoiding a wet patch on the table. 'Yer mum and dad left Ireland, didn't they? Made their 'ome in Bristol. They must 'ave left family be'ind when they did.'

Bridget sighed. In a way, Maisie's comment touched on something she'd never really thought about before. Relatives back in Ireland were never mentioned, not even grandparents, and as a consequence she had never got round to asking about them.

Placing those thoughts back for attention another time, she returned to the problem at hand. 'That's all very well said and done, but—'

Maisie interrupted. 'Never mind the past, what about the future? Your parents aren't going to be around forever—'

Bridget looked at her in alarm. 'That's an awful thing to say!'

Maisie was a picture of apology, heavy with sighs and a waving of her hands. 'Sorry, Bridge. That came out all wrong. What I'm saying is that I for one is more aware of what life is all about. You've seen some sights after a raid, just as I 'ave.' She patted Bridget's hand. 'Grab life with both 'ands, Bridge. Talk to yer mum and dad. Tell them 'ow you feel and get their thoughts on it.'

Bridget nodded. 'Thanks. I'll give it some thought.'

Maisie began to speak but was interrupted by the bloke in the uniform who was obviously drunk. He leaned on the table. They both eased away from the blanket of brown ale breath that fell over them.

'Can I buy you a drink, darlin'?'

'No. You can't.' Maisie was her usual blunt self, blunt enough for it to sink in.

He turned to Bridget. 'How about you, darlin'?'

Bridget shook her head. 'No thank you.'

Luckily, the landlord, an ex-merchant seaman who looked like an older version of Maisie's half-brother Alf, intervened. 'The ladies don't want yer attention, Jack.'

Taking hold of the man's arms, he eased him firmly but gently away from their table.

The drunk, a burly sort with a pockmarked face and dirty hair, attempted to wriggle from the landlord's grasp. Eyesight blurred with drink, he saw a smooth-looking man wearing a clean shirt and tie, hair combed neatly over his scalp, face cleanly shaven. 'Get off me you bloody poof...'

The landlord's response was to grip the man more firmly and frogmarch him to the double doors. In one big movement, he propelled him through without bothering to open them first. The landlord slapped one hand against the other in a show of finality, apologised to everyone, and suggested they had another drink on the house. Nobody refused his offer.

28

BATH

The doorman who greeted them at the door to the apartment block doffed his cap and said, 'Good morning, Mr O'Neill. I trust your journey was as good as it can be in these difficult times?'

'It was fine, thank you, Difford. Has my delivery arrived?'

The pink-faced man smiled and replied that it had. 'I took the liberty of putting the bottle on ice, sir.'

'Thank you, Difford. That was very good of you.'

Bridget, her lips parted in surprise, saw a ten-shilling note pass from Lyndon's hand into that of the man he'd addressed as Difford. The surprise had nothing to do with the money. What had surprised her was that these two, the gatekeeper of the apartment block and Lyndon, appeared to know each other.

'You know him,' she whispered as they mounted the marble staircase that swept from a stone-floored hallway, several times the size of the hallway back in Marksbury Road.

'Aha. Let me take your bag.'

She smiled at him nervously as he took the bag. Like his, it was only a light affair. She'd dared not pack too many clothes. After all, this was supposed to be a training course, not a night away with the man she loved. In a way, believing it herself helped her cope with the flighty spirits she fought inside.

Her parents and Sean had set off for Devon at midday on Saturday. She'd excused herself from seeing them off, saying she would take her away bag into work and leave with everyone else from the factory.

She hadn't met the look in her father's eyes when she'd said it but left for work at the usual time wearing her overall over a decent dress. There was another dress in her overnight bag, plus silky underwear that she'd made from fragments of material she'd bought in Miles's the drapers. Her nightdress, a very pretty thing of silk trimmed with lace, her mother had made from other fragments. The shoulder straps were no thicker than shoe laces and the lace had been cut from the hem of a discarded net curtain.

As arranged, she worked the morning and Lyndon picked her up at Bedminster Bridge a little over an hour into the afternoon. She didn't want any of her workmates to see her. Only Maisie knew what she was up to.

As he placed the bag on a very large double bed, Bridget's thoughts about what was to happen vied with her first impression of the room. The reception hall and stairs had been impressive enough. The room surpassed her expectations.

Heart thundering against her ribcage, she went to the window and, with one shaking hand, pulled back the crisp net curtain hiding the view. She found herself looking into the waters of the River Avon as they thundered in a froth of white over the weir.

'Quite a view,' she heard him say.

She let the curtain drop and turned to face him. 'Yes,' she said, her voice as low as the wings of the butterflies inside her belly fluttered. 'The river looks lovely.'

He came to her and raised her chin. 'I didn't mean the river. I meant you.'

His kiss was long and lingering. His body was hard against hers.

The bed, she thought, *will he carry me there?*

For a moment, she was too dizzy from his kisses to recall where the bed actually was.

To her surprise, he suddenly released her.

'I've ordered champagne.'

'Good gracious,' she said. 'You certainly seem to know your way round this place.'

There was a pop as the cork flew from the bottle. 'My parents own it.'

'This room?'

He handed her a glass of champagne still fizzing from the pouring.

'The management here. There are rooms and private apartments so it's both an apartment block and a hotel. Very up market.'

She hid her surprise in the first sip, then deciding it wasn't enough to help her cope with what she was hearing, took a deep draught.

'Strawberries,' he said, took one from the rich bowlful and tickled her lips. It smelt fresh as of course it should; Cheddar, where they were grown in abundance, was only a short distance away.

There were also freshly baked biscuits, a buttery flavour that melted in the mouth, slivers of smoked salmon, sweet tomatoes, a dish of cream and one of sugar.

'It's a feast,' she said. 'You're so lucky.'

His eyes, seemingly a deeper shade than normal, fixed on hers. 'I know I am.'

Blushing profusely, she bowed her head and tried to get her racing thoughts in some kind of order. This place! His parents owned it? What was she doing here? Her parents were right in saying Lyndon and her were from different worlds. She'd accepted that, but that was before she'd realised just how different.

Another thought occurred to her. 'Have you brought other women here?'

It was as though she'd hit him with a cricket bat – or in his case a baseball bat.

'What a question to ask.' He refilled his glass, then hers. 'I've only met you since I've been here. There's been nobody else. Not in this country. I fully admit to having relationships back home. I'm not a monk. But since coming here...?' He shook his head and gulped back half the champagne. 'No.'

He fell quiet, looking at her as she ran her finger round the edge of the champagne glass. Never could she have imagined feeling such jealousy. She didn't want him to have had anyone else, but they both had a past. James had broken down her barriers. She wondered what would have happened between her and Lyndon if he'd not. Perhaps she might have remained her old, reserved self. Or perhaps not.

The drained glasses clinked in celebration as he took both and placed them on the table.

'Shall we go for a walk? It's still light.'

She glanced at the daylight outside. Trees heavy with green leaves were dancing in the breeze.

'What floor are we on?'

'The third floor.'

'I'd like to stay here.' She turned to him. 'And leave the curtains open until it gets dark.'

'I'm fine with that. I've got one request myself.'

'What is it?'

He jerked his dimpled chin at their overnight bags. 'Can we get into bed without opening them?'

She smiled and although she blushed, she felt no shame.

He opened a window before they got undressed. The cool air made her bare skin tingle, not that it wasn't tingling already. When he began caressing her, she tingled even more.

'Are you OK with this?' His lips were like velvet against her ear, his breath soothingly warm.

'Yes.' Her response was short and sweet. She suspected that if they said any more, then this magic moment might be punctured never to happen again.

His hands caressed her back and buttocks, her breasts and her inner thighs. She followed suit with everything he did without fear or shame. Everything came natural between them.

The sheets were cooled by the breeze puffing gently at the net curtains from the open window. Their sighs and sweet words were brief. It was as though their bodies were speaking for them without the need of words.

Bridget closed her eyes and threw back her head, moaning with pleasure as they came together, as their love erupted on cool sheets in a cool room overlooking the street below and the thundering waters.

'I love you,' she said softly when he'd fallen asleep and night had stifled the summer light beyond the window. The moon had risen and without the pollution of lights from surrounding buildings, the sky was scattered with stars.

She stroked his face and although she had concerns about their future based on their coming from two different worlds, she refused to face it tonight. This moment would remain in her mind for the rest of her life and if this was all they would have, then so be it.

29

Lyndon O'Neill the third felt more at home in England, and specifically in Bristol, than he'd ever felt anywhere in his life. He reckoned a lot of it had to do with meeting Bridget Milligan. She was like a breath of fresh air compared to some of the girls back in his native Virginia or in New England, New York or any of the other places where his parents had a home.

Fascinated by her tales of the city, he had determined to know more, to feel that he knew as much about this country as the natives. The war was a terrible thing, but he couldn't help feeling that it had played a hand in helping him learn more, thanks to his directive from the State Department to check and report back on the morale of ordinary citizens. As far as he could see, they were holding up well. Opinions in the US varied; there were plenty shouting that Britain was finished, that they'd cave in within months and Hitler's storm troopers would be marching through Trafalgar Square in no time. He'd seen no evidence of that. Some might say he was biased on account of him having fallen in love with a native of these shores – albeit a native of Irish descent –

though he didn't think so. He'd stand by his belief, just the same as he would stand by her no matter what his parents might say.

'I'll never forget this moment,' he'd said to her, afterwards, when they'd been tangled in bedsheets. He'd ran his hand through her hair, almost breathless with the need to express himself, to tell her in no uncertain terms how he felt.

She was his love and becoming his help mate. Wasn't that what all good relationships should be?

* * *

In his job of researching the experiences of the general public at this time of great national importance, Lyndon had refused the assistance of a secretary, which his embassy was more than willing to pay for. As a direct consequence of Bridget mentioning looting in the aftermath of air raids, he was interviewing a selection of bobbies at Bedminster Police Station and as the nib of his pencil broke for the third time, he sincerely regretted that decision. Secretaries were always prepared for such emergencies. He, apparently, was not.

Yet again he made use of the desk-mounted sharpener, aware of the disparaging look of the police sergeant sitting on the other side of the desk. The desk itself was a huge, heavy affair that took up most of the room. Paint flaked from the walls in the exposed gaps between posters of wanted felons and government advice that careless talk cost lives. He was particularly drawn to one about black marketers depicting a sharp-faced guy with a pencil moustache, the brim of a trilby hat hiding one half of his face.

Sergeant Black, a man with permanently beetled eyebrows and the uneven yellow teeth of a sixty-a-day man, pulled out another Woodbine from the packet of five sitting on his desk. Such packets were normally given to employees – a slight reduction from pre-war issue. He guessed the man had somebody working in the tobacco factory. Everyone round here had somebody who did.

'So,' said Lyndon, dragging his gaze away and making a great effort not to press down too hard on his pencil and have it break again. 'You were talking about an increase in crime.'

'Bound to 'appen,' said the sergeant. He offered up a cigarette from the packet, which Lyndon refused. 'This blackout's the main problem. I don't care what they say, you can eat carrots till the cows come 'ome but it won't make any of my constables see better in the dark.'

Lyndon had numbered each relevant comment. This one was added to the growing list and he smiled as he wrote it down.

The Ministry of Food was pressing people to eat more vegetables. Carrots were abundant and used instead of sugar in jams and cakes. The public weren't entirely convinced. The Ministry had needed an item of believable propaganda and found it. When asked how he managed to fly in the blackout, a bomber pilot had responded that he ate a lot of carrots so he could see better in the dark. The faceless civil servants at the Ministry of Food had leapt on his statement. People were more likely to listen to a pilot than a stiff-necked civil servant or even a minister of the crown.

'What kind of crimes?' asked Lyndon.

He winced as Sergeant Black blew out a cloud of ubiquitous smoke, seemingly unconcerned and uncaring as to whether his guest smoked or not.

Lyndon controlled the urge to grimace as the policeman leaned closer, as though about to impart a state secret.

'There's some filthy things go on in the blackout – if you get my drift.' He tapped the side of his nose. 'Men out looking to get their 'ands on women and women, some of them no better than they should be, wandering around by themselves in the dark – sometimes way past ten o'clock! Well,' he said, leaning back into his chair and flicking ash into the overflowing ashtray. 'They gets what they deserves, don't they.'

Lyndon gritted his teeth. 'Not all of them are good-time girls. Some of them might be on their way home from war work. A large number do fire-watching and auxiliary nursing on top of their day job. It can't be easy to avoid walking home in the dark.'

The sergeant looked surprised at first. On recovering, he went on the attack. 'Then they should get an escort to make sure they get 'ome safely.'

Although he might have looked as though he was scribbling a few notes, more often than not Lyndon was actually doodling a rough sketch of the sergeant, his bloated features, yellow teeth which stuck out like miniature tombstones, brows as black as beetles – and the cigarettes of course, a continuous fog of nicotine shrouding his face.

Lyndon controlled the urge to wrinkle his nose as the foetid smell assaulted his nostrils. Virginian tobacco had a fragrant aroma when growing in the fields and was just as aromatic when being processed. The smoke from a lit cigarette and the stink of dead ash accumulating in an ashtray was a different matter. Could he bear to go on growing such a perfumed plant knowing how obnoxious it was when being smoked? He would do of course. It was his business, the source of his family's wealth, though he wondered if it would always be so.

'What other crimes get committed?' he asked, forcing himself to ignore the smoke and get on with the job in hand.

The police sergeant tapped the ash from his cigarette, too late to avoid some of it speckling the front of his dark blue uniform. He winked and his sly smile was ripe with suggestion. 'There's them women that are naturally of the night – selling themselves. Plenty of that going on in the blackout.'

Lyndon felt a surge of impatience. The police sergeant couldn't seem to drag himself away from sex and the blackout – whether the women were selling sexual favours or unlucky enough to be accosted on their way home from their duties.

'What about robbery? Burglary? Any crimes that affect the ordinary person going about their wartime duties and looking after their families?'

Sergeant Black looked a tad disappointed that he was not being asked to elucidate further on the habits of women – loose or otherwise.

'Well,' he said with a begrudging shrug of his shoulders, 'there's the spivs of course.'

'What about burglaries? I was recently told about a house that had been burgled when the family was down in the shelter. Have you come across that round here?'

The sergeant sucked deeply on his cigarette before nodding and shifting uncomfortably in his chair. 'Yeah. There's been a bit of that all right.'

Lyndon went out of his way to appear and sound totally disgusted. 'I think that's totally despicable. People sheltering from the bombs with their families whilst the dregs of society break into their house and steal their valuables. If I was the judge – or magistrate as I understand it – I'd be inclined to lock them up for life and throw away the key. Wouldn't you, sergeant?

The cigarette, smoked in double quick time, joined the rest of the detritus in the ashtray, pressed into oblivion by the sergeant's yellow fingertips.

'That ain't fer me to judge. I only find the culprit and throw them in the cell. Up to the bench what they do with 'em.'

Sergeant Black was getting annoyed. Lyndon hadn't started

out to needle him, but the more he did, the closer he seemed to be getting to the heart of the subject.

'So you don't deny this is happening?'

'Yeah. It's happenin'.'

'Have you caught any of the perpetrators?'

Sergeant Black clasped his yellow hands over his navy blue belly. 'Some. But it ain't easy.'

Lyndon's eyes narrowed. 'No. I don't suppose it's easy to patrol the streets when an air raid is going on. Your men do have to consider their own safety as well as that of the civilian population.'

The insinuation wasn't lost on Black. His face turned beetroot and Lyndon wouldn't have been surprised to see smoke coming out of his ears, let alone his mouth, where a few specks of tobacco clung to his lips.

'Now you look 'ere. I don't 'ave to put up with your questioning. Just you keep a civil tongue in yer 'ead. I know what you Yanks are like, come across some of your doughboys back in 1917. Typical of all Yanks! Think you bloody know it all!'

Lyndon added a little toothbrush moustache – just like the one sported by Adolf Hitler – onto the doodle he'd drawn.

Just in time, before he got shown the door, he reminded himself who had sent him here. He had a duty to the State Department to prepare an accurate report. Besides that, he also had a duty to look after the family business interests in this country despite the war. A little back-pedalling was in order and he did it at a rate of knots. 'I'm sorry, Sergeant, it's just that as a representative of the State Department, the fine details interest me. I greatly admire how this country is coping and I fully understand the extreme strains you and your officers must be under. It can't be easy, so please accept my apologies if I've caused offence. Don't worry, I've no powers to do anything with the information about the black market. That's your job. Mine is only to report.'

He got a wordless grunt in response. It was unclear whether his apology was accepted or not, but he didn't dwell on it. All he could think of was seeing Bridget this evening. He couldn't wait and his footsteps seemed lighter at the thought of it as he made his exit.

There was a woman in reception when he walked through, shouting the odds that she weren't no tart, that she did not run a knocking shop and that her daughter should be informed that she'd been arrested.

'Go on. She only works along the road in Wills's.'

The policeman behind the glass partition shook his head at another policeman who was holding onto the woman's arm.

'You ain't bein' charged this time, Mrs Thomas. Mavis! Let this be a warning to you. If any other of your neighbours in Sally Lane complains again that yer running a knocking shop, then you'll be up before the magistrates. Is that clear?'

The fact that Wills's was mentioned grabbed Lyndon's attention. For a moment the woman's eyes met his. He would have offered to tell her daughter if she'd been charged, but it seemed she was being let off.

He repeated all he'd heard to Bridget as they walked through the city centre, heading along St Augustine's Reach and up the Christmas Steps, a steep and ancient thoroughfare which had escaped the worst of the bombing.

Bridget frowned. 'Mavis Thomas? I think she's Carole's mother. She's one of Maisie's new girls.'

'Just thought I'd tell you so you can make sure her mother's OK.'

'And that was it?'

He suddenly wished he'd not mentioned the woman. The fact

was he wanted to talk about them, him and Bridget. Their Saturday night together had been memorable, but he certainly didn't want it to end there. 'Bridget,' he said, pausing halfway up the steeply rising steps. 'I want to talk about us.' He put his arms round her. The sunshine of the previous weekend had gone. Rain was falling, but the overhanging upper floors of some of the shops provided shelter. 'I want us to make plans for the future.'

It seemed to him she was avoiding his eyes, looking downwards. He lifted her chin with one finger. She couldn't help but meet the look in his eyes.

Pursing her lips, she said, 'It's a big step –if we move to America.'

Somewhat exasperated, he threw back his head and sighed. 'Gee! I know it would be a wrench, but that's where I come from and where my wealth comes from.'

She glared up at him, eyes blazing. 'Your wealth. If I have you, I also have to accept your wealth?'

He almost laughed, barely reining it in when he saw the look on her face. *Still*, he thought, *I have to be honest.*

'Look, honey, much as I love you, I've no intention of living in a hovel and having my kids running round with no shoes on their feet. I'm not used to that and want more for you and the children we have together. Don't you understand that?'

'I don't live in a hovel and my brothers and sisters all have more than one pair of shoes.' There was hurt in her eyes and her words were bitter.

'I didn't mean it like that...'

She stepped back and broke his grip on her shoulders. 'It seems my parents were right. We're from different worlds and never the twain shall meet.'

She spun away, her heels clattering as she dashed down the steps and back to St Augustine's Reach.

Lyndon called after her. He regretted his words, but deep down he knew he'd had to say them. He loved her, that much was true, but their relationship lasting into eternity was going to depend on whether they really could surmount the obstacles that existed between them.

30

PHYLLIS

May and June meant blistering heat and still the bombing didn't stop. Night and day they came, Italian raiders flying from Sicily, diving onto the island, attacking convoys arriving with much-needed supplies. The aircraft defending the island were three old biplanes – string bags like the ones that had flown off an aircraft carrier and did for the submarine attacking *Vendetta*.

In the operations room, long poles with magnetic tips pushed blocks across the map of the Maltese archipelago. Each block gave details of height, speed and direction. The details would be forwarded to the pilots and ground defences who would go into action en masse.

The group of islands consisted of Malta, Gozo and Comino. There was another which was too small to count. Defending the larger islands was quite enough.

Today, Phyllis's job was to type out information received from observers on a teleprinter for onward transmission to each of the airfields and the squadrons defending the islands by radio operator.

As weariness caught up with all concerned, the adjutant

announced the end of the shift. 'All alive, alivo!' His exclamation applied only to all those inside the series of war rooms. Nobody knew what to expect outside until they actually ventured out there.

Phyllis exchanged a weak smile with Vera, the other trained typist who'd got nabbed to serve abroad at this job in a very dangerous place.

'There's some that won't be alive,' said Vera as they made their way up the steps from the ops bunker, steel hats still perched on their heads.

Phyllis didn't dispute her words. She had no doubt some civilians would have lost their lives, buried in mountains of rubble. The one saving grace was that there would be few fires. Wood was pretty scarce on the island, buildings made predominantly from stone.

Pilots, ground crew and the men who manned the aircraft battery would also likely be victims of yet another raid. The worst attacks were on shipping and Phyllis had to congratulate herself that although she'd seen action, *Vendetta* had got off lightly.

Back aching, eyes stinging with tiredness, Phyllis waved her hand in an effort to disperse the thick cloud of dust they walked through, a regular occurrence in the aftermath of a raid. 'This dust. I can't wait to see a wet day again. And greenery. Long wet grass instead of all this dust.'

People began to come out from cover, some returning to exactly what they'd been doing before the raid. She and Vera eyed a woman stirring a cooking pot which she'd probably been stirring before it started, had taken it inside, and now brought it out again.

'How can she just carry on cooking after all this?' Phyllis remarked.

'Life goes on,' said Vera.

It was the end of a long hard shift that didn't always end on time. Ongoing attacks meant shifts sometimes ran into each other. Rest and recreation equated to just a few snatched moments between raids – if at all.

The overhanging verandas on traditional Maltese houses threw early-morning shade. It was hard to believe they'd worked all night.

Vera's voice was heavy with fatigue when she said, 'I've drawn the short straw. I'm back on tonight.'

'I thought you had a date,' said Phyllis as they made their way to a djhajsa – a brightly coloured water taxi that would take them to their billet in one of the handsome detached villas called Whitehall Mansions.

Vera shook her head disconsolately. 'I can't go.'

'That's a shame.' Phyllis meant it. They all needed a little romance to help them cope with air raids, shortages, heat and dust.

With help from the oarsman, they boarded the boat, along with half a dozen other tired-looking service personnel all off to get what rest they could before the next onslaught or sleep the sleep of the totally burnt out. Whatever they did, everyone knew in the tiredness of their weary bones that it would be a matter of hours between raids.

A slight breeze, warm despite the early hour, ruffled Phyllis's hair, dislodging some of the dust as it did so and she sneezed.

'Bless you,' said Vera, then went on to bemoan her lot and the fact that she couldn't make her date. 'Thing is I really wanted to see this chap tonight, but I daren't. I'll be on a charge before long if I opt out of another shift so I can't go. I just can't.'

'You're going to stand him up then.'

Vera, her cap nestling on a bed of dark blonde hair, shook her head. 'I quite fancy him but I can't get hold of him what with the raid and all that.' She looked sidelong at Phyllis, who was instantly wary, sure that a favour was about to be asked of her. 'What I was wondering, if you don't mind that is, is for you to trot along and tell him from me that I can't make it and ask if he's free tomorrow night.'

'Well...' Phyllis was in two minds. Vera was always getting out of shifts. Goodness knows how many chaps she was involved with, but it always seemed that the latest was the 'one'. 'Are you sure about this one?'

Vera looked a bit piqued. 'Of course I am. I wouldn't be asking you to do this if I wasn't dead keen.'

'What makes you think I won't pinch him for myself?' Teasing was an antidote for what they'd just been through and what they would go through again.

Vera laughed, a deep-throated sound, perhaps as a consequence of being a chain smoker. Nobody had fingertips as yellow as Vera and nobody spent so much time clearing her throat in the morning before lighting up her first cigarette of the day accompanied by a hot but weak cup of tea. 'Seems to me that being married might have put you off men for life. I've seen the glances they give you, but you don't seem to notice, so no, I'm not worried about you pinching him. So will you do it for me?'

'Well I suppose I could fit it in. I'm taking rations along to St Josephs. Tins of bully beef mostly. They mix it all up in a stew. Everything goes in.' Phyllis had told her old mates back in the tobacco factory that she was living a glamorous lifestyle, yet it was far from the truth. She'd seen war close up, people injured, hungry or dying. To her mind, it seemed callous to even think of enjoying herself, not that she would tell her old workmates that. They had enough to cope with. Spinning a few tales would not only help them cope with things back home, it helped her cope too. A lot of what she told them was pure fiction. She found she enjoyed making up what she wrote, a form of escapism for herself as well as for them. Only in her diary did she write the whole truth and nothing but the truth!

There was little entertainment going on and what there was had to fit in between raids. Most of them were way out in the sticks or took place in deep cellars filled with cigarette smoke where the drink was dubious and not necessarily distilled into a bottle with a bona fide name. One of the Maltese ops girls had asked if she'd like to help. 'Some people just can't get hold of any food – even tomatoes,' Mariana had explained. Seeing as only a night of reading or mending beckoned before yet another bombing raid, Phyllis had agreed to help out. The place where Vera's date would be waiting was not out of the way.

Vera was over the moon. 'You're a brick, Phyllis. Thanks a ton. His name's Gordon.'

Phyllis stiffened. Wasn't that the name of the officer on board the ship that had brought her here?

'What does he look like?'

'He's air force. Flies a spotter plane mostly. Ruggedly good-looking. Broad in all the right places. Brown eyes. Stands as though he owns the whole world.'

The description did not match that of Gordon. Phyllis breathed a sigh of relief. 'Right. Got it. So he'll be wearing his wings.'

'I should think so. You won't mistake him. He'll be getting off a djhajsa at the first stop along the Senglea seafront. I'll write you a note to give to him.'

* * *

There was another air raid whilst Phyllis showered and got herself ready to go out. Her uniform was dusty, and although it was strictly against regulations, she decided to chance it and wear a white cotton blouse and linen skirt. It felt cool, at least for a little while.

Once the raiders had dropped their bombs and headed back north to their bases in Sicily, Phyllis finally ventured out into the warm evening a little later than she'd intended, but hopefully Gordon would still be there. Once the message was delivered to Vera's date and the food to St Joseph's, she intended heading to where a shelf of smooth surfaced rock jutted out into the sea. It was where off-duty personnel would lay on the warm rock or take a dip into the sea. For a while it would be pleasant to look out and see a clear sky, not one littered with enemy aircraft.

Vera had given her the note to hand to the pilot officer she should have been meeting. Gordon! Phyllis smiled at her mistake and was still smiling when she came across the officer standing with his hands in his pockets, looking out at the sea.

This had to be him! Ruggedly good-looking. Quite tall. Broad-shouldered, standing with legs slightly apart.

Perhaps it was her perfume – she had just a small drop of Evening Paris left, but anyway, he must have smelt it. Whatever the reason, he turned round and looked straight at her.

'Hello. Sorry to keep you waiting.'

The crinkles that appeared at the corners of his eyes were lighter than the rest of his complexion, as though he spent time staring at the sun with narrowed eyes.

His smile widened. 'So you should be. I've been waiting here for ages.'

'Have you?'

He winked. 'Not really. I was wondering where I might get a beer round here, so I'm glad you came along.'

His accent came as something of a surprise. 'Vera didn't tell me you were Australian.'

'Oh she didn't, did she? Never mind. What's your name?'

'Phyllis. I'm on my way to St Joseph's with some food.' She held up the rucksack containing half a dozen tins of corned beef – a small contribution to help feed the hungry. 'It's not much food but all we can spare until the next lot of rations make it through.'

For a moment, their eyes held and she knew beyond doubt that he was thinking the same as she was; that it was also a case of *if* the rations got through. The convoys attempting to do so were paying a terrible price, both in loss of shipping and loss of lives.

He seemed to think something through and then come to a decision. 'Tell you what. I'll come along to this St Joseph's with you, if you promise to show me where I can get a beer afterwards. Is that a deal?'

Vera was right. He was ruggedly handsome and for a moment she was tempted. On the other hand, Phyllis had no wish to play the fool again, to get enamoured of a good-looking man only for the war to intervene. She still regretted getting involved with Sam. The whole experience had led nowhere and she barely gave him a thought nowadays. Besides, there was also that fear she held inside. Helping those less fortunate than herself helped her cope. Getting involved with another man might breach her tightened up defences.

'Look, Gordon, although a bit of help is always welcome at St Josephs, I promised Vera I wouldn't steal you from her.'

His light chuckle and wide smile brightened the whole of his face. The white creases at the sides of his startling blue eyes dissolved into his tanned complexion.

Blue! His eyes were blue.

'Oh no,' Phyllis whispered. 'You're not Gordon.'

'No and I don't want to be. I want to be Mick. That's who I am usually.' He extended his hand. 'That's my name. Mick Fairbrother. And you are?'

The breath caught in her throat and his hand gripped hers. 'Phyllis. Phyllis Harvey.'

'Well, Miss Harvey. Shall we sally forth and get to this St Josephs before the Huns in the sun come this way again?'

She opened her mouth, about to correct him and say that her name was Mrs Harvey, at the same time promising herself that she would not allow him to get too close. 'Yes. That would be nice.'

As they walked, they talked. He asked her where she came from. She told him. He told her where he came from and the fact that his parents owned a sheep station in New South Wales and that he had two brothers and one sister. One brother was serving with the Australian army and one was in the medical corps. 'Fancies himself as a doctor eventually.'

She thought that most commendable and said so. She told him about the tobacco factory but how she'd bettered herself and learned how to type.

'So I suppose once this war's over, you'll be somebody's secretary in an office.'

'I suppose so. Hopefully back with my old employer. We're all great mates there.'

He smiled at the same time as shaking his head. 'Couldn't do that myself, work indoors. I like the big outdoors – used to it, I suppose. Brought up to it.'

'Have you got lots of fields?'

He laughed and she wasn't sure why. Didn't all farmers have lots of fields?

'We own thousands of acres. Thousands of sheep. You can look from the horizon behind you to the one in front of you and not see a single wall or hedgerow. That's how vast a sheep station is.'

By the time they got to St Josephs, it seemed they were party

to the basics of each other's lives. After she'd handed over the tins
of corned beef and the clothing she and her colleagues had
collected, Phyllis was thanked by Father Anthony.

Out of the corner of her eye she saw Mick wander off beneath
a low arch to an area where a set of stone steps led down into the
crypt. She turned back to resume her interaction with the priest.

'It isn't much. I've heard the governor's wife is going to run a
drop off point where people can donate what they no longer
need.'

'Everything is welcome,' returned Father Anthony. He didn't
smile. He never did.

Just as he said it, one of the Maltese women held up what
looked like a white tablecloth. Even though Phyllis didn't understand the language, she could tell by the woman's tone of voice
that she was puzzled.

The question was directed at the priest, who frowned, then
looked at Phyllis for enlightenment with regard to the volumi-
nous item held in front of him.

Phyllis smiled at the priest's puzzlement. 'Leave it with me.
Bloomers,' she said to the woman. 'See?' She loosened the ties
dangling at each side. 'They're bloomers. Very old-fashioned
bloomers.' She held them against herself, which set all the
women laughing. 'I'll go and see how my friend's getting on,' she
said to Father Anthony.

She went off chuckling to herself, aware of Father's Anthony's
disgruntled expression.

A rush of coolness greeted her as she descended the steps
down into the crypt. When she'd first come here, Mariana had
told her that since the bombing began, it had become a refuge, a
place deep below ground with Mother Church above. Therefore
they believed it safe because the Blessed Virgin really was
watching over them.

Mick Fairbrother looked puzzled by his surroundings, the crypt itself and the tunnels snaking off into darkness lit only by candles. Phyllis knew these were the catacombs that had once housed the dead but were now turned over to house the living. Many people had lost their homes and others feared staying up top where continuous bombing made even the most basic existence impossible.

A nun who Phyllis knew was also a nurse called for help in positioning a small cast-iron bed and some other items. 'I need a strong man,' she added and directed her gaze at Mick. 'You're not doing much.' Even in a gloom that resembled November in the far north rather than midday, Sister Clare, the nun in question, had a fierce look about her.

There was a grin on Mick's face when he answered. 'I don't dare refuse.' He whispered an aside to Phyllis, 'Might get a week in the pokey if that look's anything to go by.' Then back to face Sister Clare. 'I'm your man. Just tell me where you want it.'

Refusing assistance from anyone else, Mick took the bed in both hands whilst Phyllis tagged on behind with bedding and pillows. Sister Clare ordered another nun to give her a hand, a young woman who stepped to it, quickly tucking one mattress beneath her arm and Sister Clare carrying the other.

Black water resulting from recent rainfall lay beneath the duckboards they walked over, though even they were slippery with slime underfoot. This was not the first time Phyllis had come here so knew what to expect. Ahead of her, she saw Mick looking round him, no doubt astounded that people preferred to live down here rather than up in the fresh air. On each side, the niches that had housed the long dead had been enlarged into small caves. In some, there were just a couple of people living; in others whole families.

She fancied Mick's footsteps slowed every so often as he took in the dreadful conditions, the smell of damp and frightened people, smoke from cooking fires circulating with no means of getting out, children peering out of ledges hacked out of the sheer rock.

'Next one on the right. No. Not that one,' shouted Sister Clare when Mick attempted to turn too soon. 'The next one, you fool. The next one!'

Phyllis smiled to herself. In the short time she'd been coming here to help out, it had become obvious that Sister Clare had both the figure – substantially broad – and the manner of a sergeant major. To his credit, Mick was responding with respect and also a good dash of inbuilt Australian humour.

The rocky niche he was directed into smelt different to anywhere else in the complex. Bottles marked with Red Cross labels, metal trays and surgical instruments rubbed shoulders with carefully rolled-up bandages.

'There,' ordered Sister Clare, pointing to a very specific place in the exact middle of the hollowed-out cave. 'No,' she shouted when it appeared Mick was not placing it exactly where she wanted it. 'Just here.'

'If you think a few inches are going to make a difference, sister...'

To Phyllis's surprise, Sister Clare gave the metal framed bed a good kick, then proceeded to adjust it so that it formed a chair arrangement with footrests slightly extending to either side. 'A mother giving birth has to be under this light.' Sister Clare pointed a thick finger up at the single light bulb swinging from an exposed wire. 'There is only one place for it to be and that is the right place. Understood?'

Mick saluted her. 'Yes, Ma'am, and if you want to put me on a charge...'

Sister Clare slapped his arm and stalked off, but not without Phyllis noticing the impish grin on her plump face.

'Now for that drink,' said Mick.

'As long as you're sure you're not Vera's date,' she said with a matching grin that easily spread into a smile.

Mick spread his arms. 'I guarantee I'm a free man.'

She couldn't help but say yes, but didn't match him by saying that she was a free woman.

No letter had arrived from Phyllis. Bridget and Maisie had shared their concerns on a shopping excursion to Park Street. A number of shops had been bombed and some of those left had no glass in the windows, but at least the area had not been completely flattened. Their old window-shopping haunt round Castle Street had been badly hit The only buildings of any consequence remaining were St Peters Church, the Cat and Wheel and the Bear and Rugged Staff.

Weeds were beginning to shove up through some of the bombed-out buildings and a British restaurant, one of many set up by the government – which was actually a worker's canteen embellished with a use-friendly name and housed in a marquee – had come into being at the bottom of the hill. There was a queue outside and as they only wanted tea and a slice of toast, they found a small café doing the best they could in what remained of their once larger premises.

Tables and chairs were set out a in a large bay window. Huge sheets of tarpaulin had replaced most of the walls, but it provided adequate shelter and the tea and toast were not long in coming.

Bridget felt Maisie's scrutiny.

'So what's wrong with you and Lyndon?'

'Who said anything was wrong,' Bridget replied hotly.

'You've 'ardly said a word about 'im and I 'ain't seen 'im around. Something's up. What is it?'

Bridget fiddled with her teacup, then sighed and rested her chin on one hand, elbow on the table.

'I'm having second thoughts.'

'About what?'

She looked up at Maisie. As expected, she was fixing her with a look that made her think that even if she lied, Maisie could still read the truth in her eyes.

To repeat what he said seemed almost a betrayal on two counts: one to him and one to her family.

Her blue eyes, striking in a certain light and almost dreamy in others, now focused on her fingers. She had elegant fingers that hinted at great sensitivity.

'I feel I'm between the devil and the deep blue sea. I love my family, but if I marry Lyndon, I'll have a very different life. The thing is, I won't be myself any longer. Just an ordinary girl from an ordinary background living as a rich man's wife. Will I fit? Will I cope?' She shook her head. 'I'm not sure. And what if we marry and I suddenly find out it's all wrong? Imagine how awful that will be.'

Maisie fell back in her chair. 'Bridget Milligan, you're a right chump at times!'

'What do you mean?'

Like a dog with a bone, Maisie kept on. 'What about yer mum and dad? 'Ave you told them 'e's asked to marry you?'

Bridget shook her head. She'd seen the knowing look on her father's face when she'd got back after the night away in Bath. He'd remarked that the course looked to have done her the power of good. She'd managed not to blush but concentrated on sounding confident when she said that it had been a really good course and that she'd learned a lot. The latter was true; the main thing she'd learned being that she wanted to go to bed with Lyndon for the rest of her life. It was as though their bodies had melted together. She'd been scared beforehand, but once they were lying naked, any doubts or inhibitions had flown out of the window.

'So where is he now?'

Bridget took on a resolute look and cradled her cup in both hands. 'London.'

'When's 'e due back in Bristol?'

She didn't look up when she answered and even then her voice was small. 'He's going home.'

The answer hung in the air between them. Maisie waited for Bridget to elaborate. She wouldn't push. Eventually her instinct bore fruit.

'He's going back to America. He has to report to the State Department.'

Maisie's cup clattered back into her saucer almost enough to break it.

An elderly waitress with a crooked back and slow legs, eyed her fiercely. 'You break it you pay for it,' she pronounced. 'We ain't got many left after all this bombing.'

'And there is a war on,' Maisie said in a loud voice before the woman could say it for her.

She stared at Bridget, willing her look to become so forceful that Bridget could not avoid facing her.

Bridget had hardly slept a wink all week thinking about what she wanted to do and what she felt was duty. 'You should have said yes,' declared Maisie with a cocky sideways tilt of her head.

'I need time, Maisie. I need to think about it.'

'Well, you're going to get that all right if 'e's off back 'ome. For goodness' sake, Bridge, 'ave a word with yer mum and dad. They ain't my parents, but I'll speak as I find and say they're a decent sort and love you to bits. Otherwise,' she said, reaching across the table and lightly touching Bridget's fingers, 'you ain't goin' to see your bloke for a long time – p'raps never again.'

Bridget blanched. Everything Maisie said was right. The weekend had been all she'd expected it to be. Lyndon was the sun at the centre of her universe, her future if she allowed it, but her parents and family were her past and present. She tried to explain that to Maisie whose only comment was, 'People don't last forever.' It was harsh and made Bridget wince whilst at the same time recognising a truth.

She wanted to drop this conversation, to ease away from it gently without giving a straight yes or no. Something had to be said to break the verbal stalemate between them.

She related what Lyndon had said about his visit to Bedminster Police Station. 'A woman was about to be arrested for keeping a knocking shop – a brothel. She got let off.'

Maisie frowned. 'Is this going somewhere?'

Bridget took a deep breath. 'He called her Mrs Thomas and mentioned that she lived in Sally Lane.'

Despite her determination to persuade Bridget to marry her American and escape to a new life, Maisie gasped. 'Carole's mother?'

Bridget shrugged. 'The name and address are the same.'

Maisie exhaled loudly and sat back in her chair. 'Well, that's Carole for you, all brass and brazen on the surface, but I knew something was hurtin' beneath. 'Poor kid,' she muttered. 'She's a lost one, though.'

Bridget asked her what she meant.

'Ripe for the likes of Eddie Bridgeman to make 'er into something to suit 'im. We 'ave to watch out for 'im.'

PHYLLIS

The rumble of aircraft from overhead was accompanied by the sound of gunfire from the artillery units in the many fortifications that lined the cliff tops of the Grand Harbour. Over fifteen to thirty feet thick in places, the great ramparts had been built to defend the island and the city of Valetta by the Knights of St John some five hundred years before. Thanks were owed to the man who had overseen their construction, Jean Parisot de la Valette.

Phyllis was sitting next to Vera, their backs against the wall. Both were eyeing the rations they'd been given. A little goat's cheese, two slivers of bread, four tomatoes and two figs. They laughed about Phyllis trying to give Vera's note to the wrong man.

'What a muddle this war is,' said Phyllis.

Vera agreed and went on to tell Phyllis that she'd caught up with the fellah for whom the message was intended.

Although romance was always an important subject, so was food. Vera sighed heavily before pronouncing in a serious tone, 'Phyllis, I want you to witness the most solemn vow I have ever made in my life.'

The light was dim, but Vera's porcelain beauty seemed to rise to its challenge and shine like silver.

'What is it?' asked Phyllis.

Vera poked at a tomato with a red fingernail. 'I vow that I will never ever, for the rest of my life, eat another blasted tomato.'

Phyllis smiled remembering her own promise regarding tomatoes and then her attention went back to what constituted their supper: similar to most suppers which always included tomatoes. In the warm climate, tomatoes grew like weeds as long as they were watered. Her stomach rumbled. 'I wake up in the night thinking I can smell fried bacon.'

'Oh please...' groaned the young woman, rubbing her stomach. Like everyone else, she had lost weight.

'There's some worse off than us,' said Phyllis purposefully.

'I know,' groaned Vera who had a horror of premature wrinkles and was doing her best not to frown, 'but knowing that doesn't make it any easier.'

What she said was true. Showers of dust raining down on them each time the guns rumbled or a bomb exploded nearby were nothing compared to what some others were enduring.

They'd both seen people, their houses damaged, perhaps only two or three rooms remaining, stirring a pot containing all they could get hold of that day, which included rations donated by the armed forces on top of the little they could get from official channels. Rabbits had always been in abundant supply on the island, but even these were dwindling. Fish could be plentiful enough, but enemy planes had been known to strafe even the smallest fishing boats.

The bombing was incessant. They weren't just taking their meals in the cellar: where they could be fitted in, desks and typewriters were down there with them, though sometimes they did manage to get back up to the offices to do some filing. Filing cabinets, bulging with paperwork, were just too heavy to bring down. It was a dire way to exist – regularly living, sleeping and working in the same place.

A break was needed, but it wasn't easy.

'We're going out tonight. There's a party. A bit of music too, I shouldn't wonder. Maybe even food,' Vera added, her eyes bright with excitement.

'As long as Gerry leaves us alone to enjoy ourselves,' added Phyllis.

Even the smallest social events were interrupted unless they were held way out in the countryside. From that distance, it was still possible to see the bombing of Valetta, airfields and docks.

Vera was adamant. 'There's no merchant ships expected. With a bit of luck, they'll drop a few bombs on the RAF at Ta'Quali. I reckon it's their turn anyway.'

From the very start, Phyllis fancied that her new upper-class friend led a charmed life. Not only did she come from a wealthy background, things that she wished for seemed to fall in her lap.

And so it was that the sound of explosions was at some distance, aimed at airfields in the centre and south of the island that night. It seemed her luck was holding.

'Come on.'

Phyllis was almost dragged up the steps and out into the warm air. The sun had painted the sky red. In the distance, an air battle wove elaborate patterns of pale gold and smoke grey as intricate as a spider's web.

During a lull in bombing, they took their chance and scampered down the steps to where the djhajsas and their oarsman waited patiently for members of the armed services who they knew would defy the bombers and get out to enjoy themselves.

The party was being held in a cellar beneath one of the grand Venetian palaces currently housing officers. The sea here was unsullied by oil slicks, blue and sparkling against the honey gold stone of the waterfront.

Evening had come, the cellar was cool and the air hummed with conversation, the clinking of glasses, the odd outburst of laughter dulling the strain they lived through every day.

The men wore uniform and so did most of the women, with the exception of those like Vera, who had a decent dress to show off.

A record played on a wind-up gramophone that needed constant attention, its speed slowing, the music funereal rather than dance-worthy if the handle wasn't turned on a regular basis.

She looked for Mick, hoping he'd returned early from his mission. He'd told her the night before that he couldn't make it. They'd been sitting on her favourite rock eyeing the path to the moon reflected on the water.

'Do you think we'll ever come back here – after the war. If we get through it I mean.'

He flicked his cigarette into the water. 'We have to believe we'll get through it. I wouldn't have come here if I'd thought I wouldn't.'

'Really?' His foolhardy bravery never failed to surprise her.

'It's an experience and quite frankly I wouldn't have missed it for the world. OK, it's dangerous, but I wouldn't have met you if I hadn't taken the plunge.'

'You do a dangerous job. You fly reconnaissance missions.'

'Yep. I'm up there armed only with a camera. Every time I go up I tell myself that nobody's going to shoot a bloke down armed only with a camera.'

'But they don't know that.'

He'd shrugged as though it was nothing much at all. 'I have to take my chances.'

There'd been a catch in his voice. She'd asked him when he was going up again.

'Tomorrow. First light.'

'Couldn't somebody else step in?'

His face had creased with smiles, the white lines round his eyes disappearing into the rest of his suntanned face.

'Nah! Nobody can do a better job than me, and going to a dance is not a good enough excuse'

His laugh and jolly manner were infectious. No other man had ever made her feel so fresh and carefree. When she was with him, her marriage to Robert was forgotten. At some point, she would have to face facts, but for now she felt more alive than she ever had. Besides, going home to face the situation with Robert might not be an option. The bombing raids were increasing; tomorrow might never come. As for Sam, he was long forgotten, a mere hiccup in her emotions. In the meantime, there was Mick.

She scanned the faces of the men attending. As yet, Mick was not among them. Though disappointed, she told herself there was still time. For now, she vowed to relax, drink and even dance.

Sometimes her glance was met and held, though not by Mick. There were a mix of uniforms from all over the empire; one or two were Australian. For a moment, her spirits soared at the sound of a similar accent, a certain way of speaking, but none were Mick.

She smiled back at those who smiled at her before turning away, her eyes continually searching for his blue ones. There were many who tried to talk to her, offered a drink, asked if she wanted to dance. She accepted gracefully, laughed with them, talked with them. Dwelling on one man was only for fools. Who knows how long it would last? Who knows how long *they* would last? Those were the thoughts invading her head like flies buzzing around a jar of jam. That's all they were; flies, easily brushed away, nowhere near as deadly as the day-to-day reality of the island.

A few days ago, the remains of a convoy had come in, the sides of fighting ships caved in as though they were made of nothing stronger than paper. She'd felt sick on seeing the injured being stretchered ashore, some resembling Egyptian mummies, swathed in bandages from head to toe. Goodness knows how many dead had been buried at sea, nor how many of these would end up the same way. The graveyards in Malta were full – even the more spacious military cemeteries set down in earlier centuries. Civilian dead were being buried in graves already occupied. Many catacombs had relinquished their dead, carted off in sacks, allowing the living to move in.

Yet another officer asked Phyllis to dance, but she refused. 'Not just now.'

Vera chided her for it. 'What's the point of mooning over one man, darling, when they're as plentiful as salmon all swimming upstream to get to you?'

'I'm not mooning over anybody. I refuse to ever moon again!'

They laughed, but she could tell that Vera was about to be nosey.

'Oh come on. You fancy this Mick, don't you? You really got a yen for him.'

Phyllis shot her a sideways glance. 'Sent out on somebody else's date! And I had to end up with the wrong man.'

'Not wrong for you.'

'I hardly know him.'

It wasn't quite true and neither was it disinterest, but she'd been disappointed so many times before: Robert, Alan and Sam. She feared being disappointed by yet another man. She didn't want to fall into another relationship and end up in yet another cul-de-sac. There was also the matter that she was no longer a widow. She'd explained to her commanding officer that the husband she'd feared dead had reappeared. Under what she called compassionate circumstances, she'd offered Phyllis a ticket home.

'Up to you,' she'd finally said.

As she'd stood there, it seemed as though a heavy cloud settled in her mind. Robert's voice came to her, telling her what to wear, what to think, what to do. Making love with him also came to mind, though it wasn't making love, it was being expected to lie there without moving. A respectable woman allowed her husband conjugal rights: his right to enjoy, hers to accept passively and show no sign of passion. His mother's influence no doubt. The very thought of it made her grind her teeth and state her intention to stay. Later on, she might be able to face him, but at present she could not. Perhaps she never would.

'Well, I'm dancing even if you're not,' declared Vera, bringing her instantly back to the present. A tall officer with a deep tan and glossy hair waltzed her off onto the dance floor.

Phyllis wandered over to the table where a limited range of alcoholic drinks was spread out, perhaps in a manner to hide how little there was. A naval rating poured her a beer and she thanked him.

'On yer own, are you?'

She told him that she was. 'By choice.'

'Shame.'

'I'm married.'

There. It was out. Married rather than widowed. Bitterly accepted, bitterly said.

'Serving is he?'

She nodded. 'He was at Dunkirk.'

'Ah! One of the lucky ones then, love. He got out.'

'Yes. He got out.'

She looked away. It was cruel to wish he had never got out and she felt guilty doing so. She'd not loved him, but then she'd had no rights marrying him. She'd been expecting another man's child, one she knew without doubt that she would never see again. The thing was that she'd got used to being a widow, to having a certain amount of freedom. To some extent, she'd mapped her life out; serve in this war, and then marry, have children, once she'd met somebody else. She sighed. Why couldn't he have come back at the time of the evacuation of Dunkirk?

Her dark thoughts shattered as Mick's solid shadow fell over her. 'Filling in again, are you. That's very good of you, Phyllis, putting yourself out like that.'

She opened her mouth to make comment, but he didn't give her chance. Her drink was returned to the table and his arms swept her into the middle of half a dozen couples to dance to 'Begin the Beguine'.

His arms drew her close. For the first time that day she felt totally at ease. She closed her eyes so she couldn't see the uniforms, but heard only the music. Suddenly she could be anywhere.

She smiled into his shoulder and entered into the spirit of things, that yet again she was covering for Vera, the girl he didn't have a date with anyway.

'She said she can fit you in tomorrow night if that's OK?'

'Tell her she's missed her chance. I've met somebody more beautiful and dependable. Tell her from me that I think I've fallen in love – no – not think – I *know* I've fallen in love.'

He was joking of course. That's what she told herself as she laughed and said it was funny, but she'd always thought Australians were ugly, but there just happened to be this one...

His laugh was uproarious, big enough to reach the arched stone ceiling of the party venue. His smile was broad and warm. Handsome. Blue-eyed. Tanned skin. Sunkissed hair. He had all the attributes to make him one of the best-looking men in the room.

'Glad you could get here,' he said, looking down into her face.

She felt her cheeks growing warm, told herself not to get too fond of him, but that was easier said than done. He'd come back safe and sound and that was all that mattered. 'You been to St Joseph's of late?' he asked.

'I go there when I can. Lady Gort is pressing everyone who might have something to spare to give willingly. She's quite a dragon when she's roused.'

And we've all been roped in to help, she thought to herself. Not that she minded helping out – especially the children. There were a number of babies at the shelter. She'd held them and when she'd done so, her heart had felt like breaking.

'I wouldn't mind another drink,' she said as the music came to an end.

The truth was, she didn't want to think any more about the babies she'd held. The memory of losing her own was still painful. Having another baby was the only good thing that might happen if she went back to Robert. But she didn't want to go back to Robert, to that house and his awful mother. The only part of that life she sorely missed were her friends at the tobacco factory. If only she could live that life all over again and make other choices. If only...

'I'll come with you again. I've collected a few bits of wood, OK for making toys. I've got a bit of paint too – camouflage colours, but it's all there is.'

When his smile widened, his teeth were very white, in contrast to his bronzed face.

A low rumbling sound ensued. Glasses left on tables rattled and dust disturbed by the sudden blast floated from the dry mortar between the ancient blockwork.

'Hello. Looks as though the Sparrowhawks have come back for another go.'

The Sparrowhawks he referred to were the Italian planes and what he was saying was that another raid had begun.

'Might as well get ourselves another drink. I didn't get to go up tonight, but I won't be here tomorrow.'

'Don't say it like that.'

His eyebrows arched. 'Like what?'

'Saying that you won't be here tomorrow.'

He stroked her face and gently kissed her lips. 'I'll be out and gone on a mission in no time. And when I get back, we need to talk plans.'

She watched him stride off, laughing with his countrymen, joking with whoever it was handing out the drinks. This time she was passed a glass of something pale red.

'It's supposed to be wine,' he said to her. 'Italian wine with water added.' He frowned at it, then sniffed before taking a sip, swilling it around in his mouth and turning thoughtful. 'You know what, when this lot is over, I'm going back to Oz and planting a vineyard. I reckon I can give the Italians – French too for that matter – a run for their money. No more sheep for me. I'm going to plant vines and make wine.' He grinned at her. 'Might drink a fair drop of it too. A good victualler has to commit himself if he's to be successful, don't you think?'

Up until that point, she'd half entertained telling him about the husband waiting for her back in England, the one she'd thought was dead, but Mick Fairbrother was not easily interrupted when he was in full flow. It was like being whirled round on a carousel or swooping uphill and down dale on a rollercoaster. Either way, she was left gasping for air and putting off until tomorrow what she'd thought about telling him today.

When the ceiling stopped raining dust, Mick and a few others looked upwards but were listening rather than seeing anything.

'They're going over.' He turned to her. 'Might give us chance for a walk in the moonlight.'

'Is there a moon tonight?'

That smile again. Her knees went weak.

He shook his head. 'No. Hope not tomorrow either.' The beaming expression vanished, replaced by something more serious.

'You said that you're on duty tomorrow?'

He nodded. 'Another reconnaissance trip. Up I go,' he said, tossing his head and looking upwards. 'Up I go into the wide blue yonder armed with nothing but a camera and a rolled-up chart.'

She didn't ask him where he was going because he wouldn't tell her anyway. Not that she really needed to ask. The enemy were flying their sorties from Sicily, which was only sixty miles to the north.

'You'll be radioing in?'

'I will.'

'I've been filling in on a bit of radio work.'

'That would be great. We'll fix our next date over the airwaves. Be ready and waiting.'

She laughed. 'I will.'

Shortages of staff meant she had been trained – in double quick time – to fill in when necessary. Even if she didn't get that particular duty, with luck she would hear from observers that he was nearing the coast and the radio operators would relay his message to senior command and also to the teleprinter staff.

'Reckon it's safe to go out now,' he said, his arm round her waist, firmly manoeuvring her to the steps that led up into the main hall and out into the balmy night.

The night air wasn't as dusty as usual following a raid.

'Not our turn tonight,' said Phyllis.

On the other side of the water, a plume of black smoke was spiralled skywards.

'They've been bombing the docks.' They both fell to silence as they eyed the destruction of ships and hoped to God that no lives had been lost – though there would have been. There always was.

He gave her an impromptu hug, followed by an equally impromptu kiss. 'So did you join up or get called up?'

'I joined. I wanted to get away – for various reasons.'

'Seeking adventure?'

He lit a cigarette and rested his elbows on the stone parapet, still holding warmth from the heat of the day. The smoke he blew wound lazily in front of him. He peered through it to the bigger plume on the other side of the harbour.

'I don't know about adventure. I wanted a change, though I do miss the old life.' She went on to tell him about Bridget and Maisie. 'My best friends.' She also told him about the stripping room, of Aggie Hill, of her mother marrying a Canadian colonel. 'This war has changed so much.'

'Did your mother remarrying upset you?' he asked.

'No. It was her choice and she's been alone a long time.' She looked up at the lid of stars overhead. 'We all have to follow our star – don't you think?'

He straightened, turned round and by starlight she saw the desire in his eyes.

'I'll be back by seven tomorrow. It's a date for eight. That OK with you?'

A picture of the duty rota swished past her eyes. 'I'm free.'

But I'm not free, she said to herself after he'd held her in his arms, stroked her hair and kissed her. *I'm married to somebody else, somebody I don't want to be married to.*

In time she would tell him about her true circumstances. It

might risk losing him, but whatever way the wind blew, she had to be honest with him. She would not make the same mistake again – not with him; especially not with him.

Tomorrow I'll tell him, she said to herself. *Tomorrow when he gets back from this mission.* And he would get back. She was sure of it.

Lyndon had not lost his temper when Bridget had refused to
marry him. Neither had he called it quits.

'I'll be in touch,' he'd said to her in that sad moment when
he'd headed home.

Time had rolled on. Summer had come and gone and the
crisper air of the fall as they said in the states, or Autumn as they
said in England, was colouring the leaves.

He'd written to her asking her forgiveness for being so crass
about her background and what had seemed to him obvious
benefits of marrying into a rich and influential family.

Forgive, forgive, forgive me...

He'd gone on to beg her not to pair up with anyone else and
that he would be back but just didn't know when. She'd told him
about using the scarf to swaddle a newborn. It had taken her time
to tell him. He'd told her it didn't matter. A scarf was easily
replaceable.

Peace reigned at home; peace in New York, peace at home in
the house he'd grown up in. His father's study was of the old-
fashioned type, pictures on the wall of ancestors. Nobody was

quite sure whether they were family ancestors or auction purchases. As far as Lyndon's father was concerned, they suited him and the study. Both were set in their ways and any proposed updating by his wife was fiercely resisted.

Lyndon took a deep breath before closing the door behind him. No amount of furniture polish could compete with the smell and smoke from the fat Havana protruding like a chair leg from his father's mouth.

His father looked delighted to see him, the cigar now settled onto the edge of a cut-glass ashtray. He tossed his head and clucked his pleasure. 'You've done a fine job, my boy. You're making your mark in the world.'

His father stood up and shook his son's hand as he might for a man of business and status.

'I'm glad you think so, sir.'

After pouring and toasting with two measures of whisky, his father sat back down. Lyndon had the distinct impression that his father had been kept informed by his friends at the State Department. He also suspected his father of pushing his name, determined that unlike him he would not remain merely the owner of the biggest tobacco plantation in Virginia. His eyes were on Washington, maybe even on the White House.

Lyndon wasn't so sure he wanted the same. On reflection, it might get him back to England in some official capacity, in which case it was worth thinking about.

They talked some about the international situation. His father reiterated his own long-held views that the US might be persuaded into the war at some stage. 'Though I think it's less likely now Hitler has broken his pact with Stalin. Fascists and Communists were always awkward bedfellows.'

* * *

It was some days later when Lyndon was in Washington for debriefing that he went back to his hotel and wrote another letter to Bridget. In it he outlined that his report had been well received, that he was missing her, that he would return and they would marry. He also referred to the night they'd had in Bath:

We go together like peaches and cream. Nothing else matters.
I've told Dad my intentions. He told me to please myself and,
when it comes to it, he'll tell Mom.

His eyes darkened as he thought about that night in Bath. The passion was still there, so strong that it woke him up in the middle of the night. Their eyes, touch and bodies had been for each other. When he closed his eyes, he could still smell and feel her. When he opened them, he felt a great sadness. This war was going on too long. He wanted it gone. He wanted to be with her.

Despite his feelings, he presented a cool and collected picture to the State Department official. There was good coffee on offer; he did admit how much he'd missed it. 'Unavailable in England,' he said as his request for a second cup was honoured.

'You'll get all the coffee you want in the Philippines.'

'Philippines?' It was the last thing he'd expected. 'That's a long way away.'

The official gave no sign that he'd noticed Lyndon's dismay. 'That's where we'd like you to go. You can indulge in even more decent coffee on the way there. A ship from our base in San Diego to Pearl Harbour, our base in Hawaii and then a flight on to Manila.'

'How long will I be there?'

The official perused the thick file sat in front of him. 'Three months at Pearl Harbour. That should take you up until Christmas. Then on to the Philippines. We'd like you to do a similar appraisal there to the one you did in England.'

He didn't refuse. In fact, he felt like a boy about to step into an adventure book he'd been reading. Adventure books from his boyhood still lined his bookshelves at home. His mother had once had them removed, but a root around in the attic and they were back in their usual place.

Back in his hotel, he flipped the letter he'd written from hand to hand. Bridget would be disappointed that he wouldn't be arriving back in England any time soon. *But this*, he thought, *is an opportunity*.

Possessed by this boyish sense of excitement, he tore the letter up, took a fresh sheet of paper and a pen and wrote again.

Most of it was pretty much as before, asking her how she was doing before dropping in the crunch line.

...My country seems to need me more than I thought they did. I'm off to Manila in the Philippines via our naval base in a place called Pearl Harbour, Hawaii, where they want me to do some fact-finding on the morale and attitude of the local population. I'm to include Japanese residents whose empire's been making some pretty big noises in the Far East. They reckon on it taking me about three months before I go on to Manila. I'm not sure what I'll find in either of these places. Hopefully, it's not a war...

34

CAROLE

Carole pouted at her reflection in the mirror. She'd been reading a fashion magazine – such as it was. Fashion was becoming a rare commodity. Uniforms were taking over. She smiled down at the open page of models, hands placed on their hips, which were thrust forward in an exaggerated pose.

'I can do that,' she said, piling her hair on top of her head with one hand and resting the other on her thrust-forward hip.

She smiled at herself, applied bright crimson lipstick to her mouth, then smiled and posed some more.

A polite knocking from downstairs was followed by her mother's exclamation on opening the door followed by a muffled conversation, then a harsh shout.

'Carole! You're wanted.'

Before hammering off down the stairs wearing a pair of black court shoes that were a tad too big for her, she pouted one last time at the mirror. She looked stunning. Just like a film star.

Eric was standing nervously on the doorstep. He had invited her to a dance at the services club in Little Paradise, not far from Sally Lane. Despite her comments to Pauline about not being seen out dead with him, here she was again. But there it was and she didn't know how, Eric had got tickets.

* * *

His back turned to the bar, Eddie Bridgeman eyed a mass of different uniforms pouring into the services club. Up on the improvised platform – wooden pallets covered with dark brown felt – a band of West Indian musicians were setting up their instruments. Trumpets, saxophones, a double bass and trombones were exactly the instruments he wanted to see. Swing had made its way with the American bands across the Atlantic. Everybody wanted to hear it, to dance to the music and live for the moment.

It had taken a little bribery to get the contract, but Eddie Bridgeman knew the right people, those with an open palm who held the purse strings for a franchise like this. Eddie congratulated himself on having experience in the nightclub game. People wanted entertaining. What better bloke to provide them with all they wanted? Music, booze and birds.

The band started up and the lights were dimmed. Eddie loved the atmosphere, the blue smoke subduing the glare on light bulbs only half dulled by fringed lampshades.

It was an hour or so later when he spotted her, a vision in blue gliding round the dance floor as though she was old enough to be in here. The little minx had got hold of some tickets, or more likely the young oik that was with her. He didn't look much older than she was. Too young to be a proper man; *Not like you, Eddie old chum!*

The thought of Carole's slim young body caused a stirring in his loins. Angie had come back along with the prospect of some sexual relief, but she'd only stayed long enough to grab some stuff she'd left behind. He didn't know where she went after that and didn't much care. She was no longer to his taste. Too old for his liking. In the meantime, there was this ripe fruit in front of him ready for the plucking.

Though underage, he knew she was drinking, which suited him fine. He turned to the barman, a grizzly sort of sour expression but quick with the service. She was drinking port and lemon. With an eye to taking advantage later, he told the barman to go heavy on the port and light on the lemon – basically a ratio of three to one.

He kept his eye on the clock and on her. The dance floor was crowded, but he could see her footwork wasn't as accurate as it had been. She was more than tipsy.

The dance was scheduled to finish at eleven, but her being young he reckoned she'd leave before that. The young chap she was with had also been plied with too much beer for his own good.

Tonight, Eddie thought to himself. *I'm going to have her tonight.*

He moved cautiously round the edge of the dance floor, nodding at those he knew, brushing off the eager hands of young women who knew who he was and what he could do for them. Tarts mostly. They weren't what he liked. It was fresh fruit like Carole that turned him on.

His timing proved spot on. He saw the young chap place Carole's coat round her creamy white shoulders. The dress was seductive. She must know that. It was all her fault, dressing like that to entice. And she had enticed. He was hot for her.

Carole waved her hand when the young lad said something to her. He guessed what it was when he peeled off towards the gents' toilets and she carried on through the lobby towards the heavy serge blackout curtain and the double doors.

It wasn't that dark a night, thanks to a full moon touching

everything with silver. Nothing the government could do about that.

He saw her leaning with one hand against the wall and she seemed wobbly on her legs.

He thought about saying something, but what was there to say? Best to take her by surprise.

Before going outside, he told a bouncer to stand guard and not to let anyone out for at least fifteen minutes. That was all it should take.

* * *

Carole felt sick. Her head was spinning. She wished she hadn't drunk so much. She wished the moon wasn't so bright, wished she was home in bed, wished she wasn't so close to Sally Lane and her mother.

At first, the sound of footsteps didn't register. The realisation that she wasn't alone didn't hit until his hands were on her shoulders, slamming her against the wall face first, then hoisting up her skirt, a hand ripping at her underwear, another holding her face against the wall to stifle her screams.

For a moment it seemed as though the moonlight had changed from silver to gold as a beam of light flashed over them.

'What the 'ell's goin' on yer?'

Recognising her mother's voice, Carole forced her face away from the wall.

Eddie recognised her too. 'Get lost, Mavis. You're too old for me now... Christ!'

He clutched the nape of his neck, his legs buckling as he reeled backwards from the force of the blow she landed him. One hand grasping the rough stone of the old wall, he steadied himself and scowled into the light from Mavis's torch no doubt the source of the heavy blow on his neck.

'I'll pay you for 'er,' he shouted at Mavis. 'I want 'er and I'm going to 'ave 'er.'

Bleary-eyed and not yet clear what was going on, Carole did her best to stay on her feet.

Suddenly her mother was laughing a bitter laugh. What with the torchlight, it was just possible to see the grotesque expression on her face, the sheer disgust directed at Eddie Bridgeman. 'Don't you get it, Eddie? Are you still that thick?'

Rubbing the nape of his neck with one hand and doing his flies up with the other, Eddie frowned. He was getting angrier. 'What you on about, you silly cow!'

Her look was so intense that the bags beneath her eyes smoothed out. Her lips quivered as the truth came out.

'We were childhood sweethearts, Eddie. You were my first love, but you used me. You ruined my life. Don't you get it, Eddie? Don't you get it? You're 'er dad, Eddie. Carole's your daughter!'

It was hard to distinguish the look on his face and when Eric appeared, the moment for saying anything else was gone. Eric sought Carole, who clung onto him like a drowning sailor might a lifebuoy.

'Come on, Carole,' his voice trembling. 'I'd better get you home.'

Neither of them looked back to where Mavis and Eddie still stood in the darkness, Mavis laughing in his face and calling him a stupid bugger, and Eddie, for the first time in his life, feeling disgusted by his own urges.

35

BRIDGET AND MAISIE

Despite his parents' protests, Sean still hankered to work on the farm, any farm, not necessarily the one in South Molton. 'It's what I wants to do,' he proclaimed adamantly. 'Anyway,' he said, throwing a winning smile at his mother, 'it's safer in the country. I gets well fed there too. And I'll be there for the others.'

His mother had to concede he had a point, though told him without holding back that she'd cry buckets when he did leave.

Looking a little peeved, he promised to take a bit more time thinking about his options. 'But I do wants to make me own money and the sooner, the better. After all, I wants to get married some day.'

His parents had exchanged a secretive smile. Their boy was beginning to grow up.

Bridget told Maisie this over half of warm shandy in the Engineers' Arms. It wasn't their usual place for a night out, too big a place to ever feel cosy. The old pubs in the centre of town close to Castle Street had always been their favourites. Bridget had loved the low ceilings and the feeling of history that both the Cat and Wheel and the Bear and Rugged Staff still retained. In times gone by, the centuries old pubs had been surrounded by the classy shops of Castle, Wine and Mary le Port Street. All those lovely streets were now ruined. Somehow it saddened them even to think of it, let alone wandering round the fenced-off ruins where weeds were pushing up despite the cold winds of winter.

Maisie noted that Bridget was unusually thoughtful. She was given to a lot of thinking about one thing or another. This evening, her eyes were downcast, her fingers fiddling with her glass.

Bridget knew that Maisie was looking at her with that knowingness in her eyes. Not admitting what was on her mind would lead to a whole host of questions. Or statements. Maisie was good at discerning something was wrong.

Bridget sighed. 'I've had a letter from Lyndon. He won't be coming back here any time soon.'

'There's a war on.'

'I'm going to punch the next person who says that.'

'Fancy giving me the details?'

Bridget shook her head. 'Not at the moment. He's going to be so far away, in a place called Manilla.'

'Never 'eard of it.'

'He's stopping off first at a place called Pearl Harbour in Hawaii.'

'Never 'eard of that – oh wait a minute. Ain't that where they wear grass skirts and do hula dancing?'

'Yes. Hula dancing,' muttered Bridget. Maisie sounded funny but she was in no mood to laugh.

On seeing her downturned mouth, Maisie did her best to reassure. 'At least you've had a letter. We've heard nothing from Phyllis.'

Bridget frowned. 'Let's hope she's all right, but I am worried. It's been three months since we heard from her.'

The last letter they'd received had mentioned about her voluntary work – though goodness knows how she managed to fit that in with her work with the WAAF.

'Strange she doesn't say much about Robert – next to nothing in fact,' Bridget remarked.

Maisie agreed.

The opening of the pub door brought in a draught of cold December air. On seeing who had come in, Maisie caught her breath. 'Bloody 'ell. Talk of the devil.'

Bridget looked. Wearing his heavy army overcoat, head down, shoulders stooped, Robert Harvey had entered the bar. She swivelled round and opened her mouth to call him over.

Maisie's hand landed on hers. 'What d'ya wanna do that for?'

'He might have heard from Phyllis through official channels,' whispered Bridget. 'She's still his wife.'

The implication was that something very bad had happened. If it had then Maisie had to concede that Bridget was right. As her lawfully wedded spouse, the forces would track him down and he would know first.

Bridget waved. 'Robert?'

Haunted eyes in a tired face flinched as though he didn't quite recall who she was. Recognition eventually dawned. After paying up and the beer being poured, he came over and greeted them.

'It's Bridget, isn't it?' He looked at Maisie as though not quite sure who she was.

'I'm Maisie Miles.'

'Oh yes.'

Bridget, who had seen more of him than Maisie, maintained an impassive expression. 'So how are you?'

In the past, he would have boasted of all the grand deeds he'd done – whether they were that grand or not. This Robert, the one that had been in the heart of battle and gone missing, was lighter in weight as well as bravado.

'Getting better,' he said in a far quieter voice than she remembered. He fixed his eyes on his drink.

Bridget remembered him as something of a bully, a man who liked to have the last say.

For her part, Maisie couldn't help thinking that he no longer resembled his mother quite as much as he'd used to.

Robert flinched at the loud slamming of the pub door.

Bridget locked eyes with Maisie. The sound was as loud as gunfire. Her father had mentioned men reacting like that years after the battle responsible for that reaction was over

It did occur to Bridget to ask him about Phyllis, but she suspected his constitution was too fragile to cope. Instead she asked after the health of his parents, though goodness knows the next time she ran into Hilda Harvey would be far too soon.

'OK,' he said nodding, taking a sip, nodding and taking another.

'Keeping busy?'

'Keeping busy. Yes.'

The next sip he took seemed to revive him a little. He looked up for a fraction before his gaze returned to his drink.

'She's getting the back room ready.'

'That's nice,' said Maisie, not having a clue as to its significance.

'For Phyllis.'

Bridget met Maisie's shocked expression with one of her own.

'You've heard from Phyllis?' she asked cautiously, fearing what she would hear next.

Robert nodded. 'Yes. The War Office sent a telegram to say she's been injured.' He said it as one might for a friend, certainly not for a spouse.

'Badly?' asked Maisie, her blood suddenly turning cold.

'She was out cold for quite a time. Recovered now, but has problems. She'll be home just before Christmas.'

Bridget too felt the warmth draining from her body. It sounded as though Phyllis was badly injured. There was also the prospect of her coming home. How would that go? She had hated living with his parents.

She spotted Maisie's head twitching in a subtle shake, warning her not to say anything.

'We're glad to hear it,' Bridget finally said.

'Yeah,' said Maisie. 'It'll be lovely to see 'er again.'

She managed a false smile and both watched as Robert swigged back the rest of his drink in a couple of gulps and got to his feet. He said nothing, not even goodbye, as if he'd forgotten they were there.

'Are you thinking what I'm thinking?' said Bridget.

'He don't seem that concerned. Is that what you were thinking?'

'No, though I get your point. He's different than before. My dad said that the experiences of war affect you for years. It's affected Robert, that's for sure. It don't sound as though she's written.'

'We didn't get the chance to ask.'

Maisie sighed into the dregs of her drink. 'Well that explains why we ain't 'eard anything of late. Must be difficult for her to know what to say, seein' as she thought he was dead but now she knows he is alive...'

'She hasn't written to us and that worries me. I'm wondering just how badly she's been injured. Let's hope we hear from her soon.'

The fog was clearing from Phyllis's mind. Misted details were becoming clearer. She'd known she was in a hospital when she'd first come round but hadn't quite known what hospital or where.

36

PHYLLIS.

The fog was clearing from Phyllis's mind. Misted details were becoming clearer. She'd known she was in a hospital when she'd first come round but hadn't quite known what hospital or where.

'Where am I?'

'St Andrew's Hospital.'

The name hadn't been familiar. She couldn't remember a hospital of that name in Bristol and said so.

The nursing sister, a member of Queen Alexandra's Imperial Military Nursing Service had informed her that she was still on the island of Malta.

'You were almost buried under a fall of masonry during a raid. You were knocked out. Don't you remember, my dear?'

'No.'

Even to Phyllis's own ears, her voice sounded small and far away, like an echo rolling round in her skull.

The woman's smile was sympathetic. 'Never you mind, dear. It'll all come back in time and then you can go home.'

She'd closed her eyes after that and slept. She slept a lot. When they were open, it was almost wearying, watching the nurses bustling between beds, their starched headgear floating out behind them like the wings of a giant butterfly.

So much sleeping. It was during that sleep that her subconscious pushed Robert to the surface. She remembered being married to him, living with his family, receiving the news that he was likely killed in action. Tears sprang to her eyes when she also remembered the baby she'd lost.

'I remember,' she said pre-dawn when the ward was only just easing into life. 'I remember,' she said again in a hushed voice.

One day, a young nurse whose uniform she didn't recognise came to see her.

'I'm a member of the First Aid Nursing Yeomanry,' she replied when Phyllis asked her outright. 'I've been looking after you for a while.'

'Have you?' For the life of her, Phyllis had no recollection of the fresh-faced young girl, but she did know about the Yeomanry – the FANYs, as they were referred to.

'There's a handsome Australian wanting to see you. I told him I'd see if you were up to it. You don't have to see him.'

It was hard to remember everything. Her memory was coming back in bits and pieces. Strangely enough, there was one memory that kept emerging as a bell – helping a priest out alongside an Australian. Mick! The name came back in an instant, along with eyes of cornflower blue, a tanned countenance and a quirky smile that lifted one corner of his mouth.

Of course she'd love to see him.

'Right,' said the young nursing yeoman. 'Let's get your pillows plump so you can sit up better.'

He came in bearing a bunch of grapes, a scarcity unless you had a decent plot of land and plenty of water.

She latched onto his smile as though it would somehow save

her from drowning – though in what she couldn't quite grasp. After all, she wasn't at sea.

He kissed her on the forehead and placed the grapes on the ledge beside her.

'You had quite a belter.' He nodded at the bandage that was in place round her head.

'A blow on the head?'

'A real belter of a blow on the head.'

She groaned and held a hand to her brow. 'I couldn't remember a thing.' She smiled suddenly, almost coquettishly. 'I remembered you though.'

'I would have got here sooner. Sorry about that.'

He looked pensive.

She smiled at him as he took hold of her hand. 'I know who you are.'

'Of course you do.'

'I mean it. It's a bit like having a jigsaw inside my head. All the bits are cluttered up and take some sorting out.'

'If you never remember anything else, I'm sure glad you remember me.'

'How long have I been here?'

She was sure the nurses had already told her, but some of the more trivial things tended to slip her memory.

Although he smiled, his expression was concerned. 'Six weeks.'

She gasped. 'Six weeks.'

'You're doing well, but you need a lot more rest. They're talking about sending you home before Christmas. If you want to go that is...'

His voice trailed away, along with the sparkle that had been in his eyes.

'Home?'

She tried to recall what home was like. Bits of it came back. Some bits were welcome. Some were not.

'Oh, this just came for you.' He took a letter from his breast pocket. 'It's from home.' Vera said it came this morning. She's drawn duty, so I offered to bring it. Thought you'd like to read it as soon as possible.

The writing seemed vaguely familiar. As it came to her who had written, the frown lifted from her brow and a whole host of memories crowded her mind.

She laughed. 'Maisie! One of the girls I used to work with.'

With shaking hands, she opened up the letter and began to read. It was dated four weeks previously. Weeks when she hadn't known who and where she was.

A quick note. The air raids have petered out. We had a few rogue enemy raiders taking pot shots at anything they fancied, but that's stopped too. Lyndon has asked Bridget to marry her. I've got my own first aider to accompany me when needed.

The record club isn't so well supported as it used to be, mainly because without any heavy raids, everyone prefers to go home.

A NAAFI type place with drinks and dancing has opened up in Little Paradise. Me and Bridget ain't been there yet, but it's on our to-do list. I could do with a new dress first. Bridget's mum is a dab hand at altering something old to make something new.

Robert told us that you've been injured and that he expects you home before Christmas. We both hope you're recovering and look forward to seeing you again.

Anyway, get well soon.

Love from me and Bridget.

'It's from Maisie and Bridget, the mates I used to work with at the tobacco factory.' Her eyes shone. 'Isn't that wonderful? I remember them.'

'Sounds good to me,' he replied, his countenance and shoulders relaxing, glad to see her responding so well to a single letter. 'Any chance of them sending over some cigarettes?'

She flipped playfully at his arm. 'Everyone asks that question.'

He took hold of her free hand in both of his. 'Phyllis, it's so great to see you looking so much better. It's been hard to concentrate with you lying here, not knowing anything about anything.'

'I need to write back to them.' She looked at him, then back at the letter, biting her bottom lip as she considered what she had to do. 'There's something I have to tell you, Mick. Something that might make you change your mind about me.'

'I don't like how serious this sounds.'

'It is serious, but it has to be said.'

'I love you, Phyllis. That's the most serious thing I need to say.'

The suddenness of the statement took her off balance for a moment. She took a deep breath before getting back on track.

'I love you too, Mick. I want to be part of your future – if we get through all this, that is.'

His lopsided smile touched her heart. 'If you're not here, Christmas is cancelled for me. You don't have to go, do you?'

It ached to shake her head, so she kept to words. 'I don't want to go home. I do have the option to stay, but it depends on how you react to what I'm going to tell you.'

Mick heaved a great sigh of relief at the same time running his right hand through his straw-coloured hair. 'Well go on, Phyllis, I'm all ears.'

37

BRIDGET AND MAISIE

Quarter past five and the girls of the tobacco factory were pouring out of the main door, keen to get home, have supper, get changed and go out on the town.

Bridget and Maisie were coming out arm in arm, unaware that someone was lying in wait to take them to task.

Hilda Harvey, her dark eyes more sunken than ever in her deep sockets, was waiting for them.

'You two!' She stepped in front of them. 'Scarlet harlots, the pair of you. It was you who told her not to come back. Don't deny it. I know it was.'

Looking totally flabbergasted, Maisie and Bridget stopped in their tracks.

'I'm sorry,' said Bridget, in as polite a manner as she could muster, 'but I don't know what you're talking about.'

'Oh yes you do,' hissed Hilda, pointing a black gloved finger into her face. 'She was supposed to come home for Christmas, but you two told her not to. And don't deny it. It's typical of papists conspirators like you.'

'I ain't a papist whatever you call it,' shouted Maisie.

A crowd of factory girls had gathered round, curious to find out what this was all about and somewhat surprised at Maisie and Bridget being referred to as scarlet harlots.

The thin lips of Hilda Harvey, Phyllis's mother-in-law and Robert's mother, stretched hideously over small, sharp teeth. 'You told her not to come home. You turned her against my Robert. Vengeance is mine,' she spat, her eyes narrowed, her sallow cheeks turning purple with rage.

'Stop it! Just stop it!'

Even Maisie was surprised at how loud Bridget shouted and the way in which she stepped forward so her face was close to Hilda's.

'We've not heard from Phyllis for months, so how could we tell her not to come home? All we know is what Robert told us, that she was injured and coming home for Christmas.'

'You have not seen my Robert! You're lying.'

'We saw Robert in the Engineers' Arms. He told us then. If you don't believe us, ask him.'

'Hilda! Hilda! What are you doing?' Tom Harvey entered the fray, grabbing his wife's arm, his comfy old face rife with concern.

She shook his hand off and glared at him. 'They're saying they didn't tell her not to come home. I don't believe them,' she exclaimed, her back ramrod straight, her piercing eyes fixed on Bridget and Maisie.

Bridget spoke directly to Tom, Robert's father. 'We saw Robert in the Engineers' Arms. We've had no word at all from Phyllis, so how can we tell her not to come back?'

'I know,' said Tom in a quiet voice, immediately turning his attention back to his wife. 'Come on, Hilda. Let me take you home.'

'Get your hands off me!' In one rough movement, Tom was

hurled to one side. Hilda Harvey's sticklike body was stronger than it looked.

She stalked off, coat flying out behind her, leaving Tom Harvey looking totally helpless. Realising he could do nothing more, he turned to Bridget and Maisie.

'Hilda's a bit highly strung. Robert's not the same as he was and she's taken it badly. She doesn't mean what she said. It's just her way of coping.'

* * *

That night turned out to be a mellow autumn night. The air was dry but turning crisper with the prospect of winter being on the horizon.

They'd arranged to meet at their old haunt, The Catherine Wheel, one of the few remaining buildings on Castle Green.

Bridget's mother had made Maisie a smartly fitted velvet jacket from an old curtain. It was dark red and went well with a tweed skirt cut down from an old one given her by her grandmother. Feeling as smart as a magazine mannequin, she caught the bus into town and made her way to the old pub where the ceilings were low and cigarette smoke as thick as soup.

There was just enough light left for her to see Bridget standing outside the pub door waiting for her. The moment she clapped eyes on her, Bridget waved enthusiastically. There was something white in her hand.

'It's from Phyllis,' she cried excitedly. 'She's all right.'

Maisie breathed a sigh of relief. 'So is she coming home for Christmas?'

Bridget laughed. 'Not ruddy likely. You'll have to read it, but basically she's saying that she's never coming back. She's met somebody else and told him everything. He's willing to wait and so's she. Isn't that marvellous?'

Maisie agreed that it was. She breathed a deep sigh. 'You know, Bridge, I'm looking forward to Christmas. There won't be much on the table, but who cares? We're still 'ere.'

'Yes,' said Bridget thoughtfully. 'We're still here. That's something to celebrate in itself.'

'Right!' said Maisie. 'So let's go in and have a drink. We bloody well deserve it.'

* * *

Far away in the Pacific Ocean, Lyndon O'Neill the Third had arrived at Pearl Harbour in Hawaii. The sun was shining and both sea and sky were an incredible shade of blue. It looked like paradise on earth, yet there in the harbour were the battle wagons of war.

The State Department had assured him that his three months here would be a doddle.

'All being well, you can then fly on to Manilla.'

It was the 'all being well' bit that threw him. His father had informed him in grave tones that the government tended to hold their cards close to their chest. 'Too much information upsets the populace and produces irate letters to the newspapers.'

He accepted that they weren't telling him everything, that there was disagreement about what was likely to happen next.

He'd read about Japanese atrocities in Nanking, China. Some people declared the truth was unsubstantiated. He accepted there was nothing he could do, so pushed the big picture aside, concentrating instead on the smaller and more personal picture.

In the quiet of a hotel room where the sea could be glimpsed through the fronds of palm trees, he picked up a pen and began to write.

Dear Bridget,

 Please forgive my crass remarks. I still love you and hope you still love me...I've now arrived at Pearl Harbour and expect to still be here at Christmas...

MORE FROM LIZZIE LANE

We hope you enjoyed reading *Fire and Fury for the Tobacco Girls*. If you did, please leave a review.

If you'd like to gift a copy, this book is also available as an ebook, digital audio download and audiobook CD.

Sign up to Lizzie Lane's mailing list for news, competitions and updates on future books:

http://bit.ly/LizzieLaneNewsletter

If you haven't yet why not discover the first in the series, *The Tobacco Girls*.

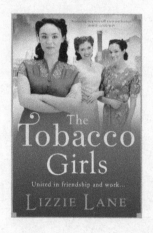

ABOUT THE AUTHOR

Lizzie Lane is the author of over 50 books, a number of which have been bestsellers. She was born and bred in Bristol where many of her family worked in the cigarette and cigar factories. This has inspired her new saga series for Boldwood *The Tobacco Girls*.

Follow Lizzie on social media:

facebook.com/jean.goodhind
twitter.com/baywriterallat1
instagram.com/baywriterallatsea
bookbub.com/authors/lizzie-lane

ABOUT BOLDWOOD BOOKS

Boldwood Books is a fiction publishing company seeking out the best stories from around the world.

Find out more at www.boldwoodbooks.com

Sign up to the Book and Tonic newsletter for news, offers and competitions from Boldwood Books!

http://www.bit.ly/bookandtonic

We'd love to hear from you, follow us on social media:

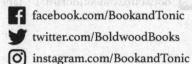

facebook.com/BookandTonic

twitter.com/BoldwoodBooks

instagram.com/BookandTonic

9 781800 485082